Christmas
under a
Starlit Sky

Also by Holly Martin

TOWN CALLED CHRISTMAS SERIES

Christmas Under a Cranberry Sky (Book 1)

WHITE CLIFF BAY SERIES

Christmas at Lilac Cottage (White Cliff Bay Book 1)
Snowflakes on Silver Cove (White Cliff Bay Book 2)
Summer at Rose Island (White Cliff Bay Book 3)

The Guestbook
One Hundred Proposals
One Hundred Christmas Proposals
Fairytale Beginnings

HOLLY WRITING AS AMELIA THORNE

Tied Up with Love
Beneath the Moon and the Stars

FOR YOUNG ADULTS

The Sentinel
The Prophecies
The Revenge

Christmas under a Starlit Sky

HOLLY MARTIN

Bookouture

Published by Bookouture

An imprint of StoryFire Ltd.
23 Sussex Road, Ickenham, UB10 8PN
United Kingdom

www.bookouture.com

ISBN: 978-1-78681-093-9
eBook ISBN: 978-1-78681-092-2

To the wonderful team at Bookouture,
thank you for being amazing.

CHAPTER 1

When Neve envisaged seeing her ex-boyfriend for the first time since their break-up, she had never imagined it playing out like this. She kind of thought, if she ever saw Oakley Rey again, she would be dressed in a sexy, floor-length dress and looking utterly fabulous. She wouldn't be standing there with tears falling down her cheeks at seeing him again and she wouldn't be dressed as an elf with red and white tights and oversized green pointy shoes with bells on the ends.

She couldn't believe he was here. He should be at some super-glamorous, glitzy party in California but instead Oakley Rey, Hollywood superstar, was climbing out of a helicopter on the tiny remote Juniper Island, the northernmost island of the British Isles.

She wiped her eyes and watched him stride across the grass towards her. Her heart physically ached. There was a part of her that wanted to run straight into his arms, but it was outweighed by the part that had her pointy elf shoes glued to the ground. He looked amazing. Incredibly he had bulked out in the nine weeks since they had been apart, somehow looking so much bigger and more muscular than she remembered. He looked strong, confident and every inch the Hollywood star.

His eyes locked with hers as he moved towards her and it was almost as if they were the only people in the world before she suddenly remembered that she was standing in the grounds of the Stardust Lake Hotel. Her unexpected reunion was about to be witnessed by probably half the guests as they all peered out their windows to see who had arrived in the black, sleek helicopter. It was Christmas Eve, every lodge at the hotel had been taken up by the guests and journalists that had arrived for the grand opening a few days before. And worse still, her family was standing there with her.

Her mum and dad stood frozen to the ground to the right of her, while Gabe, her brother, had his arm round her shoulders, trying to offer some comfort at the shock of seeing Oakley again. She heard Gabe's girlfriend, Pip, asking quietly who the man was and Gabe telling her it was Oakley, confirming that she wasn't having some kind of hallucination. No one moved, no one said anything, and there wasn't a single word in her head that she could utter to encapsulate her feelings over seeing him again.

In the end Neve's four-year-old niece broke the silence.

'Oakley!' Wren squealed with delight and ran forward to greet him as Neve herself should have done. Wren launched herself at him and Oakley dropped his bag and caught the bundle of arms and legs and threw her up in the air before catching her again. She let out a shriek of joy and giggled as Oakley threw her over his shoulder and hung her upside down. He adored Wren, always had, and the ache in Neve's chest grew to something almost tangible as she watched them play and laugh together. He would make a wonderful father. One day – he was too young now. At twenty-six, his lifelong dream of being a movie star was about to be realised and a child would get in the way of that.

With Wren still slung over his shoulder, Oakley walked up to them so that he was within touching distance. Every bone in her body screamed at her to take that last step, lean her head against his heart and feel his arms around her, with his head resting on top of hers as he always used to hold her. But she couldn't.

For a second, all his confidence seemed to falter at a lack of any reaction from her, but as he clocked the tears in her eyes, he smiled, sadly. 'Hey, Freckle,' Oakley said, softly.

His voice, his name for her on his lips. It was enough to send the tears straight back to her eyes again. How could she ever think she could let this man go?

When there were still no words forthcoming, Gabe cleared his throat. 'Hi Oakley, erm. . . It's good to see you again.'

Oakley tore his eyes away from Neve to address her brother.

'Hey, Gabe, I think this belongs to you.' Oakley handed over a giggling Wren to Gabe. 'I hope you don't mind me landing there. We were heading to the airport when I saw you guys walking over to the hotel. I didn't want to waste any time getting to my girl.'

My girl. Neve swallowed, painfully.

The helicopter suddenly took off with an ear-splitting noise and as it faded into the distance, silence descended on them again.

Gabe spoke again, clearly trying to fill the gaps. 'We weren't expecting you. All our lodges are full. We have houses down in the village where you could stay for a few days but I think we've filled a few of them for the New Year's Eve ball. We could—'

'You don't need to worry, I'll be staying in Neve's house,' Oakley said, simply.

Her heart thundered against her chest at that thought.

'I don't think that's a good idea,' Gabe said, clearly uncomfortable about him showing up like this and not knowing what Neve's reaction to it would be. She couldn't help him out. She had no idea what her reaction should be either.

Her mum, Lizzie, stepped forward and to Neve's surprise she embraced Oakley in a hug. 'It's so lovely to see you again. We're all heading over to have some lunch. You'd be very welcome to join us but I expect you and Neve have some talking to do.'

Lizzie stepped back and then with meaningful looks at the rest of her family she ushered them all away from Neve and Oakley.

Luke, her older brother, hovered for a moment, his hand on Neve's back. 'You OK?'

Neve nodded. Luke gave Oakley a meaningful glare then walked after the rest of his family, leaving her alone with the man who had stolen her heart.

Oakley stared down at her, his face breaking into that gorgeous heart-stopping smile. 'You don't look too happy to see me. I did promise I'd spend Christmas with you, you know I never break a promise.'

She cleared her throat. 'That was before we broke up.'

He stepped closer, so close she could feel his warmth, his wonderful scent that reminded her of sweet roasted chestnuts, close enough to see the flecks of toffee gold in his warm chocolate eyes.

'We never broke up, Freckle, we were just. . . taking a break.'

She wanted to kiss him, to lean up and press her lips to his. How could she feel this way? She'd chosen to break up with him and it had been nine weeks. She was supposed to be over him by now. It wasn't supposed to still be hurting like this. She had missed him so much.

Clarity came when her eyes found the small scar on the side of his head. The scar she knew he'd got while filming a scene in his latest movie. Mere days after she had read about it online, she had switched on her computer to find that he had been rumoured to be seeing the pretty red-headed doctor who had stitched him back up. One of many women he had been linked with over the last few weeks. She didn't know why she tortured herself daily with reading the Google alerts for him, but he was like an addiction for her and if she couldn't be with him then that had been her poor substitute.

She stepped back out of his proximity and immediately felt cold without him.

Unperturbed, he turned and grabbed his bag. 'Which way to your house?'

'You're not staying with me. I have one bed and one shower.'

'Looks like we'll have to share then,' Oakley said, walking off.

She marched up to him. 'We are not sharing anything. Lord knows whose bed you've been sharing for the last few weeks! I'd like to keep my sheets clean, thank you very much and—'

She let out a yelp as he wrapped a hand round her waist and tugged her up against him, his brown eyes shadowed by his eyebrows as he scowled at her. 'Is that what you really think? That I've been working my way around the female population of California in your absence? There's been many a woman who has flashed me a pretty smile and her phone number or in some cases her room number. Not one of them interested me. Not one of them made my pulse race like you do. Not one of them made me laugh as hard as you do. They weren't you and being with them would not even have scratched the surface of what I got from you so there was absolutely no point. You are the only one I want and I'm here to get you back.'

He released her and walked away towards the lodges.

She watched him walk up the path ahead of her. He made it sound so simple when in reality it wasn't. He lived in California, she lived here at the Stardust Lake Hotel. He was about to become a huge Hollywood star, she was a hotel manager. Their worlds couldn't be any further apart. And the biggest problem was the secret she carried inside of her, the secret she had kept to herself for the last ten days. If he knew that he would run a hundred miles away from her.

He turned back briefly. 'Which house, Freckle?'

They needed to talk, she knew that. As Neve noticed a few guests peering out their windows at what was transpiring, she knew they needed to talk in private and the only way she was going to get that was by taking him to her house.

She pointed. 'That one in the corner with the holly wreath on the front door.'

He turned and walked towards it.

She would tell him and let the cards fall where they may.

❄

Adam Douglas looked out of his office window as the helicopter took off, shattering the tranquil peace of the island for a second time. Oakley Rey was here and while he was happy for Neve that they would hopefully be able to sort out their differences, he had a good mind to go down there and give Oakley a piece of his mind for landing so close to the hotel. If only he could get off the phone. He watched Oakley talking to Neve and decided for her sake to let it go. He tuned back in to what was being said on the other end of the line.

'. . .I'm ever so worried,' said Deborah, the owner of the chocolate shop in the village.

Adam sighed and rubbed his head. 'How long has Ivy been missing?'

'Well, as I said, she always goes out for a walk at about seven in the morning. She's normally back after an hour. We've been so busy with the shop I didn't realise she hadn't come back. We've been round to her house but there's no answer.'

Adam glanced at his watch. Ivy, the woman who ran the painting shop, had been out for nearly five hours. The hotel had an agreement with the villagers that their shops must be open between the hours of ten and six and although he didn't know Ivy personally, he knew that all the shop owners in the tiny village were reliable and wouldn't just not open unless there was a really good reason for it. It was freezing outside – if she had gone out for a walk and fallen over somewhere, she'd be at risk of hypothermia now as well as any injuries she had sustained from the fall.

'I'll get a search party together, any idea where she goes?' Adam asked.

'No, I don't, I'm afraid.'

'OK, can you keep an eye out for her and if she comes back to the village, can you call through to the hotel and let us know?'

'Of course, I'm sorry to bother you, I didn't know who else to call.'

'It's no bother.'

He finished the call and phoned through to the reception asking Iris to contact the boys from the maintenance team, the porters and round up anyone else who was free. He asked her to put together some basic rescue bags including blankets, water, a walkie-talkie, some snacks and a first aid kit.

He pulled his coat and snow boots on. There were never problems like this to sort out at the hotel he worked at as deputy manager in London. The worst thing he had to sort out there was a mistake with a reservation, a wedding not up to the high standards of a bridezilla or men who were using the hotel for extramarital affairs and their wives finding out. He had been on the island for four days, on a secondment from the London hotel to help Neve with the opening of Stardust Lake Hotel, and he was already realising how different life was going to be for the next few months on this tiny island.

The hotel accommodation was made up of lots of ski lodges instead of rooms, and instead of spa facilities and a pool there were snowmobiling and sledging activities and a giant ice palace where the New Year's Eve ball was to take place in a week's time. The only way onto the island was by boat or plane, whereas normally everyone who arrived at the hotel in central London came by taxi or a chauffeur-driven car. The weather was brutal – it had snowed every day since he had arrived and the cold coastal winds were harsh and cruel. And he had Shetland ponies that ran riot around the village, apparently stealing things from the villagers and the tourists.

The village was another thing to contend with. He had met many of the villagers a few days before – wonderful, colourful, mostly elderly characters. Many of them telling him excitedly about the predicted spectacular show of the Merry Dancers over the Christmas period. It had taken him a while to realise that they were talking about the Northern Lights. Deborah had told him the meanings of the different colours. He remembered that a red aurora was a foretelling of love, which brought a whole new meaning to the expression, 'Red sky at night, shepherd's delight'.

The town called Christmas was to be an almost year-long Christmas and winter-themed market. Most of the people in the village were islanders who had lived there all their lives. Gabe Whitaker had come along and converted all their houses into wooden ski lodges and somehow persuaded them all to run individual little shops selling crafts and food straight from their front rooms. Although they were supposed to be independent shops, Neve had explained to him that the islanders were to be treated almost like hotel staff and would need to be looked after, especially the older folk, who might need hand-holding during the first few weeks of the hotel opening.

And that was another thing that was causing him a headache. Neve. He'd known her for eight years and she was the most organised and efficient person he knew. Nothing fazed her, she never got upset, she was fiery and took no crap. But since he'd got there she had been in a complete state, crying all the time, she'd been sick several times as well and, although he knew she was upset because of her break-up with Oakley, he strongly suspected she was pregnant and that was the reason why she was an emotional wreck.

And now he had a missing old lady to contend with too.

He ran down the stairs to the reception and spoke to Iris and Jake, the receptionist and porter, co-ordinating the search. He grabbed his rescue bag as Iris made up a few more and then headed outside, just as Gabe, Luke and their parents walked up the steps with Pip and Wren, probably heading for lunch.

'Ivy Storm has gone missing,' Adam said, not bothering with any preliminaries. 'She went out for a walk around seven this morning and hasn't come back. I've organised a search of the island, around the south, east and north. Can you guys take the west side and I'll cut through the middle road?'

Gabe's dad, David, scooped up Wren. 'We'll take care of Wren, you guys go and find this lady.'

Gabe looked at his parents apologetically and Adam knew that he had planned to spend the whole day with Pip, his parents and his daughter.

'Sorry, Princess, I won't be long,' Gabe said, pressing a kiss to Wren's forehead.

'It's OK Daddy, you need to find Ivy and make sure she is safe,' Wren said, with all the wisdom of someone five times her age.

Iris came out and handed bags and walkie-talkies to them. Luke agreed to take the coastal path and Gabe and Pip said they would head to the west.

'Shall I go and get Neve?' Gabe asked.

Adam looked over at Neve and Oakley, who were standing talking to each other as if they were the only people in the world that existed.

'No, they need to talk. We can handle this one without her.'

He watched as Oakley marched over towards Neve's house and Neve followed him.

He turned back to Gabe, Pip and Luke and they all split up in search of Ivy. Adam headed towards the road that cut straight through the middle of the island. Snow started to fall again and he looked up and cursed the sky. He only hoped they would find Ivy soon.

CHAPTER 2

Oakley looked around the resort as he walked up to Neve's house. It had changed so much since he had been up there with her in the spring. The little snow-capped wooden ski lodges looked cosy and inviting, some of them with trails of smoke drifting from the chimneys. Behind the lodges, up on the hillside, he could see the cluster of glass igloos, some of them glowing gold against the backdrop of the sparkling snow. He'd seen the spectacular ice palace as he'd flown over, which was another new addition. He knew Neve had worked so hard to get everything ready for the opening and he was so proud of her and what she had achieved.

He glanced back at her, smiling at how adorable she looked in her elf costume. Her long, black hair cascaded over one shoulder in loose curls and he longed to run his fingers through it again. She looked pale, paler than normal, which was saying something when she normally had skin the colour of fresh fallen snow. Her freckles, peppered over her cheeks and nose, seemed darker than usual. Maybe she was ill or maybe just shocked to see him turn up here like this. She'd be even more shocked when she found out the reason why he'd come. He smiled at the thought, though nerves and fear slammed into his stomach as soon as he allowed himself to think about it.

Oakley pushed the thought away and walked up the stairs to her front door. He let himself in and looked around as he dumped his bag on the chair.

Inside it was small and cosy, decked in wood panelling with colourful rugs and cushions. There were two bright blue sofas facing each other either side of a log fire and a Christmas tree dressed in silver ribbons and twinkling lights stood in one corner. Open wooden stairs led up to a mezzanine bedroom; he presumed the bathroom was up there too. There was a small kitchen area at the back. It was nice, but there was something about the place that suggested this was somewhere that Neve stayed, not lived. There was nothing personal about this space, no photos, no trinkets or ornaments. It lacked anything of her personality at all.

'Nice place.'

Neve closed the door behind her and leaned up against it. Why did she look scared to have him here?

'Can I get you a drink, or something to eat?' she said.

She was being so polite to him and he hated it. Their relationship had always been filled with chemistry and passion. He wanted to grab her, kiss her hard, taste her, run his fingers over her silky skin and then drag her down in front of the fireplace and show her how very impolite he could be. This politeness made him worry that maybe he'd left things too late. Maybe they really were over.

She was still waiting for his answer.

'Burger and fries would be great. It feels like I've been travelling for two days to get here and even in first class the airplane food is bad. I'll take a beer too, please.'

'Burger and chips,' Neve corrected, and he was relieved to see the small smirk playing on her lips.

Oakley laughed. 'I've been stateside too long.'

Neve pushed away from the door and picked up the phone, presumably dialling through to reception. She put the order in for food to be delivered and when she put the phone down she turned back to face him.

God, he had missed her so much. He should never have let her go, he should have fought for her when she had broken up with him. He should have called before now, talked to her, but his stubborn pride had prevented him from begging her to come back. But now he would get down on his knees and beg and plead for her to give them another chance, pride be damned. He loved her and he needed her in his life and he had no intention of leaving here without her.

Silence stretched between them. How had it come to this? When they were together they would talk for hours barely drawing breath and now things were awkward between them. He looked around the room, he needed to say something and he knew he couldn't lead with the main reason for his trip.

He glanced at the fireplace and walked over, getting to his knees as he built and lit a fire. Maybe if the room was warm and cosy it might make them both relax a bit.

Neve was watching him, he knew that, and as he glanced over his shoulder he saw her staring at his bum. He smiled, a sliver of hope blooming in his heart.

He stood up and wiping his hands down his jeans he stared at the flames as they flickered and danced in the fireplace.

She came over to stand next to him and that gave him hope too.

'How's it been going here at the hotel?' Oakley asked. 'I know you were helping to oversee the development of it for months when you were in London, flying back and forth between the two hotels, you worked your arse off. Did everything go smoothly for the opening?'

'It couldn't have gone better. The ice palace is a big hit, people love the glass igloos and the village with the Christmas market. People have been hiring the snowmobiles or hiking around the island and the grand opening and the Christmas carnival were a huge success. I'm so pleased for Gabe, all his hard work paid off.'

'All *your* hard work too. He is very lucky to have you.'

'I'm lucky to have *him*. He gave me a home when I had nothing, gave me a job. I owe him so much.'

'I think you've paid your dues.'

It annoyed him that she felt this huge sense of loyalty to her brother. She worked her arse off for him. Gabe was a good man and Oakley respected how he looked after his family and his staff, but he didn't want Neve's loyalty to him to stand in the way of her own dreams.

'Oakley, we need to talk.'

He looked at her and saw real fear in her eyes. What on earth did she want to say that had her looking like that? Not unless she had moved on with someone else already. That would put a real dampener on his plans.

He lifted a curl of her black hair off her face and tucked it behind her ear. 'I'm listening, Freckle.'

❋

Her breath caught in her throat at his touch and any words she had been trying to say dried in her mouth.

With his blond hair curling at the back of his neck, his white shirt open at the collar and his tanned chest peeking out the top, he was a sight for sore eyes.

'You look good, Oakley.'

He grinned as he appraised her. '*You* look amazing.'

'I'm dressed as an elf.'

'You still look amazing. Always do.'

She sighed. He was such a charmer and, like many women before her, and probably many women after her, she had fallen for it, hook, line and sinker.

'I'm going to get changed. One of the porters will be bringing over the food shortly.'

'Do you need any help getting out of that costume, Freckle?' Oakley called after her as she walked up the stairs.

'I'm sure I'll manage.'

'Well, give me a call if you need me.'

Neve walked into her bedroom and sat down on the bed, glad to have the space from him. He was here in her home. The last time she'd seen him, he'd been just about to jet off to Hollywood to start filming the latest comic book superhero blockbuster with Oakley in the title role of Obsidian. And now he was here, on this tiny remote island off the coast of Scotland with a permanent population of sixty-three people, probably a hundred if you counted all the hotel staff staying there. The last time she had seen him, she had broken his heart by ending things between them and, as he had stormed out of her bedroom and slammed the door behind him, she had felt her own heart breaking too.

She let her head fall into her hands.

Neve had first met Oakley when he was filming in London, starring in a supporting role in a British romcom. He had lived at the hotel she had been deputy manager for at the time and stayed there for ten months. He had been this cheeky, smiling man with the exuberance of an oversized puppy. Never a bad word to say about anything, despite the fact that on many occasions he came back to the hotel after a day's filming so exhausted he could barely stand. Every woman fancied him but for reasons she would never know, he had eyes only for her. She had resisted him at first – he was an actor who probably turned on the charm to any woman who caught his eye and, not being one for casual relationships, she certainly didn't want to go down that road. She had also been wary of getting involved with a celebrity again, someone in the public eye. Her last boyfriend had been an Olympian and he had broken her heart spectacularly so she and Oakley had become friends. They'd had breakfast together every day that his filming schedule would allow it and dinner some days too. Slowly that friendship had developed into something more and then quickly progressed, at least for her, into a full-blown love affair. She loved him, she couldn't deny that, and having him here was bringing back all the pain she had suffered after he left.

She quickly got changed and went downstairs, just as Jake, the hotel porter, arrived with the food. She watched Oakley with Jake and smiled. Jake was clearly stunned to be serving food to a Hollywood star, although he was trying to remain professional. Oakley was treating Jake like he was his best mate, chatting to him about Christmas and the hotel as if it was the most normal thing in the world.

Neve walked down the last few stairs and approached them.

'Thanks, Jake. Is everything OK over at the hotel?'

'Yes, there's no problems. Adam told me to tell you he's looking after everything today and not to worry about coming back to work this afternoon.'

'Adam's here?' Oakley said, his smile disappearing. Adam, her assistant manager, was the one person that Oakley didn't like. Their close friendship made him uneasy.

'He came up from the London hotel to give me a hand with the opening. He'll be here for a few months.'

Jake, recognising the tension between her and Oakley, excused himself and left them alone.

'Might have known he would follow you up here,' Oakley said, throwing himself down on the sofa as he started to tuck into the food.

'Adam is a good man. I wish you weren't so down on him. Besides, Gabe asked him to come up here to help, not me. There's been so much work to do to get this place ready and I've. . . not been well the past few weeks and. . .'

'What do you mean, you've not been well?' Oakley's eyes filled with concern.

Neve hesitated before she spoke. 'I've just had a sick bug, it's nothing to worry about. And there's nothing going on between me and Adam. Which is more than I can say for you and your beautiful co-star, River Andrews.'

'You know there's nothing between me and her. You know most of that is rumours started by my mum. The press love it and the attention doesn't hurt to build an early following for the film.'

Oakley took a big bite of his burger.

'Oh yes, your lovely mother,' Neve said, dryly. 'She made it very clear that she didn't like me.'

'Of course she likes you.'

His mum hated her and had pretty much told her so. Of course Oakley didn't know that.

'She told you to make sure you were never photographed with me. She didn't want you to be seen with me, something you took heed of. We rarely went out and when we did it was all in secret.'

His face fell. 'Is that what you thought? You know that the press take pictures of something as simple as me eating an ice cream, or buying a t-shirt. They hound the women I'm seen with and dig into their pasts and you're angry because I wanted to protect you from that? I recognised that what we had was unique and special, for the first time in my life I was in love and I wanted to keep that private and not have it ruined by the press harassing you. It was never about me not wanting to be seen with you.'

Neve swallowed the emotion clogging her throat. Was that true? Had he really done that to protect her?

'And who I date has nothing to do with my mum. I will date whoever I want, I've told her that.'

'Doesn't stop her interfering though. I'm surprised she even let you come over here.'

'I fired her as my manager.'

Neve sat down on the sofa opposite him. That was a big statement from him. His mum had always been the third wheel in their relationship. She had been his manager since he got his first movie role at the age of fifteen and helped him to secure several large TV parts after that. Without his dad on the scene and just one sister, they had always been close and he had been happy for her to make the decisions on which path his career should take. It was only in the last year or two that Oakley had started to resent her interference and his mum had blamed Neve entirely for that.

'She wants the best for me but she's too controlling. I was happy for her to take the lead when I was a kid, I didn't know any better, but the time has long since passed where I need someone to make my decisions for me. I didn't want it to affect my relationship with her. She wasn't happy but we've reached an understanding. We're better off as mother and son. Don't mix business and pleasure.'

'That's something I should have taken heed of,' Neve said. 'You were a guest in my hotel, I shouldn't have got involved with you.'

'We were meant to be together, Freckle, there's no shouldn't about it.'

She watched him as he finished his food. She had never felt before what she felt for Oakley. Even with Zander, the man she thought she had been in love with many years ago, it was never like this. The intensity of her feelings for Oakley was all-consuming. As much as she wanted to, she couldn't just switch those feelings off.

Oakley licked his fingers clean and shoved the plate aside. He beckoned her across the room with his finger and that gorgeous smile.

She stayed where she was. It was safer that way. 'What are you doing here, Oakley?'

'I told you, I want you back.'

'Well, I don't want to get back together, so you had a wasted trip.'

He stood up and sat down next to her, slinging his arm around her shoulders. She didn't have it in her to protest. She belonged in his arms. His warmth, his scent, it was an intoxicating mix. He hadn't shaved for a few days and he had golden stubble across his jawbone. He looked delicious and right now she wanted nothing more than to kiss him, to feel that stubble against her cheeks or her throat as he worked his kisses down to her collarbone.

'You don't want me here? You're not happy to see me?' Oakley said, clearly unperturbed by her comment.

'No.'

Without warning he pressed his mouth to her neck, right against her pulse point, and she let out a soft involuntary moan of pleasure at his touch. She knew he could feel her pulse hammering against his lips.

He pulled back slightly and the dark look he gave her made her breath catch in her throat.

'I think you're lying. I think you want me as much as I want you.'

'It's just lust and sex though, Oakley, you can't base a relationship on that.'

'I think lust and sex is a great basis for a relationship.' He smiled as he placed a kiss on her shoulder. She sighed, closing her eyes for a moment. 'Freckle, if I really wanted just sex, I could have stayed in California where there's free sex on tap. I want something more than that. I want you. It's always been you.'

He picked up her hand and kissed the inside of her wrist.

If he kept this up, her restraint would be shattered very quickly.

She took her hand from his mouth, though she didn't move from his side. She couldn't.

Oakley looked at her. 'Why did you really break up with me?'

'You know why. It never would have worked, you're over there, I'm over here. I'd only be holding you back. Your acting career is just taking off and you need to be available. Travelling back and forth would not be good for you, you'd be tired, it would affect your filming schedule, you might miss auditions or callbacks. It would interfere with your career and I never wanted that.'

'You would never have held me back, we could have made it work. Was that really the reason or was it because of the rumours of me and River being together?'

That hadn't helped either. The insecurities she had that she wouldn't be enough for him had been poked at like an old wound when she'd seen them together.

'There were photos of you and her together everywhere. Laughing, joking. . .'

'Holding hands? Did you see photos of me holding hands with her, like I held your hand?'

She swallowed. 'No.'

'Kissing? Hugging? Making love? Were there any photos of that?'

She shook her head. In reality she knew he hadn't cheated on her, but it still didn't stop those insecurities from surfacing, didn't stop her wondering if he found River more attractive than her. And how long he would be faithful when he could have any woman he wanted.

'Because there weren't any. There is no affair, there never has been. We were together simply because we had both been cast in this movie and wanted to meet before filming started. There has never been anyone but you since I walked into your hotel nearly a year ago. I want you back, Freckle. I've missed you so much.'

'Nothing has changed. I'm here, you live in California. You'll be travelling all over the world. We're never going to see each other. And every day I open up the newspapers or go on the internet and see you with another woman. It kills me, wondering if you're lying next to them in bed, holding these women like you used to hold me. Telling them you've never felt this way before.'

Annoyingly, tears formed in her eyes again. Damn her over-emotional body for betraying her like this.

Oakley smiled, sadly, and brushed the tears gently away. 'I'm not Zander.'

'I know,' she said, quietly. 'But I've been through this before. I know what it's like to date a celebrity who has women throwing themselves at him. It gets pretty hard to say no. And Zander wasn't even that famous. You're Oakley Rey, you're on the cover of every magazine, there are whole forums dedicated to discussing how hot you are and what women would like to do to you. There are memes and gifs circulating social media of your naked bum and you taking your top off. Pretty soon you're going to realise you can have any woman you want and it's much more fun playing the field than waiting around for months until you see me again.'

'I'm not going to cheat on you. It hasn't been hard for me to say no for the last few weeks because I only wanted you and these other women never came close. And as for the rest, we'd make it work. I told you that.'

'How? We'd see each other for a few weeks here and there. How could we ever have any kind of future like that? How could we have a proper relationship?'

'People who work in the forces see their partners for less time than we would see each other and they seem to make it work OK. I'm not saying it would be easy but if it's worth it, if what we have is worth fighting for, then we'd make it work somehow.'

'What about children, Oakley? How would that work? You'd come back and play with the baby for a few days before jetting off to some far-flung destination for a few months.'

'Children are a long way off for us, Freckle. I don't think we need to worry about that just yet.'

'I'm thirty-one. Babies and marriage might not be in your immediate future but they are in mine.'

'You could come with me on location – lots of actors and actresses travel with their husbands and wives.'

'And do what, just sit in the trailer waiting for you? I have a job here, my family are here.'

'Well, at least we'd be together,' he said and she opened her mouth to protest. He cupped her face, running his thumb over her cheek and stalling all other words in her throat. 'Look, it's Christmas Eve. I fly out New Year's Day. We have just over a week. Could we just, if only for one day, pretend that we don't have this big insurmountable problem between us? Could we spend Christmas Day as friends and talk and laugh like we used to? I've missed that so much. And come Boxing Day, we can talk about how we could make this work. Maybe come up with some kind of plan. And if we can't sort something out by New Year's Day, if the long distance and the travelling really is too hard to work around, then I'll leave and I promise you'll never hear from me again.'

Neve swallowed as she stared back at him. He had flown thousands of miles to be with her over Christmas and to get her back. He wanted this to work and for a moment she let all her doubts be pushed to one side. She wanted this to work as well and for a second or two she focussed on the tiny ray of hope that maybe they could be together. 'I've missed you too.'

'So we can be friends then. We were good friends before we got together. Even if we can't do anything else, we can do that.'

She considered it for a moment and even though she knew she was a fool for agreeing, even though she knew it would break her heart all over again when he had to leave in a week's time, she found herself nodding anyway. 'OK, just friends?'

Oakley nodded and held up his hands in a boy scout salute. 'I'll be the perfect gentleman, I won't even try to squeeze your bum or anything.'

She smiled. There was no way they could remain as just friends for the duration of his stay and with him sitting next to her, fixing her with that heart-melting smile, she was having a hard time remembering why she was holding back.

CHAPTER 3

Adam scanned the landscape, trying to see anything out of the ordinary. There were snow-capped hills and trees as far as the eye could see but no bodies of injured old ladies. There were a few hikers climbing one of the taller hills in the distance and he wondered, not for the first time, whether Ivy had just decided not to open the shop today and gone exploring round the hills instead. He had half the hotel staff out looking for her and she might just be out for a nice stroll around the hills.

He glanced over at a small herd of Shetland ponies just off the road. They were gathered close together and for reasons he couldn't put his finger on he knew something was off about them. They seemed restless and upset, when normally they were lazy and so chilled out they were practically sound asleep standing up.

He headed off the road and towards the herd. They eyed him as he got near but they didn't move away as he expected them to. As he grew closer he realised they were standing on the edge of a narrow ditch and to his surprise he could see the flanks of one of the ponies inside the ditch.

Crap.

Missing old lady and now a trapped pony too. Could his day get any weirder?

He got closer and froze. Slumped over the belly of the Shetland was a young woman, her long chestnut hair cascading over the pony. Her face was pale, her eyes closed. Although his day had just got weirder, he knew it had also just got a whole lot worse.

He grabbed his walkie-talkie and put out a call to the rest of the search party.

'This is Adam, no sign of Ivy yet, but there's a girl just off the middle road trapped in a ditch under a pony.' He looked around, trying to find some landmarks to give to the party, but it was just hills and fields and trees in every direction. 'I'm maybe half a mile from the hotel, maybe a little more. I'm not sure if the pony is alive but neither of them are moving. I'm going to need a snowplough or a JCB or something to lift this thing off her and we'll probably need an air ambulance too—'

'Oi, Hero, *I'm* Ivy and I don't need an ambulance,' came a voice from behind him. Adam whirled round to see the girl looking at him, her hair a tumbled mess of dark curls, her large grey eyes filled with anger. 'I'm not going to hospital.'

He quickly spoke into the walkie-talkie again. 'Sorry, the girl *is* Ivy. Hold off on the air ambulance for a moment. She's conscious, but I'll still need some help getting her out from under the pony.'

'We'll be there as soon as we can,' Gabe said.

Adam shoved the walkie-talkie back in his pocket and moved closer to the edge.

'Ivy, sorry, I was expecting—'

'Someone older… I know, it happens all the time. Thank God for my surname, Storm, which is at least a little cooler than Ivy. Took you bloody long enough to find me, I've been sitting underneath this pony for hours.'

'Are you OK, are you hurt?' Adam sat down on the edge of the ditch, ready to lower himself down.

'Don't come down here, it's really muddy, you'll never get back out again.'

Adam decided to take his chances and, ignoring her warning, he jumped down into the ditch. Ivy rolled her eyes.

The pony was alive too, breathing heavily, though it had plainly given up attempting to get out.

'Are you hurt?'

'No, I'm OK, I just can't move.'

Adam moved so he was next to her. She was trapped by her legs but she didn't look as though she was in any pain. He knelt down beside her and tried to lift and roll the pony off her, but, as he'd suspected, the pony was too heavy for that.

She was way too calm though and he didn't like that.

'Are your legs not crushed?'

'No. Actually, I'm kind of standing, the ditch is deeper where I am. He's sort of lying over me, not on me. I can move my legs, I just can't get the manoeuvrability to get out. The mud doesn't help. If you'd stayed at the top of the ditch you might have been able to pull me out.'

Adam stood back up and looked up at the side of the bank. It was wet, snow-covered and, as she'd said, very muddy. He reached up to get a handhold but his hands just slipped off the edges.

He sat back down next to her. 'Looks like we're both trapped.'

Ivy rolled her eyes again and he couldn't help but smile. She was very pretty, even though she was covered in mud. Her grey eyes had that smoky pewter look to them which made her look interesting. If he had to guess, he would say she was from Greek or Italian heritage, she had that exotic Mediterranean look to her.

She shivered suddenly and he remembered that she could be suffering from hypothermia. He delved in his bag and pulled out the blankets, wrapping one round her shoulders and another round her front. He yanked his hat off and pulled it over her head. But she surprised him by suddenly cuddling up to him, wrapping her arms around him and resting her head on his chest. He hesitated a moment before he draped an arm around her shoulders.

'Don't get any funny ideas, but I'm so cold, I'd cuddle up to anything right now, including this stinky old pony.'

He held her tighter, rubbing her shoulders through the blankets. 'What happened?'

'I was just out for a walk and I heard this commotion from over here. I came over and I could see this fat thing on his side, struggling to get out. I hopped down to help him out and as I was pushing him, I slipped. The pony was panicking and I somehow ended up underneath him and wedged against the side. Thankfully he's given up struggling now, he was just making the situation worse.' She closed her eyes, hugging Adam tighter. 'I didn't think anyone would find me.'

Her voice sounded vulnerable for just a moment, showing a small chink in her prickly armour.

'Well, I'm really glad I found you.'

'Don't get any ideas that I'm going to jump into bed with you to thank you for being my hero.'

He smirked. 'That was the furthest thing from my mind.'

'You're not my type.'

'What type am I?'

'That tall, dark, sexy type, cute smile, cute bum. That type does nothing for me,' Ivy said. Her eyes were still closed and her voice seemed to be getting a bit slurry. 'I might make you a thank-you cake.'

'Hey, don't go to sleep on me.'

'I'm not.' Her voice was definitely getting quieter now, almost as if she had been holding on for someone to find her and now she knew she was safe, she could relax.

He shook her gently and when she didn't respond, he shook her harder. Still nothing.

He pulled off his glove and stroked a finger down her cheek, trailing his thumb across her lips. Her eyes fluttered open and she looked up at him blearily. For a second he considered kissing her, knowing he'd probably get a slap if he did, but at least her anger would wake her up. Almost as if she knew his intentions, she straightened slightly so her head was no longer on his chest, though he still kept his arm around her to keep her warm.

'So you own Kaleidoscope, the painting shop in the village. What is it you paint?' Adam asked, needing to keep her talking.

'Pictures,' she answered, obtrusively. She leaned her head back and closed her eyes again.

'What kind – landscapes, portraits, modern art?'

'Finger paintings, and if you tell me I'm too old for that, you can kiss goodbye to your cake.'

'Tell me how you do it. I presume it's a bit more than stick men with smiley faces.'

She smiled and after a moment she opened her eyes and looked at him. 'You really want to know?'

'I'm interested, finger painting sounds fascinating.'

She grinned. 'You're such a liar but as you asked, I'll bore you with it. I generally paint on sheets of plastic, enamel tiles or glass, anything with a shiny, glossy surface. I use card and canvas too occasionally but I don't get such a good effect. I'll pour the paint on or sometimes spray it using cans of spray paint, then I'll use my fingers to get the effects I need. I'll dip my fingers in different colours, spread it across the painting. Mostly I'll do landscapes that way, sometimes I'll do portraits of people, but lately Gabe has asked if I can do Christmas-themed pieces. I can go back to landscapes in the spring. I love it, the feel of the paint on my fingers, the different effects I can get with my nails, or the pad or side of my fingers.'

He smiled as she talked, he loved how passionate she was about it. Her whole face came to life when she spoke about her art.

'Sounds wonderful. I'd love to see it.'

'I'm sure it's not your thing at all.'

He felt a bit annoyed by that. 'You know nothing about me, you have no idea what my thing is.'

'So, tell me, Hero, what *is* your thing? Are you a guest at the hotel and you just fancied playing rescuer to the little old lady?'

'I'm the assistant manager.'

Ivy stared at him. 'You're the assistant manager here. How come we've never met? Didn't think it was important enough to meet the common folk in the village then?'

'Good God, you're arsey. On second thoughts go to sleep, please. I might get some peace and quiet for a while.'

Ivy fell silent for a few moments. 'I'm sorry.'

'It's OK.' He didn't really mind; if he'd been trapped under a pony in the freezing cold for several hours, he wouldn't be in the best of moods either.

'No, it isn't. You're sitting in a freezing, muddy ditch with me, trying to keep me warm and awake. You're being really nice and I'm being a complete bitch.'

'You're not being a complete bitch. . . Maybe half a bitch.'

She laughed, running her fingers absently through the pony's fur. The pony seemed to be sleeping now, loud snores were coming from it.

'My ex-husband is getting married today,' she said, quietly.

'Ah, that has to hurt.'

'I don't have any feelings for him. I don't love him any more, he was a complete arse but. . .'

'It feels like you've been replaced, or like he has moved on with his life whereas your life has stood still,' Adam said.

Ivy stared back at him. 'It's exactly that.'

Adam nodded. 'I was never married but I've been in your shoes.'

'There was a group of us – his friends and their wives – and since we started divorce proceedings four of them have had children. I lived in a tiny bedsit in London for six months, barely going out. They all carried on going on holiday together, meeting up. Everyone has moved on with their lives.' She sighed. 'She's pregnant, Callum's new bride. Our divorce was finalised six months ago and he's found a new wife and got her pregnant already.'

'You guys never had kids?'

Pain briefly crossed her face and Adam guessed this was a sore point too. 'I'm sorry.'

'No, it's OK. We didn't have children.'

She didn't elaborate or give any more details and he knew when not to push.

'What about you?' She quickly diverted the subject but that was not something he was particularly comfortable talking about either.

'My relationship was a very long time ago.'

He hoped that would be the end of it. She must have sensed he didn't want to talk about it as she was silent for a few minutes.

'I don't even know your name.'

'Adam Douglas. I'm on secondment from a hotel in London, I'm just here for a few months to help Neve out with the opening. I only arrived on Wednesday, which is why you haven't seen me. I did come down to the village the other day to introduce myself to everyone, but one of the guests fell over and I had to help her back to the hotel before I had a chance to meet everyone. I'm sorry you got missed.'

'I'm sorry too.'

He looked down at her and she stared up at him, her pretty grey eyes unwavering. Something lurched inside his chest.

Suddenly he could hear shouts and he knew the cavalry had arrived.

Adam stood up and whistled loudly to attract their attention. He grabbed his walkie-talkie.

'Head for the cluster of ponies, we're over there, about a hundred yards from the road.'

'OK, we're coming,' Gabe said.

'Well, it was nice meeting you,' Ivy said. 'You can get back to your very important job of being an assistant manager again now. Sorry to interrupt your day.'

'Best interruption I've had since I arrived here. Besides, I'm looking forward to you paying me back.'

She stared at him in shock and he laughed.

'You said you were going to make me a cake.'

She smiled. 'I said I might.'

Just then Gabe and Pip arrived at the top of the ditch.

'Hey Ivy, are you OK?' asked Gabe.

'Yes, I'm fine, thanks, just a bit cold.'

'We'll have you out in just a moment.'

Audrey, a pretty redhead who lived in the village, appeared at the top of the ditch. Luke stepped up beside her. He looked very concerned, though Adam knew he was probably more worried about the pony than Ivy.

'You all right, pet?' Audrey asked.

Ivy nodded.

Adam could hear the sound of large machinery getting closer and a moment later the large JCB they used for shovelling snow appeared at the edge of the ditch too.

'Right, let's get some rope around the pony and we can lift it off,' Gabe said.

'I want some rope around Ivy too,' Adam said. 'As soon as we can I want to pull her out of the hole. The pony might get scared once we start to lift it and might kick out. I want Ivy out of there before that happens.'

'Agreed,' Gabe said.

They attached two ropes to the shovel part of the JCB and passed the other ends down to Adam. He slid them underneath the pony.

'Can you reach under the pony, see if you can grab the ropes?' Adam said to Ivy.

She put her hands under the pony's belly and, after a bit of fumbling around in the mud on both their parts, she managed to grab the ropes off him.

The pony suddenly woke up and started shifting around. Adam leaned over it, putting all his weight on top to try to prevent it from struggling, talking soothingly to get it to calm down.

'Get me some more rope for Ivy,' Adam called, frantically. They had to get Ivy out of there soon.

They threw another rope down and Adam leaned over the pony to tie it under Ivy's arms, then he passed both ends back up to Luke.

'Here, help me out,' Adam called up to Luke.

Luke grabbed his hand and, with one swift yank, pulled Adam out of the ditch. The man was huge and he no doubt could scoop the pony up as easy as scooping up a baby. They probably didn't need a JCB after all.

Luke took one end of the rope tied to Ivy and Adam took the other.

Adam called across to the driver. 'Just lift the pony a little bit, we need to get Ivy out first.'

The driver nodded and raised the shovel a little, shifting the pony just a few inches. As soon as they could, Luke and Adam tugged on the rope holding Ivy and she slithered out the ditch.

Adam scooped her up and carried her a few metres away from the ditch and the possible threat of kicking legs while Luke and a few others took over getting the poor pony out of the hole safely.

He laid her carefully on the ground. 'Are you OK?'

'I'm fine, thank you.' Ivy struggled to get up and Adam helped her, but as soon as she was standing up, she slumped against him and he quickly caught her.

'Sorry, my legs and feet are just a bit numb. I'll be OK in a minute.'

'Look, the hotel isn't far. Why don't I take you back there and you can have a shower and warm up?'

She nodded and he was gratified that she wasn't going to argue against it. She seemed fine and probably didn't need a doctor but he would feel better once she was indoors and warm again.

Gabe came running over to see if Ivy was OK. Adam quickly explained his plan and Gabe suggested they take the snowmobile that someone had used to get there.

Adam helped Ivy back towards the snowmobile and helped her on. She was a lot shorter than he was and very petite, like a little doll with bags of attitude. He sat behind her, bracketing her arms with his as he held onto the handles and took off towards the hotel.

When they got there, Adam helped her off the snowmobile but when she seemed unsteady on her feet, he scooped her up again.

'I do not need to be carried like a baby,' Ivy protested.

Adam sighed and put her down and supported her by holding her arm instead. They walked into the reception area and up the two flights of stairs to his temporary bedroom directly above his office. Gabe had promised him use of one of the lodges after

Christmas but for now he had a bed and his own bathroom and he was happy with that.

He left her standing in the bedroom and went into the bathroom, turning the shower on so the water was warm, not hot. Then he walked back out and found her exactly where he'd left her, still shivering like crazy.

'I've got the temperature of the shower turned down low, you need to turn it up slowly. It's not good for your body to go from extreme cold to extreme hot very quickly. When you're used to the warm, you can turn it up slightly then. I'll put out some clean clothes for you and send some food up. I'll be downstairs in my office if you need me, it's the first door on the left.'

'I might need some help getting out of these clothes, my fingers are numb.'

Adam's feet were welded to the floor. She was incredibly pretty and there was something about her that he felt drawn to, but there was also a vulnerability that she was determined to keep hidden and it felt like he'd be taking advantage of her to undress her, despite the circumstances.

He swallowed. 'I'll send one of the girls who work here up to help you, I don't think it would be appropriate for me to—'

'Adam, it's just a body. I'm sure you've seen lots of naked women in your time, and I've been poked, prodded and examined by so many doctors over the years that I'm certainly not embarrassed by being seen naked any more. I'm freezing, will you please help me? You can keep your eyes closed if you are that repulsed by me.'

Adam quickly moved in front of her and started to undress her.

'Believe me, being repulsed by you is not the problem here,' he muttered.

He pulled her t-shirt off and swallowed down the groan when he briefly saw the black lacy bra, edged with pink ribbon, before he looked away.

Adam pulled down her tracksuit bottoms, feeling like he was some kind of pervert as he knew he shouldn't be enjoying this. When he revealed matching black knickers and a sparkly belly button stud shaped like a snowflake he knew it would be a while before he forgot that wonderful image. Away from the horse and all that mud there was an amazing scent to her, a tangy sweetness of clementines.

He didn't think it was necessary to take her underwear off too, so he guided her into the bathroom and waited until she was under the shower. She started rubbing her body, trying to get warm, and he watched her for a moment. When he spoke, he knew his voice was strangled. 'Can I help you with anything else?'

She turned to look at him, flashing him a brilliant smile. 'Are you offering to scrub my back for me?'

'No, of course not,' he lied, wondering if she would need help with any other body parts too.

'I think I've got it covered.'

Adam quickly left the bathroom and got changed. He laid out some clean clothes for her on his bed and then went back downstairs to his office. He closed the door, sat down at his desk and let his head fall into his hands.

Getting involved with someone here was not part of his plan. He was here for three months and then he would be going back to the bright lights and prestige of working as deputy manager in one of the best hotels in London. Getting involved with anyone, anywhere, was not part of his plan at all. But Ivy lived and worked down in the village and he worked up here in the hotel. It would be quite easy to avoid her. So why did he feel disappointed by that fact?

CHAPTER 4

So much for holding back. Oakley was stretched out the length of the sofa and Neve was lying on his chest as he played with her hair. She didn't have any recollection of getting into this position, they had been too busy talking for her to notice, but he had clearly used his superhero powers and arranged it by stealth. Right now, in their little bubble of pretending that everything was fine between them, she couldn't be happier so she was disappointed when there was a knock on the door.

'Just pretend we're not here,' Oakley whispered, theatrically, and she laughed as she got up.

She opened the door to find her brother Gabe and his girlfriend Pip standing on top of the steps. They were holding hands and Neve couldn't help but smile at how sweet they looked together, despite only really being together for a little over a week.

'Is Oakley still here?' Pip whispered and Neve nodded, knowing the man himself was only a few feet away and could probably hear what was being said. 'We didn't want to interrupt but we just wanted to make sure you're OK.'

Neve smiled and reached out to take Pip's hand. She had missed her so much while she had been away and now Pip was back for good, Neve was looking forward to rekindling the sisterly relationship they'd had before. She lowered her voice. 'I'm fine, thank you. I don't know what the future holds for us but right now I'm actually really happy he's here. You don't need to worry.'

'If you would prefer that he stayed in the village we can put him in one of the spare lodges down there,' Gabe said.

She shook her head. 'That's not necessary, me and Oakley have a lot to talk about and we're not going to be able to do that if he's all the way down in the village. I appreciate your concern, but I promise you we're fine.'

Both Gabe and Pip's eyes lifted upwards and Neve knew Oakley had come to stand behind her. He moved to her side, a huge smile on his face as he slung an arm around her shoulders in a sign of togetherness that they hadn't quite reached yet.

'Hello, we didn't properly meet before. I'm Oakley,' he said, offering out a hand to Pip.

'Pleased to meet you, I'm Pip.' She shook his hand.

Oakley's eyes glanced down to Gabe and Pip's joined hands and he smiled too. 'Do you work in the hotel?'

'Pip is our official photographer, she has an incredible talent,' Neve said, warmly.

'Oh that's cool, I can never take a decent photo. Mine are always blurred or have a big finger across the middle of it. You'll have to show me some of the photos you've taken of this place. It looked great when I flew over the top of it.'

'I'd be happy to show you, *if* you're still here after Christmas,' Pip said, pointedly.

Neve suppressed a smile at the sudden protective streak from her. Growing up, it had always been Neve who had looked after Pip.

'Well, we just wanted to make sure you were both OK,' Gabe said, awkwardly. 'You know where we are if you need us. Will you both be coming to Christmas lunch tomorrow? We're having it in my house and then we can do presents and games afterwards. The whole family will be there.'

'Of course, we wouldn't miss it for the world,' Oakley said.

Gabe smiled. 'OK, well, we'll see you tomorrow, around one.'

He flashed another look of concern at Neve and she smiled at him reassuringly as they turned to leave. She closed the door and turned to face Oakley.

'Gabe got a new girlfriend?'

'An old girlfriend, to be precise. Pip was Gabe's first love. We all grew up together and I adored her. Then a horrible accident and a terrible misunderstanding led to Pip running away. They met up again for the first time about a week ago and fell in love all over again. She's so good for him, she makes him so happy. She's great with Wren too. I think this is forever for Gabe. I imagine they'll get married really quickly and Wren will probably want to wear an Elsa dress if she's bridesmaid.'

Oakley laughed. 'I'm happy for him. And if they can get back together and fall in love again after all those years apart, maybe there's still hope for us.'

He threw himself down on the sofa, stretching out along the full length of it, and indicated to her to resume where she had been lying before they were interrupted.

'You need to see her photos, the ones of Stardust Lake Hotel are incredible,' Neve stalled. Now their little bubble had burst, she wasn't sure if she should lie with him again when they were supposed to just be friends.

'Maybe you can show me around and I can see the resort for myself,' Oakley said, snagging her hand and pulling her gently towards the sofa.

She was slightly annoyed at how little resistance she put up as she lay down on top of him again.

'I'm going to be busy over the next few days with the preparations for the New Year's Eve ball.'

'A ball?'

'Don't worry, I won't ask you to dance with me. I know that isn't really your thing.'

'I'd love to dance with you, Freckle. I'm not very good at it, but I promise you I'll dance with you at the ball.'

'It's a masked ball.'

'If I'd known you were having one of those, I would have brought my superhero mask.'

Neve laughed. 'I don't think that's the kind of mask we imagined when we came up with the event, though I suspect some of the kids will be wearing Batman masks.'

'Now that is something I definitely want to see. And I totally understand if you're busy, I don't want to get in the way of your work. I can certainly show myself around.'

'I can take some time to show you around. We can take the horses out, I'm sure they would appreciate the run.'

'You have Shadow and Knight here? I might have known you would never leave them in London.'

'I couldn't. I never rode them enough when I was in London, I was hoping that might change now I have somewhere beautiful to ride them. Gabe wants to offer horse rides in the summer, so I'll be taking small groups out when the other horses arrive.'

Oakley smiled fondly at her. 'I bet you'll love that. Horses have always been such a big part of your life.'

'I love them. I can't ever imagine not having one.'

'What about your job? Are you happy here? You always wanted to work with horses, do you think you will stay working for Gabe for the foreseeable future?'

Neve hesitated before she spoke. It was true that she couldn't say she truly loved her job. She was good at it and there was something almost comforting about going to work and knowing what was expected of her and how to do it. It was only supposed to have been a temporary thing to get her back on her feet, raise enough money to pursue her dreams, but here she was some eight years later, having worked her way up from receptionist to hotel manager with no plans to ever move on.

'You told me that you always wanted to open up your own riding school and offer lessons to disabled children. That was your dream. Do you not see yourself pursuing that one day?' Oakley said. 'I'd hate to see you settle, to drift through life doing something you are good at, that perhaps pays well but isn't something you love.'

'Gabe needs me here.'

'What about what you need?'

Neve smiled. 'Everything is simple in your world, isn't it? If you have a dream, pursue it—'

'And if you love someone, never let them go. Simple rules, but very effective.'

Her breath caught in her throat and he caught her hand, intertwining his fingers with hers.

'What are you afraid of, Freckle?'

For the longest time she didn't answer but she had always been able to talk to Oakley about stuff she had never talked about with anyone else.

'That dream seems tainted somehow.'

'How so?'

'I told you that Zander, my ex, was an Olympian who slept with everything that moved.'

'He broke your heart.'

'He did but he also took that dream from me too.' She played with a stray thread on the sofa. She didn't want him to think less of her because of the mistakes in her past, but she wanted him to know where her fears came from and that she was scared of making the same mistakes again. 'When my grandad died, he left us all a shedload of money. My parents sold their farm, bought a caravan and used their share of the money to travel the world. Gabe invested in hotels, Luke bought a house and I bought my own farm with a plot of land to build the riding school on. My dream was in my grasp. But I was so in love with Zander, well, I thought I was. I was dazzled by him. And his dream of going to the Olympics was in his grasp too but he needed funding, sponsorship. He persuaded me to loan him the money he needed. I took a huge loan out against my house, gave him the money I intended to use to build the riding school. He promised he'd pay it all back.'

Oakley looked furious. 'And he didn't. He betrayed you, took your money, broke your heart and dumped you. No wonder you were so reluctant to get involved with me. But why didn't you tell me this before?'

'I was a fool. And that's not something I wanted anyone to know. I was so young and naïve and so in love, I would have given him the moon. Then I found out he was sleeping with one of the girls on the team. He'd played me and I only realised afterwards that he had only started showing an interest in me after I'd inherited the money. That had been his intention from the start. We broke up and I demanded that he give me my money back but he just stopped taking my calls and refused to see me. In the end I gave up as I just felt so humiliated every time I tried to get in touch. I couldn't afford the loan on my house and had to sell it to pay it back. I ended up with nothing and that's when Gabe gave me a job and somewhere to live. I could have had my dream and I gave it all away.'

'So you just gave up on your dream? You tried once and you didn't succeed so you're not going to try again?'

'It's not as simple as that,' Neve protested.

'Yes, it is. If it's your dream then never let it go, you keep fighting for it. By giving up on your dreams, you're letting Zander win. And that asshole doesn't deserve to win anything. If we ever got back together, I'd never stand in the way of your dreams. I'd help you to realise them.'

Neve smiled. 'I'd never want to stand in the way of your dreams either.'

'See, we're perfect for each other.'

She smiled. He was right, she had been holding back from her dreams for too long. But leaving her job and going after them was going to be easier said than done. She decided to change the subject. 'So, tell me about the movie, how's it been?' she said, as he took her hand.

She watched the smile spread across his face and her heart soared because of it.

'It's been amazing, everything I ever hoped it would be and more. The days are long and it's hard work and sometimes there are hours in between takes. But every day I get up and go to work in Warner Brothers Studios, working with some of the biggest names in movie history. I put on this incredible costume, and sometimes the only thing I'm acting against is a green screen with a football on a stick, but I love it. I count my lucky stars every single day that I'm doing this. I thought I had made it when I was filming on the streets of London for almost a year, but this is a whole other story. I've always wanted this.

'When I was six years old and went to see *Superman* in the cinema, I asked my mum if Superman could really fly. She told me he was an actor, that it was just a film and that the film studios made it look like he could fly. I knew then this was what I wanted to do. I wanted to fly like Superman, fight dragons and travel through time and space. Last week we actually filmed a scene where I flew. It was ridiculous, I had a harness, we did the whole thing in a green studio with a huge fan blowing wind in my hair, and I could not stop smiling the whole time we were shooting it. They had to keep stopping filming because I was grinning so much and I was supposed to be angry. I'm having the time of my life and I never want this journey to end. Getting this job is honestly the second best thing to ever happen to me.'

Neve couldn't help but smile at his enthusiasm and love for his job. 'I'm so happy for you, I couldn't be more excited that you're living your dream. You deserve this success, you've worked so hard to get here. . . Wait, *second best* thing to happen to you? What was the first?'

He grinned. 'Meeting you.'

She laughed. 'Oakley Rey, you're such a charmer.'

'It's true.'

She shook her head, smiling fondly.

The smile faded from his face as he grew serious. 'When I met you, I knew that you were the person I wanted to spend the rest of my life with, the other half of my heart. You *are* the best thing that has ever happened to me. We have to work out some way that we can be together because I can't even begin to think about my life without you in it.'

'I don't want to lose you either but. . .'

He placed his fingers over her lips. 'No buts, Freckle. I promise you we will work this out.'

She rested her head on his chest and closed her eyes as he wrapped his arms around her and held her tight.

Maybe he was right, maybe they could work this out. Right now, she never wanted to let him go.

❉

Ivy swirled the paint across the sheet of glass, creating a Christmas tree with her fingers. It wasn't turning out anywhere near as good as she hoped and she knew that was because of Adam.

She had come to this little island, as far away as she could possibly get from her ex-husband, to get away from life for a while and partly to get away from men. The possibility of having another relationship was not a thought that had entered her head. A relationship would lead only to heartbreak and her feeling like a complete and utter failure. She never wanted to be made to feel like that again. She had been here for a few months before the hotel opened and men hadn't been a problem. Most of the men in the village were either twice her age or happily married and all the men who worked at the hotel had mainly stayed around the hotel so she had enjoyed an almost solitary existence. But now Adam had arrived and her promise to herself not to get involved with anyone was rapidly weakening.

Ivy didn't know what it was about him that had her questioning her 'no men' plan. It wasn't the sweet, protective way he wanted to look after her, she knew that. She didn't need anyone to look after her, she was fine on her own. And it wasn't the way he just laughed off her sarcastic comments, almost as if he saw through her spiky exterior to the person she was underneath. She didn't like that person – she was too soft and likely to get hurt and the only way to ensure that didn't happen was to push people away – but Adam had seemed unfazed. It wasn't the way he had seemed genuinely interested in her painting either. She painted for herself, because she could get lost in the sensations and the creativity of making something with her hands. If she made money from it that was great, but she didn't do it for anyone else's approval.

Ivy sighed as she added a swirl of gold to the glass. She was all alone in her little workshop and she was lying to herself.

She hadn't seen Adam since he'd left her in the shower and it bothered her more than it should. She had stood under the shower for ages, until her body was warm and the pins and needles had faded completely. Afterwards she had dressed in the clothes he had laid out for her, eaten the food one of the porters had brought up for her and still he hadn't returned.

Eventually she had wandered down to his office, but the door was closed and she had heard him talking on the phone so she'd left him to it. She'd gone back to her lodge, after checking in with Deborah from the chocolate shop next door, and slept a little while and then reopened her shop for the evening crowd but still there had been no sign of him. But then why would he come to see her? He had done his job as assistant manager, he'd joined the search party and got her out of the ditch. What possible reason would he have for coming by? He had a hotel to run and it was Christmas Eve, he probably had far more important things to do.

It was getting late now and as her painting didn't remotely resemble a Christmas tree, she decided to wipe the glass clean and go to bed.

The wind chime near the front door suddenly tinkled, indicating that it had been opened. She always meant to lock the door once the shop was closed but she never remembered. In that sense she was too relaxed for her own good and one day it was going to come back to bite her.

Ivy peered round the doorway leading from her workshop into the main shop and couldn't help the grin from spreading on her face. Adam was standing there, looking insanely sexy, dressed in a thick black winter coat and jeans that showed off his broad thighs.

As he closed the door behind him and walked towards her, she couldn't decide if her relaxed attitude to keeping her door locked had finally come back to bite her or all her Christmases had come at once.

❆

'I was just passing,' Adam said, knowing it was a terrible excuse and knowing she knew it too. He just wanted to see her. Though judging by the huge smile on her face she clearly didn't mind the impromptu visit. 'Thought I'd see if you'd made me that cake yet.'

She laughed, loudly, and he loved the sound of it.

'Not yet, I think you've had a wasted trip.'

Adam shook his head, not taking his eyes off hers for a second. 'I got to see you so it definitely wasn't a wasted trip.'

Her smile faltered a little and he decided then and there he wasn't going to play games with her. He took a step closer, relishing in her sweet, clementine scent.

'I got caught up with work and when I came up to see if you were OK, you'd gone. I've been thinking about you all afternoon.'

Her eyes widened with surprise. 'I've been thinking about you too.'

She clapped her hand over her mouth, clearly shocked that she had been so honest with him.

'I just wanted to make sure you were OK.'

She swallowed. 'I'm fine.'

Ivy looked down at the paint on her hands and peeled off some of the dried bits. It seemed he made her nervous and he didn't know whether to be delighted or saddened by that fact. He stepped back a little. 'You're in the middle of painting, it looks incredible. Can I watch you finish it?'

She waved her hands, dismissively. 'This is awful, I've been too distracted to do anything decent. I don't suppose your presence here will make things any better, but you can watch me attempt to rescue it if you're really interested.'

He smiled. 'If this is bad, then I can't wait to see the good stuff. It looks amazing: the shadowing on the branches, the way the baubles stand out so much – you have a real skill here.'

'Those are some of my better ones.' Ivy gestured to a row of paintings stacked up against the wall. Some of them were snowflakes, some were ponies in the snow, others were of the ice palace or the reindeer. They were all detailed and beautiful pieces. 'Those aren't for sale though, they're all Christmas gifts for the villagers. I was going to take them round tomorrow.'

'That's very kind, they must have taken you ages to do.'

She shrugged. 'They've all been so welcoming, looking out for me, inviting me for dinner. I wanted to do something to repay them.'

She turned her attention back to the painting in her hand. He watched as she danced her fingers across the glass, sometimes using her nails, sometimes bending her finger and using the pointy parts of her joints and ligaments. Her fingers moved so quickly, as if she instinctively knew which parts of her hand to use to get the different results. She dabbed her fingers in different colours and swirled and twisted the patterns across the glass until the tree gleamed with trails of gold, ruby and silver. It looked so real he wanted to reach out and touch it. In a matter of minutes she had produced something that the best artists in the world would take weeks or months to create. She had a rare and beautiful talent.

She stepped back to admire her work and pulled a face. 'Not one of my best, you can have it if you want.'

'It's perfect, I would love to have it.'

She handed it to him and he held it reverentially, twisting it so that it caught the light.

'Thank you, doesn't mean you can get out of making me a cake though.'

She laughed. 'Why don't you come upstairs with me to the kitchen and I'll make a cake while you wait? Then all my debts are paid.'

Adam stared down at the glass for a moment. He didn't want her to feel obligated to make a cake for him, especially this late at night – he wasn't even that keen on cake – but if it meant that he got to spend more time with her then that was definitely a good thing.

'I want a chocolate cake,' he said, trying to keep the smirk off his face. 'With *three* layers.'

She laughed loudly. 'Coming right up.'

CHAPTER 5

Neve stood in her bathroom and leaned her forehead against the door. She and Oakley had talked all day and all night. They had ordered more food, neither of them willing to leave the little bubble they had made for themselves. And now, on the other side of the door, Oakley was waiting for her in her bed.

There had been no suggestion from either of them that he should sleep on the sofa. She had announced she was going to bed and he'd gotten up and followed her up the stairs as if it was the most normal thing in the world. What on earth was she thinking?

She usually slept naked but she had to put the brakes on this somehow. Walking out there with no clothes on and getting into bed with him was just handing herself to him on a plate.

She glanced around the bathroom and saw Oakley's shirt lying over the chair where he had discarded it to have a quick wash. Slipping it on, she relished the wonderful smell of him. She wrapped her robe over the top. Feeling a little less vulnerable, she opened the door, walked out into the bedroom and froze.

Oakley was sitting up in bed waiting for her, naked from the waist up. The duvet was covering his legs and hips so she couldn't tell if he was wearing anything at all. He looked divine though. He'd clearly been working out for his new superhero role and the muscles on his arms, chest and stomach were toned and well defined. She couldn't help but smile at his mischievous grin.

'Are you wearing any clothes under that duvet?'

'You know I always sleep naked, Freckle,' he said, innocently. 'You know I get too hot otherwise. You normally sleep naked too.'

'Well, one of us has to be sensible. We're supposed to just be friends, remember.'

She dumped her robe and felt Oakley's eyes appraise her in his shirt.

'Where's the fun in that?' he said as he lifted the duvet slightly for her. She climbed in next to him and briefly saw a flash of his legs, showing he was indeed completely naked and, by the looks of things, ready for action.

She laughed. 'You promised nothing would happen.'

'I didn't promise that I wouldn't be turned on by the prospect of sharing a bed with my beautiful girl. And I didn't promise nothing would happen, just that I'd be a perfect gentleman and we could be friends. We can be friends who make love, I'd be happy with that arrangement if you are.'

Neve giggled. 'I bet you would.'

She lay on her back as she stared up at the ceiling. It felt so good to be lying here with him, just like they used to. She was having a hard time remembering why she was resisting him. He was here for one week and she was kidding herself if she thought that she could lie in bed next to him for that length of time and not let anything happen between them. And as he was only here for a week, shouldn't she be grabbing him and making the most of it now? But nothing had changed, she had to remember that. For all of Oakley's requests to pretend that this problem didn't lie between them, it did and to go back to making love and being together would just make everything harder when he left again in a week's time. And what if they got back together, when would she see him next? How much time could she realistically take off from work to go and visit him? Would flying to see her every spare chance he got grow tiresome or distract him from his job? Could she really trust him to turn down the advances of all those pretty women when he was apart from her for months on end? And what about the secret she promised she would tell him? That would change everything.

She rolled onto her side and switched out the light. 'Goodnight, Oakley.'

He was silent for a moment before she heard him shifting around in bed behind her. She felt his warmth cocoon her as he lay on his side directly behind her. He leaned forward slightly and kissed her shoulder.

'Is this code for you wanting me to spoon you? Because we both know how much you love that sexual position.'

She couldn't help it, she burst out laughing. 'Goodnight, Oakley,' she said, more firmly this time.

She felt him shrug. 'OK, well, just let me know. I'm here all week.'

He rested his hand on her hip for a moment and then slid his hand round to her stomach, pulling her against him, so her back was against his chest. Her breath stalled. As his breathing became heavy, his hand stayed over her belly and it brought tears to her eyes. In a perfect world, this was how it would be. Lying next to each other every night, cuddled up close, his hand protectively over his unborn child as slowly it grew bigger and stronger. She wanted this more than anything. She had a new dream now and she was going to fight for this one.

❆

Ivy stood in her kitchen as she threw ingredients into the blender. Her heart was racing at having Adam here. He scared her and attracted her in equal measure. She didn't want to get involved in a relationship but that didn't stop her heart from wanting the complete opposite. He smelt so good. Even with him leaning against the unit on the opposite side of the kitchen, she could smell this scent that reminded her of fresh rain-soaked grass and the sweetness of toffee. He was talking to her about the plans for the New Year's Eve ball and the plans for the hotel in the coming year and she was impressed that, although he was only there for a few months, he was still taking his position very seriously, not just killing time.

She threw the eggs, flour and milk into the blender on top of the creamed butter and sugar, put the lid back on and fired up the blender to mix them all into a light creamy batter.

She opened the lid and took the melted chocolate off the stove, pouring it into the batter.

Adam came up behind her to inspect what she was doing and her heart danced in her chest.

'Smells delicious,' he murmured, his warm breath on her neck making her heart go into a gallop. Why did he have such an effect on her? He made her laugh and it had been a long time since she had found anything to make her smile. He was sexy and good-looking and charming, but she had been the victim of a charming man before and that had ended badly. She refused to let herself get hurt again. But he'd been hurt too and there was something about him that made her want to trust him.

She flicked the blender on and squealed as she belatedly realised that she hadn't put the lid back on. Thick gooey chocolatey batter splattered across the room, all over her and Adam. The mixture hit her in the face and she quickly turned the blender off.

Silence descended over the room, the only sound the noise of the cake batter dripping off the cupboards and onto the unit tops. Ivy didn't dare turn round to look at Adam, who hadn't said a word. She wiped her face and then slowly turned around.

He was staring down at himself aghast. It was all over his face and clothes.

She reached up and wiped a finger through the chocolatey mess on his cheek, then popped the finger in her mouth and sucked off the mixture.

'Tastes delicious too.'

He smirked and the smirk quickly turned into a loud laugh, deep and masculine, and as he continued to laugh, she couldn't help laughing too.

He moved closer to her and removed a chunk of batter from her forehead before putting it in his mouth.

'Mmm, it does taste good,' he said, his eyes on her as he sucked it from his fingers. He suddenly bent his head and kissed the side of her temple, gently sucking the mixture into his mouth. 'Tastes *very* good.'

All humour had gone from his voice now and Ivy couldn't remember how to breathe as he trailed his mouth down the side of her cheek, kissing the chocolate batter off her skin. He reached the corner of her mouth and kissed her softly there. He paused for a moment, waiting for any kind of reaction from her, waiting for her to stop him but she couldn't.

He kissed her gently on the mouth, his hands moving to her waist. She tentatively kissed him back, tasting the chocolate on his lips, and as she let out a soft involuntary moan, he slid his tongue inside, tasting her too.

His kisses were so soft and so not what she was expecting from him. He was taking his time, being really gentle with her as if she was someone to be cherished. She had never been kissed like that.

He pulled back slightly and leaned his forehead against hers. His eyes were closed and he was breathing heavily.

For a moment, a wonderful, blissful moment, she felt contented and happier than she had felt for a long time. She had only just met this man but everything about the kiss had seemed so perfect, so right. But that peace didn't last long. A few seconds later all her fears and doubts slammed back into her brain.

She put her hands against his chest and attempted to push him away, though he held onto her. He opened his eyes, studying her carefully, completely unfazed by her reaction.

'I don't want a relationship,' she blurted out.

He didn't bat an eye. 'Neither do I.'

'I've just come out of a messy divorce.'

'I know.'

'You leave in three months.'

'True again.'

'So what was this?'

He shrugged and kissed her softly on the forehead. 'A Christmas kiss.' He stepped back. 'Let me help you clean this mess up.'

'No, please, don't,' Ivy said, quickly rebuilding the wall that he had just knocked down. She needed some space from him now.

'OK.' He moved to the sink, quickly washed his face and hands and then moved to the stairs. 'It's Christmas Day tomorrow, do you have any plans?'

She shook her head. 'Deborah or someone will probably invite me round for lunch.'

'Our chef will be putting on a huge Christmas banquet. I thought the villagers had all been invited.'

'I was, but...'

'Being on your own seemed a better idea. I get that. You could join me, I'll be eating at twelve o'clock. We can sit in the corner and ignore everyone else. As assistant manager, I don't think I can get out of it.'

'I'll think about it.'

He smiled. 'Don't think too hard. It's just lunch after all.'

She couldn't help but smile too. 'OK. I'll bring the leftover cake.'

He grinned. 'I'll look forward to it.'

He waved goodbye and left and Ivy let go of the breath she had been holding.

What was she doing?

❄

Adam stepped out onto the street and looked up at the cranberry sky, the Northern Lights dancing and flickering across the darkness. It was rare that the aurora was this colour and he wanted to run back inside and drag Ivy out to see it but he knew that she needed some space from him. That kiss had surprised them both.

No one was out to see the show from the Merry Dancers and somehow it made it all the more special.

The front door of the lodge opposite suddenly opened and Luke came out from Audrey's house.

He watched Luke give Audrey a hug and then step out onto the street.

That was an interesting partnership. Luke was so closed-off and Audrey had seemed so bubbly when he'd met her a few days before. But Audrey had been there with Luke today, helping him with the pony, so it seemed they were friends at least.

Luke started walking back to the hotel and jumped slightly when Adam stepped out from the shadows and fell into step beside him.

'Great show tonight.' Adam gestured to the sky and Luke looked up as if seeing it for the first time. 'Red is a foretelling of love apparently.'

Luke looked back over his shoulder at Audrey, who was watching him leave and then turned back to Adam. 'Did you come from Ivy's house?' he asked, pointedly and deliberately changing the subject away from him and Audrey. 'I saw you two at the ditch today.'

'What did you see?'

'You, her, together,' Luke said.

'There was no together.'

'The red Merry Dancers seem to think otherwise. It's a bit late for you to pop by for a cuppa.'

'I could say the same about you and Audrey.'

'We're friends.'

Adam sighed. He had no idea how to define what he had with Ivy. They seemed to have bypassed the friend stage completely. 'It's silly, anyway, to allocate meaning to a colour in the sky. Love has nothing to do with it.'

'Exactly,' Luke said as he looked back over his shoulder again and Adam found himself looking back at Ivy's house too.

'It's never easy, is it?' Adam muttered.

Luke shook his head. 'I wish it was.'

CHAPTER 6

Oakley woke up as the clock downstairs softly chimed midnight. The room was lit with the silvery glow of the moon and a soft red glow from the sky and for a second he looked around the room in confusion before he realised where he was, at Stardust Lake Hotel with his beautiful girl in his arms. As he snuggled in closer to her, his heart leapt as he realised it was Christmas Day. Today was the day he was going to put his plans in motion and, though he had talked himself in and out of this on the long flight over from the States, after spending the day with Neve and talking to her, he now had more confidence in it and he suddenly didn't want to wait any more.

He nuzzled into Neve's neck and kissed her. She stirred in his arms, though she didn't open her eyes.

'Wake up, Freckle, it's Christmas Day.'

She groaned and rolled onto her back to face him. 'What time is it?' she asked, sleepily.

'About a minute after midnight.'

She giggled and reached up to stroke the stubble on his jaw. 'God, I love you.'

He froze, his heart leaping into his mouth. She had told him she loved him before. They'd been together for ten months and the 'love' word had come up very early. He'd thought they were forever and then she'd broken up with him. He wasn't sure if the reasons she'd given about her breaking up with him because of his career were the real reasons or whether there was something more behind the break-up. He had feared that maybe she just didn't see a future for them any more. The fact that she still loved him made his heart soar.

She realised what she just said and her smile faltered. But he wasn't going to let her talk her way out of it.

'You love me?'

She swallowed and then wrapped her hands round his neck. 'I always have, always will.'

He needed no further words of encouragement as he bent his head to kiss her. Her lips were soft and pliant as he pressed his mouth to hers. Her mouth opened slightly, letting out a breathy moan, and he slid his tongue inside, tasting and devouring her. The taste of her was sublime, sweet and tangy and something he knew he would never get enough of. He ran his hands through her silky black hair. She moaned again, her kisses urgent and needful.

He moved on top of her, kneeling either side of her, and started to undo the buttons on the shirt she was wearing. He felt sure she would stop him any second so he was surprised that when he'd undone the last button she shrugged out of the shirt desperately and then slid her hands over his back.

'God, Oakley, you've got so big.'

He leaned back so he could look at her and frowned with concern. 'You've lost weight.'

She did look thinner, though her breasts looked somehow bigger and her belly softer and slightly more rounded. He ran his hand over it and her breath hitched. She caught his chin and tugged him back to her mouth. He kissed her again, running his hand over her breast, and she gasped against his lips.

He lay down carefully on top of her, taking his weight on his forearms but needing to feel her skin against his as he kissed her.

She was so soft, so warm, her skin velvety smooth. He needed her now.

'Oakley, please.'

'Condoms,' he muttered, tearing his mouth from hers as clarity pierced the fog of desire in his brain. 'I have them in my bag.'

He quickly climbed off the bed and rummaged in the bag until he found them. He threw the box onto the bedside table, snagging one from the box and quickly rolling it on.

'Don't want me getting pregnant, do you?' Neve said and he wasn't sure but there seemed a note of bitterness in her voice.

He kissed her as he manoeuvred himself on top of her. 'One day, Freckle. You are going to look so beautiful, carrying our baby inside you. You can come on set with me and in between takes I will give you massages and rub your feet and rub baby oil into your gorgeous bump. But let's leave that a few years, shall we? I'd like to get a ring on your finger first and marry you and take you on a year-long honeymoon as soon as filming is finished. We'd take a boat and explore the world, just me, you and the stars. And then we'd come back to our house and after a few more years of making love to you every morning and night, when I'm a bit older and hopefully wiser, we could have a baby or maybe five babies – hell, a whole football team of little sprogs.'

'You have it all planned out.'

'I have lots of plans when it comes to you.'

'Babies don't come to order.'

He kissed her and smiled. 'I don't think we need to worry about any of that just yet.'

He trailed his tongue from her belly button up to her collarbone and any other words about babies or any possible reservations about making love to him were lost in a strangled noise in her throat.

He leaned over her and she wrapped her legs around his hips, urging him closer. He slid carefully inside her, a groan bursting from his throat as he kissed her. Her hands clutched at his back as he moved against her, writhing underneath him.

He pulled back slightly so he could look at her.

'I can't wait to take that step in our relationship but give me a few more years first.'

She looked sad at this and he kissed her on the forehead.

'I love you, Freckle.'

The sadness in her eyes vanished completely. 'I love you too.'

'That's all we need. The rest we can work out along the way, I promise you that.'

She kissed him, sliding her tongue inside his mouth, urging him on with her long legs. He moved against her and as she clung to him, he knew he was right. Whatever would come their way, they would find a way through it all so they could be together.

❄

Ivy stepped out of her lodge onto the street, with her bag half-filled with the Christmas paintings she had made for the other villagers. Snow covered the street in a sparkly blanket, tiny flurries falling through the air, catching the light of the early Christmas Day sun. The lodges were all quiet and still; no tourists would be coming down today. It looked so pretty and peaceful and Ivy couldn't help but smile, though she knew Adam was partly responsible for the grin on her face. She had no idea what was going to happen between them, but for now she wasn't going to worry about it. Live for the moment. She was going to have Christmas Day lunch with a lovely man and she would just enjoy that and not worry about what the future held. Nervous and excited, she was enjoying having that flutter of butterflies again. The sensible part of her brain was trying to tell her it wouldn't be that simple. There were issues that had to be sorted out before she could think about starting a relationship with Adam but her happy heart was in charge today and for once she was going to take a day off from worrying that she could never have a normal relationship again.

She took a deep breath and walked to the end of the street. She'd get the hardest visit over with first. Though the village was predominantly made up of a much older generation, there were a few middle-aged couples with teenage kids and then her, Audrey, Antoine, Joy and Finn representing the 'young uns' as Deborah called them. She knocked on Joy and Finn's door. They were a happily married couple with a daughter of five years old and another baby on its way. Rebecca, their daughter, would have been up for hours and had probably opened all of her presents already.

Finn came to the door and smiled when he saw her. 'I thought you were one of the tourists then, I was going to tell you to clear off,' he said, opening the door for her so she could come in. 'Happy Christmas, Ivy. Go through, Joy will be delighted to see you. Rebecca has her playing with My Little Pony at the moment, so I'm sure she will be thankful of the reprieve.'

'I've just come to give you both a Christmas gift, I won't stay long,' Ivy said, stepping inside and keeping the smile fixed on her face.

She walked into the lounge area at the back of the shop and watched a heavily pregnant Joy playing with her daughter. The burning ball of emotion clogged her throat and jealousy slammed into her gut. She would never have that.

Joy looked up at her and her face broke into a huge smile at seeing her. She heaved herself up and waddled over to give Ivy a big hug. Guilt sliced through Ivy's emotions. Joy was so sweet and friendly and Ivy hated that she would often actively avoid visiting the couple because of the emotions it always stirred up in her. Ivy hugged her back, closing her eyes against the wide-eyed Rebecca, who was sitting on the floor behind Joy, watching them.

'Happy Christmas, Ivy,' Joy said, squeezing her tight.

'Happy Christmas. How are you feeling?' Ivy pulled back and forced herself to look at the large pregnant belly between them.

'Ready to pop at any second and I've still got a month until my due date.'

'Well, I hope you're taking it easy and Finn is looking after you.'

Joy grinned. 'He does everything for me, I barely have to lift a finger. I'm so glad you're OK. I heard about what happened with the pony yesterday.'

'Oh, I'm fine. I was more cold than anything else.'

'And Adam was there to rescue you. He seems nice,' Joy added, casually.

'He is.' Ivy left it at that; she certainly didn't want to talk about her tentative relationship with Adam, if she could even call it that.

Joy smiled and clearly decided to let the subject drop. 'Did you want to stop for lunch? Finn has cooked so much food.'

'No, I'm fine, really. I just came round to give you a present. I have loads of other presents to deliver this morning, so I won't keep you.'

Ivy delved in her bag and pulled out a large parcel marked with their names on the gift tag.

'Is this one of your paintings? You know how much I adore them.' Joy ripped the paper off and held the painting up to the light. It was of a couple, carrying a small child and a baby. Joy was a woodcarver and she had many such pieces in her shop of faceless couples and families with elongated bodies and limbs entwined and Ivy had used Joy's work as inspiration for this painting. 'Oh Ivy, I love it! I made you something too, though I haven't wrapped it.'

Joy moved to the drawers on the side of the room and grabbed a carving and brought it back. It was a small, incredibly detailed carving of the Golden Gate Bridge. 'I saw the photo of the bridge in your house, so I figured it must be special to you.'

'Thank you, it's perfect. The Golden Gate Bridge is somewhere I really want to visit one day, it's a reminder of dreams not yet realised,' Ivy explained.

Joy smiled. 'It's good to have dreams. Don't let go of them.'

'Some dreams are impossible,' Ivy said, quietly, glancing briefly at Joy's large belly again. 'I should go, I have lots of presents to deliver. Hope you all have a lovely day.'

Joy gave her another hug and Finn gave her a wave from his position on the carpet, playing with Rebecca. Ivy hurried out onto the street.

Once she was alone, she breathed a sigh of relief.

She hoped that one day it wouldn't hurt so much to see people with children. One day she could talk and play with other people's children and it wouldn't hurt at all. But for now she would just continue to fake being OK with it and pretend that seeing babies and small children didn't burn a hole in her heart.

Ivy had spent five years trying for a baby, five years of heartbreaking disappointment every month. And as all their friends – well, Callum's friends – got pregnant with their first, second and even third child, her womb had stayed resolutely empty. It had never got any easier to deal with.

She'd had all the tests, the doctors had declared there was nothing wrong with her, except there must be because even IVF had failed to produce a child. She was broken, damaged goods, and Callum, her ex-husband, had made it very clear it was all her fault and how disappointed he was in her. And clearly it was her fault because he got his new wife pregnant easily enough.

That was the worst thing about getting involved with Adam, because if it ever turned into something serious she would have to tell him that they could never have children. And when was the right time to bring up something like that? Right now, in his eyes at least, she was someone he liked, someone he found possibly attractive and desirable. She didn't want that to be replaced with looks of disappointment and eventually revulsion. She couldn't bear that to happen again, and especially not with Adam.

But it wasn't going to be something serious with him, this was just a little bit of fun and she was entitled to have that. He would leave in three months so she need never worry about the future. She would enjoy what he was offering and never expect or hope for anything more than that.

She sighed, knowing she was deluding herself if she thought it could be anything casual with Adam. Already it felt like something more and they'd only kissed once.

Ivy spotted Audrey leaving her lodge and, needing some happy relief, she called across to her. Audrey waited for her as Ivy hurried over. Audrey was a couple of years older than Ivy and they had become friends when they had both arrived on the island a few months before. Audrey was bubbly, permanently cheerful, and literally lived in a sparkly world, making fairy lights in jars and glitter lamps to sell in the village. They had chatted over a glass of wine on a few occasions and, although they hadn't delved too deep into their personal lives, Ivy had got the sense that Audrey had developed a soft spot for Luke Whitaker after helping him with the ponies and reindeer over the last few weeks. Although as far as she could see the feelings weren't reciprocated.

'Where are you off to?' Ivy asked, already guessing the answer.

'Oh, nowhere,' Audrey said, vaguely, touching a necklace she was wearing, one Ivy hadn't seen her wear before. It was an opal and marcasite star and looked antique.

'That's a beautiful necklace.'

'Oh,' Audrey blushed. 'Luke gave it to me.'

Ivy was unable to stop her eyebrows disappearing into her hair. Maybe she was wrong. As Audrey was clearly not wanting to talk any further about it, Ivy decided not to pursue it and changed the subject slightly by handing over the present she had made.

'I made you something.'

'Oh, thank you. I have something for you too, but I'll pop by later to give it to you,' Audrey said, tearing at the paper. She stopped to admire the painting of a herd of Shetland ponies and a couple standing hand-in-hand nearby. The couple were seen from the back so it was impossible to see who it was, though the huge size of the man and the red hair of the girl were big clues. 'This is wonderful. Is that. . . me and Luke?'

'It's a couple who like horses,' Ivy shrugged, nonchalantly.

Audrey grinned and threw her arms around Ivy's neck. 'I love it, thank you.'

'I hope you have a lovely Christmas Day,' Ivy said, meaningfully. 'Will you be going to the banquet later?'

'No, I think we'll. . . I'll be having a quiet lunch.'

Ivy suppressed a smile.

'What about you?' Audrey asked.

'I'm probably having lunch at the hotel.'

'With Adam?'

Ivy smiled. 'He asked, so. . .'

Audrey nodded. 'Well, I hope you have a lovely day too.'

Audrey put the picture just inside her shop and after locking the door, she gave Ivy a wave and headed off in the direction of the hotel.

Ivy watched her go with a smile, wondering if soon they would both have news to share with each other.

❄

It was mid-morning by the time Ivy reached Deborah and Stephen's house, the last house in the village. Despite it being Christmas Day, everyone had taken the time to chat with her and she'd had more cookies, sweets, mince pies and slices of cake foisted on her than she could count.

Ivy knocked on the door and when Deborah answered, she pulled her into a big hug.

'Merry Christmas, my dear,' Deborah said, holding Ivy tight. 'We didn't know if you'd be joining us for lunch but you'd be very welcome.'

Deborah held the door open and Ivy stepped inside the warmth of the lodge. Even though the chocolate shop wasn't open that day, the sweet, mouth-watering smells of chocolate still hung in the air. Stephen got up from his seat near the fire, wearing a dazzling Christmas waistcoat decorated with large satin holly leaves. He came over to give her a hug too.

'Oh thank you, but I have plans,' Ivy said.

'I hope those plans don't involve sitting in the house on your own,' Deborah said.

Ivy smiled and Deborah's face suddenly lit up.

'Do your lunch plans involve that nice new manager, Adam?'

Ivy blushed. Was nothing secret in this village?

'Now, Debs, don't embarrass the poor girl,' Stephen said. 'Just because we saw him leaving her house last night, it doesn't mean they're together.'

Ivy felt her mouth fall open. 'You saw him leave my house?'

'The Merry Dancers were out last night, red ones no less, which as we all know is a foretelling of love. We were watching them and then suddenly we saw Adam come out, looking very happy with himself. We wondered if the Merry Dancers had been working their magic again.'

'He just came to see if I was OK, after being trapped in the ditch yesterday.' Ivy cringed at being the subject of gossip.

Deborah offered her a chocolate. 'Of course, dear, and the Merry Dancers might have been presiding over someone else. We saw Luke come out of Audrey's house too. Now everybody has been dying for them to get together for months so maybe, with a little bit of magic from the Merry Dancers, it might happen after all.'

'Luke was round Audrey's house?' Ivy said, momentarily latching onto the piece of gossip, before realising that Audrey wouldn't appreciate being the subject of the village news either. But for him to be visiting her so late at night certainly said something.

'I know, it's wonderful, isn't it, dear? Stephen saw him hug her. She deserves to be happy again, they both do. What about you, have you found your happiness?'

'I'm having lunch with Adam,' Ivy said, knowing that juicy little piece of gossip would be circulated around the village by the time she had finished her pudding so she might as well get it out of the way now. 'We're just friends, nothing more.'

Deborah clapped her hands together excitedly, practically whooping with joy. 'I think that kind of friendship is exactly what you need right now.'

Ivy sighed. 'I brought you guys a present.'

She handed over the last of her parcels and Deborah took it from her and Stephen shuffled over to see what the present was too. Deborah tore at the paper and gasped at the picture of the Merry Dancers twirling and swaying across the sky above Stardust Lake.

'It's beautiful,' Deborah cooed.

'Ivy, this is just splendid,' Stephen said, taking the painting from his wife and holding it up to the light.

'I painted the emerald sky,' Ivy said. 'So not a prediction of love, I'm afraid.'

'Oh, but the emerald sky is the symbol of marriage,' Deborah said, seriously.

Ivy stared at her for a moment and then she burst out laughing.

❄

Neve woke with her face pressed into Oakley's throat, one of his arms tight around her shoulders, the other holding her bum.

She smiled. What a perfect start to Christmas Day.

After having the day off yesterday she knew she would have to go and give Adam a hand today, even if only to relieve him for a few hours so he could enjoy Christmas too. And although, judging by the sun in the sky it was already late morning, right now there was nowhere else she wanted to be.

Oakley had given her so much hope the night before. The fact that he had plans for their future was something she never thought possible. He'd even mentioned marriage. He wanted children with her, a whole football team, and yes, he had said he wasn't ready to start a family yet and yes, he'd mentioned that he wanted to wait a few years several times but he'd also said he loved her and that they would work out any problems that came their way. It wasn't ideal that she was pregnant now – she had her job in the newly opened hotel, he was just starting filming on a movie that would take close to two years to finish – but they would find a way to make it work, she was sure of that.

And although she had promised Oakley they would spend Christmas together without talking about the problems that faced them, she knew she had to tell him today and then they could start discussing how they would make it work. Since she had found out nearly two weeks earlier, she had been in turmoil about what to do. Should she tell Oakley and risk him staying with her just because of the baby and have him end up resenting her, or not tell him and raise the baby on her own? She knew he had a right to know but she hadn't managed to pluck up the courage to pick up the phone and tell him. But now there was hope. Where before the prospect of being pregnant and alone terrified her, now she had hope for the future. He loved her and it really was as simple as that.

She kissed his cheek and he blinked a few times, rubbed his eyes and then looked at her, his face lighting up into a huge smile when he saw her.

'Happy Christmas,' Neve smiled.

'Happy Christmas, Freckle.' He kissed the tip of her nose and then untangled himself from her arms and got out of bed. 'I have a Christmas present for you.'

Neve watched him stroll across the room, completely naked, and she wondered if that was her present. He grabbed his jeans and pulled them on and then rummaged in his bag.

'I have two presents actually, but one is too big to wrap up.' He grabbed a square box from his bag and turned back to face her. He eyed her sitting naked in the bed, waiting for him. 'Maybe you should put a shirt on. I won't be able to concentrate on anything if you're sitting there, looking all naked and beautiful.'

He passed her his shirt and she slid it on, doing up a few cursory buttons. He stood, appraising her legs with obvious hunger.

'Maybe you should put on some jeans too,' he suggested, passing her the jeans.

She rolled her eyes but did as he asked and, happy that she was suitably attired, he brought the silver-wrapped box back to the bed. It was quite a large box, probably holding a watch or a necklace.

'I didn't buy you anything,' Neve said, feeling the weight of the box and then tugging at the paper.

'You don't need to – if you love this present, that will be good enough for me.'

She grinned and opened the black box.

Her heart stuttered and then stopped beating altogether as she stared at the square-cut diamond ring nestled against the black velvet.

'I love you, Neve,' Oakley said, softly. 'I love to be with you, to talk, laugh and dance with you. I simply cannot imagine my life without you in it. Will you do me the honour of becoming my wife?'

Neve stared at the ring, no words in her mouth.

He took the ring out of the box and slid it on to her finger. It fitted perfectly and looked incredible there but doubt filled her mind.

'We. . . we can't just get married,' she said, her mind racing a hundred miles an hour.

'I've bought a house in California, that's your other present. It's about an hour from the studios and is in the most beautiful countryside.'

'I can't move to America. My job is here, my family are here.'

'I know you have your job and things are busy at the moment for you, but maybe in a few months' time, when things settle down, you might want to come and live in it with me.'

'And do what? Sit in it all day long and wait for you to come home?'

He looked hurt. 'No, it has over three hundred acres of land and stables for around thirty horses. I thought you could open up your own riding school, just as you always wanted to do.'

She stared at him in shock. Her life's dream and he had just handed it to her on a plate. Could she take it? Could she leave her job at the hotel and move to America for good? Marry Oakley, have her happy ever after? It seemed too good to be true and for a brief moment she couldn't think of a single reason to say no.

'We can hire staff to help you with the horses and I can pay for all the specialist equipment you would need to teach disabled children. I'd help too. You know I can ride and I'd help to look after and train the horses.'

Doubt clouded her mind. She would have to leave Gabe, he'd have to get a new manager, and she hated to let him down like that. She'd miss Gabe and Luke and the thought of not seeing her little niece every day filled her with an immense sadness. Her parents too – even though they didn't visit as often as she would like due to their world travels, she didn't want to miss out on seeing them altogether. But she couldn't let this opportunity go. This was a way for her and Oakley to be together. Maybe if she stayed for a few months, until Gabe had a replacement, until all the problems of the new hotel had been ironed out, then maybe she could join Oakley in the spring.

But before she agreed to anything she knew she had to tell Oakley her secret. He had to know what he was letting himself in for.

'Say something, Freckle. Yes would be good, but I'll settle for any words right now.'

'Oakley, I'm pregnant.'

CHAPTER 7

Oakley stared at her in complete shock, his jaw slackening as pure and utter fear filled his eyes. He scrambled off the bed, hands in his hair as he stared at her. In her entire life, she had never seen anyone look as terrified as Oakley looked right then. His eyes were wide, his pupils dilating, his breath was shallow, goosebumps erupting on his arms. His body was going into total fight-or-flight mode.

He didn't want this. He didn't want her baby. Tears filled her eyes.

The thought of him hating her baby, *his* baby, was too much to bear. Her half-brother Luke had grown up knowing that his mum hated him and didn't want him around and long after he had come to live with his dad, Neve and Gabe, Luke had been devastated by the betrayal. She couldn't put her baby through that.

Her mind cast back to the night before and how many times he had said that he wasn't ready for kids yet, that maybe he'd be ready in a few years' time. Whenever they'd had sex, he always, always used a condom. There was never a time that he forgot. Which made her discovery even more surprising, clearly for them both.

This couldn't have come at a worse time for him, he had just started work on a major Hollywood movie and a screaming baby did not fit in with that. She knew there was quite a bit of travelling involved in this film; he would feel guilty about leaving her. And what about after the filming was done and he got offers for another film? Would he turn them down out of loyalty to her, or would he stay so that he could help look after the baby and would he grow to resent her for that?

Suddenly everything he had said about his job slammed into her mind, about how much he loved it and how it was everything he ever dreamed it would be. He had worked so hard to get to this point, she couldn't let it ruin his career.

When Zander had betrayed her all those years before, she had vowed that she wouldn't let anyone else's dream ruin her own. Here were all her dreams wrapped up in a neat little bow – the riding school, raising a child with Oakley, being married to him – and she knew she had to let them go. For him.

'The baby isn't yours.'

As soon as she said the words she wanted to take them back. For a moment, just a split second, she was sure she saw relief flood his eyes before anger took over. She had never seen Oakley angry before, but he was suddenly livid.

'The baby isn't *mine*?' he choked out.

The horrible poisonous lie lay in the air between them and she couldn't take it back. She had said it for him. She had wanted to release him from his responsibility to her and the baby because for a moment it had seemed the best thing for Oakley, but in doing so she had hurt him so much more than she had when she had broken up with him nine weeks before. She felt sick, blood rushed in her ears.

'Whose baby is it?'

'It doesn't matter, it was one night, a silly drunken mistake. I was upset about you and. . .' she trailed off, knowing she was making the situation so much worse.

'I can't believe this. All this time all these women were throwing themselves at me and I turned them all down because I was in love with you, because with some stupid skewed sense of loyalty I didn't want to betray you. And now I find out you've been sleeping with someone else behind my back. Whose baby is it?'

Tears formed in her eyes, her perfect future was ruined.

'Is it Adam's?' Oakley asked, his voice low and furious.

Oh God, what a horrible tangled mess. How could she have got this so wrong? It was a terrible idea. She should have just said that he didn't need to be a part of the baby's life if he didn't want to, though knowing Oakley he would have stayed with her regardless. And then hated her for it in years to come.

Her silence clearly spoke volumes.

'I'm going to kill him,' Oakley said, storming from the room and thundering down the stairs.

'No, Oakley, wait.'

Neve got up and ran after him but as she reached the top of the stairs her foot slipped and she pitched forwards. She let out a wail, her arms and legs flailing everywhere as she fell heavily on her knee. She fell sideways, her arm smashed into the steps below and her head crashed into the bannister. Oakley spun round, his eyes widening in fear, and he launched himself at her to catch her. She tumbled down two more stairs before he caught her in his arms.

'Christ, Neve, are you OK?'

Pain slammed into her body from everywhere. She felt woozy and sick and she could taste blood in her mouth. But her hands went to her belly and she let out a sob of pain.

'Oakley, the baby!'

After that she knew no more.

※

Adam walked around the dining room checking the tables – the decorations and the place settings were perfect. There was going to be a great banquet for all the guests and villagers and although many of the journalists had flown home after the grand opening to spend Christmas with their families, the dining room would still be full to capacity.

He knew Neve would be over soon to help supervise the banquet too, despite Oakley's arrival. There was no way she would miss something as important as this.

The staff had made sure everything was flawless. Gabe had ensured he had the very best people working there and Adam was very impressed that they had set everything up without a hitch. There was going to be live music in the form of a harpist and violinist. Every place had name cards, there were little snowflakes next to those with dietary needs and even a children's menu too. Rich smells of turkey, vegetables, Christmas pudding and brandy sauce drifted out from the kitchens. It was going to be a great event and every eventuality had been catered for.

He glanced over at the table in the corner set for him and Ivy. There were candles ready for lighting and although they were designed to create a Christmas ambience, they also lent a romantic atmosphere to the room. He was looking forward to his lunch with Ivy immensely and although he wasn't sure why he wanted to pursue anything romantic with her when he was leaving in a few months, there was something about her that made her impossible to stay away from. He enjoyed talking to her and spending time with her and that kiss was not like anything he had experienced before, he wanted to do that again. It had been so long since he had been involved in a relationship that to take these first steps after all this time seemed almost alien.

He looked at his watch. It was just past half eleven and he knew the first guests would be arriving shortly. It was also just under half an hour until he sat down to lunch with Ivy and he wanted that to go more perfectly than the rest of the banquet.

Suddenly the doors to the dining room burst open and Iris, the receptionist, was standing there, looking very tearful.

He rushed over to her. 'What's happened, are you OK?'

'It's Neve, she's just fallen down the stairs. She's unconscious.'

He stared at her, the news was like a kick to the stomach.

'Shit. Have you called the air ambulance?'

'Jake's calling them now.'

Adam ran out to the main reception to see the young porter was on the phone. His hand was shaking and he was clearly struggling with answering the questions the operator was asking him.

He turned back to Iris. 'Is Oakley with her?'

'Yes, I spoke to him. He didn't stay on the phone very long, he just said she fell and she was unconscious and that we needed to call an ambulance.'

Adam took the phone from Jake and quickly and calmly explained the situation and where the helicopter pilot could land to get the easiest access to Neve's lodge. He finished the call and turned back to Iris, who was quivering like a leaf. Damn it, she was so organised and efficient that he often forgot she was only seventeen.

'Do Gabe and his family know?'

Iris shook her head, tears filling her eyes.

He placed a hand on her shoulder. 'She's going to be OK. Oakley's with her and the ambulance is on its way. Give Cora a call, explain what's happened and get her to come over to oversee the lunch. It's important that our guests have the most minimal disruption possible. Neve wouldn't want us to cancel the lunch because of her so everything is just going to carry on as normal and I need you to be able to help with that.'

He knew he had to distract Iris now. He couldn't let her just fall apart.

'I'm going to see Gabe,' he turned to Jake. 'Look after Iris for me.'

Jake nodded and Adam rushed out.

He ran over to Gabe's lodge and knocked on the door. Inside, he could hear squeals of laughter from Wren as she no doubt played with her abundance of new toys.

Gabe opened the door with a huge smile on his face. Adam could see Pip and Wren playing with Winston their dog in the lounge. He hated to be the one to wreck this sweet, happy family Christmas but of course Gabe had to know. Gabe's smile fell off as he saw Adam's face.

'There's been an accident, Neve's fallen down the stairs and she's unconscious. We've called the air ambulance and it's on its way.'

Gabe paled and when he spoke his voice was choked. 'Where is she?'

'In her lodge. I don't know any other details. Can you tell your parents and I'll tell Luke?'

Gabe nodded, numbly, and behind him Pip and Wren had gone very quiet as they had either heard what had happened or sensed something was wrong.

'The ambulance is going to land over there,' he pointed. 'I'm going to get Boris and Mikael to help with keeping people away from the area. Go and tell your parents and I'll meet you back here shortly.'

Gabe nodded again and turned back to face his family to explain that Christmas Day had now been cancelled.

Adam ran over to Boris and Mikael's house. They had a child too and they wouldn't exactly be happy to have their special day disrupted either.

He knocked on their door, and Boris came to answer it. With his blond hair and blue eyes he looked like he should be a model, not a groundsman. Boris was smiling too and Adam wondered how many people's Christmases he was going to ruin that day. He quickly explained what had happened and by that time Boris's husband, Mikael, had arrived on the doorstep with their son, Chester.

'I need you guys to co-ordinate the arrival of the helicopter, make sure none of our guests get in the way and then, Mikael, I'm sorry to ask but I'll need you to fly Gabe and his family to the hospital in Lerwick. I'm not sure how many passengers the helicopter will be able to take but I suspect it'll just be the one and I imagine Oakley will take that seat.'

'Of course,' Mikael said. 'We will do anything to help.'

'Boris, can you get a car ready to take Gabe and his family to the airport?'

Boris nodded.

Adam waved his thanks to them and raced back to the hotel. He grabbed a snowmobile and took off down the track towards Luke's cottage.

The husky puppies were jumping and chasing each other around the small garden as Luke stood on the front doorstep, sipping a mug of coffee and watching them. He clearly enjoyed this solitary existence away from the hotel and away from everyone. Adam knew Luke was close to his family and had probably planned to spend the afternoon with them but for him starting Christmas Day with just himself and a bunch of puppies for company was probably as close to perfection as it could get. When he pulled up outside the cottage, it surprised Adam that Audrey stepped up beside Luke, having come from inside the house. He knew she hadn't spent the night with Luke, having seen him leave her house the night before, but for her to be there on Christmas morning said something about their relationship – although he wasn't sure what and there was no time to get into any of that now.

Adam got off the snowmobile and quickly walked into the garden. Audrey grinned at him and gave him a wave but Luke didn't look too pleased to see him. He would be even less pleased in a second.

'Neve's been involved in an accident. She fell down the stairs and she's unconscious. The air ambulance is on its way.'

Luke went very still and when Adam glanced down he noticed Audrey clutching Luke's hand. He seemed almost frozen, unable to move or speak.

Audrey stroked his arm. 'Luke, you need to go to her.'

Luke nodded, suddenly seeming to come out of his reverie. 'Can you take care of the puppies?'

'Of course, I'll make sure I get them in.'

Luke stepped outside without any shoes, obviously moving in shock, before Audrey stopped him.

'You need shoes and a coat,' she said.

'There's no time.'

'There's plenty of time,' Adam insisted. 'It'll probably be half an hour before the air ambulance can get here.'

Luke looked angry at this. 'Why will it take so long?'

'Because it has to come from one of the other islands.'

Luke nodded as Audrey tugged him back inside to get his things.

A few moments later Luke came hurrying back out and he and Adam got on the snowmobile.

'What happened?' Luke asked as they roared back towards the main hotel.

'I have no idea. Oakley was with her but I don't know any details.'

Adam pulled the snowmobile to a stop outside Neve's lodge and with still no sign of the helicopter, he and Luke ran inside.

There was no sign of Gabe or the rest of his family either, but Adam suspected he was still getting Wren dressed and talking to his parents. Neve was lying pale and unresponsive on the sofa and Adam cringed that Oakley had obviously moved her after her fall. Oakley was kneeling next to her, talking to her, trying to persuade her to wake up. She looked so pale and vulnerable and Adam's heart sank. They had been friends for eight years and she was such a strong person but right now she looked as weak as a kitten.

Luke immediately went to Neve's side.

'I tried to catch her,' Oakley muttered, not taking his eyes off Neve's face. 'She fell so quickly and I tried to get to her.'

Luke took her hand and Oakley shifted slightly to make room for him but as he did so, he glanced up at Adam and his face turned to one of hate. Oakley suddenly launched himself across the room at him and before Adam could say a word, Oakley had him pinned up against the wall by his throat.

'This is all your fault. I knew it, I knew you wanted her and you waited until she was upset and vulnerable before you got her drunk and took advantage of her. I should kill you for this.'

Luke leapt up and grabbed Oakley, yanking him away from Adam with apparent ease. 'What the hell is going on? Whatever your issues with each other, now is not the time.'

'She's pregnant,' Oakley said, his voice choked with emotion. 'She's carrying your child. We were supposed to be forever and you ruined that.'

Adam stared at him incredulously. Although he had strongly suspected that Neve was pregnant, he had no idea where Oakley got the impression that the baby was his. In all the years he had known her, they hadn't so much as shared a kiss. They had both been hurt in the past and the way they had dealt with it was to throw themselves one hundred percent into their jobs. There had never been anything remotely romantic between them – she was his friend and that was as far as it had ever gone. Oakley had always assumed something was going on between them but it was a big leap to go from that to believing they had slept together and she was carrying his child. Unless... Neve had told him that. But what possible reason would she have for lying? It would be very easy to tell Oakley that he had never slept with her but if Neve had told Oakley that for a reason, Adam didn't want to undo the lie. His loyalty was to her, certainly not to Oakley.

He swallowed, choosing his words carefully. 'I had no idea she was pregnant.'

'She didn't tell you?' Oakley said.

Adam shook his head, honestly. In fact he had asked her outright if she was pregnant a few days before and she had flat out denied it.

'Are you going to marry her?' Oakley asked.

'No,' Adam said. It was one thing pretending the baby was his, quite another to pretend to be husband and wife. What a complete mess.

Oakley went for him again and if it wasn't for Luke, he would have succeeded.

'So you're going to leave her to look after the baby on her own?'

This was getting more and more complicated. 'I will make sure she and the baby are OK,' Adam said. 'But I have no intention of marrying someone I don't love and who doesn't love me. That would be a mistake.'

The fight seemed to go out of Oakley at this and as a deafening noise erupted outside, signalling the arrival of the helicopter, they both knew that this argument would have to keep.

'I need my shoes,' Oakley said, disentangling himself from Luke's arms and running upstairs.

Luke stared at Adam as if he'd quite like to punch him as well.

'I haven't slept with her,' Adam whispered. 'We've never even kissed. If she's pregnant, that baby is his.'

'Then why didn't you tell him that?'

'Because I wonder if Neve told him that the baby is mine for a good reason. Or it could be just a big misunderstanding but I want to speak to Neve first before I discredit her.'

Luke nodded.

'I'll go and talk to the helicopter crew,' Adam said, leaving the house just as Oakley came running down the stairs again.

Adam spoke briefly to the helicopter crew just as Gabe and his parents went running into Neve's house. He explained how she had fallen, had been unconscious since the fall and was pregnant, probably around ten weeks.

They ran in, carrying a stretcher and, knowing there would be far too many people inside Neve's small lounge already, he waited outside.

A few minutes later, the helicopter crew returned with the stretcher between them. Oakley was by her side as they carefully manoeuvred Neve towards the waiting helicopter, her family bringing up the rear.

Oakley climbed on board before they had even loaded Neve in there, ensuring there would be no question over him not going with her.

They carefully placed her on board and her family gathered round, obviously concerned. Adam hung back a bit but stood close enough that he could hear what was said as the pilot briefly told Gabe which hospital they would be heading to and then advised them to stand back.

The Whitakers shuffled backwards out of the way and a few minutes later the helicopter started its engines and took off. They all stared after it in numb shock.

Adam stepped forward. 'Mikael is going to fly you to Lerwick and I'll make sure there is a car waiting for you at the other end. He'll come back here but as soon as you need to come home, give us a call and we'll come back out and get you.'

'It's Christmas Day,' Gabe said, weakly. 'The guests…'

'Will be fine, I'm going to take care of all of that. You don't need to worry. I have a car waiting to take you to the plane now.'

'I need my bag,' Neve's mum, Lizzie, muttered, tearfully.

'That's OK. You guys take your time to get yourselves organised and get your things,' Adam said, calmly. 'Whenever you're ready, the car will take you there.'

'I just need to say goodbye to Wren,' Gabe said. 'Pip is going to stay with her, I didn't think it was a good idea to bring her to the hospital.'

He looked at Adam to see if he agreed with him. But Adam was certainly no expert when it came to children. He guessed that Wren would be upset by the events too and she was old enough to know something was going on even if they hadn't been entirely truthful with her. She might be even more upset that Gabe was leaving her when she would want to go and see if Neve was OK too, but if that's what Gabe thought was best, he wasn't about to tell him it was wrong.

'That sounds like a good plan and I'm here if Pip needs any help.'

Gabe nodded numbly and walked off towards his house while his parents rushed off towards the lodge where they were staying. Only Luke remained.

'Is there anything you need to get?'

Luke shook his head as he watched the helicopter disappear into the sky. 'She's always wanted a child.'

Adam bit his lip, he couldn't let any emotion take over now, not yet. He had to stay calm for Gabe and his family. 'I know.'

'It will destroy her if she loses this baby.'

'She's strong and Oakley is too. That baby is going to come out wearing a superhero outfit, just like his dad, and be up and running by the time he's a few weeks old.'

Luke smiled, sadly. 'I hope so.'

Adam sighed. 'And if the worst happens and she loses the baby, we will all be here to support her and help her through it. She won't go through this alone.'

Luke nodded. 'No, she won't.'

Gabe came running back out of his house, just as his parents returned, and Adam escorted them all over to the waiting car. Boris was waiting for them with the doors open and his son, Chester, standing next to him.

'Can you stay with Adam?' Boris said to Chester. 'I'll be back in fifteen minutes.' Boris stood up and addressed Adam. 'I won't be long. Take him to play with Wren if you want,' he said, handing the small boy over into his care.

Chester took Adam's hand and before Adam could say anything, Boris ran round to the driver's side and the car roared off down the road, taking Gabe and his family with it.

He looked down at the boy, who stared up at him with wary, wide blue eyes.

Adam smiled, to try to put the boy at ease. 'Daddy won't be long. Did you get some nice presents from Santa this morning?'

Chester nodded. 'I got Transformers and a red bike and a *Frozen* magic wand, just like Wren's, and an Incredible Hulk costume and *Star Wars* pyjamas and a water pistol and Lego and roller skates and spaghetti.'

'*Spaghetti?*' Adam asked, in confusion. Surely he had misheard or Chester had used the wrong word.

'I love spaghetti, it's my favourite thing in the world, and Daddy cooked it and made it different colours and then let it go cold and wrapped it up for me so I can play with it, though not on the sofa or on the carpet but I can play with it on the kitchen floor if I want. I like the way it feels and tastes but Daddy said not to eat this stuff, this spaghetti is just for playing with, but I'm having spaghetti on toast for my Christmas lunch when everyone else is having turkey and I can eat the spaghetti at lunch but not the spaghetti that I can play with. Do you want to see my spaghetti?'

Adam couldn't help but smile at how Chester was quite obviously more excited about the spaghetti than the brand new bike or other toys.

'Sure, let's go and see your spaghetti.'

Adam looked up to see that a man, one of the guests, was waiting for him. He had a camera round his neck.

'Sorry to bother you, I can see you're busy,' the man said. 'I'm Ben Eustace, from the *Daily Oracle*. I couldn't help but notice the air ambulance arriving. Is everything OK?'

'Everything is fine. One of our staff had a fall, it's nothing to worry about,' Adam said, walking past him towards Boris and Mikael's house.

'And was that Oakley Rey I saw getting on the helicopter? I'd heard rumours he was here, but that was quite a surprise to see him.'

'I can't discuss the identity of the guests in my hotel.'

'I'll take that as a yes. And what was the name of the member of staff he was with?'

'That's none of your business,' Adam snapped.

'Well, as Gabe Whitaker and his brother Luke have just gone off to the hospital with two people I presume are their parents, I'm guessing the girl on the stretcher was Neve Whitaker.'

'Yes, it was,' Chester said, helpfully. 'Daddy said that she banged her head but that she is going to hospital and that she will be better soon.'

The journalist looked delighted by this piece of news.

'And what is the relationship between Oakley and Neve?'

Adam carried on walking.

'Did I hear mention of a baby too?' the journalist called after him. 'Is the baby Oakley's?'

Adam walked up the stairs to Boris's house as Ben followed from a slight distance.

'A superhero baby, the world is going to love this. Will they call it Obsidian Junior?'

Adam let the door slam shut behind him and resisted letting out a string of swear words.

Chester looked up at him again. 'Is Neve really having a baby with superpowers?'

Adam sighed. 'Why don't you show me this spaghetti?'

Chester ran off to the other side of the room and Adam sat down on the sofa. When he had thought every eventuality had been catered for, he couldn't possibly have imagined that his day would have turned out like this.

CHAPTER 8

Ivy sat at the table in the corner and checked her watch for the hundredth time. Adam had definitely said twelve o'clock, yet it was gone half past twelve and there was still no sign of him.

The other guests were sitting at tables, finishing off their delicious starters, laughing and joking, pulling crackers, and Ivy was utterly alone. If she was going to spend Christmas Day alone, she could have done so in the privacy of her own house instead of sitting at the table for everyone to see.

Something was going on, she knew that. The waiters and waitresses were whispering to each other whenever they got the chance but she thought it was more than likely they were excited about the rumour that Oakley Rey had landed here the day before and they were wondering if he was going to turn up for the Christmas Day lunch.

She stopped one of the waitresses as she rushed past.

'Sorry, I was just wondering if Adam was coming or if you know where he is?'

'He's busy right now, but I'm sure he will be along shortly.' The girl hurried off again, balancing plates and bowls in her hands.

Ivy checked her watch again. As assistant manager for the hotel, it was bound to be busy for him, especially as it was Christmas Day, she understood that. Her stomach gurgled hungrily, made even worse by all the wonderful smells and delicious plates of goodness that kept on passing by her table. Should she start her lunch without him? Surely he wouldn't mind. She'd have her starter and by then he'd be there and they could enjoy the main course together. She waved the waitress over and asked her to bring the first course out. As the girl rushed off to the kitchen, Ivy looked back over to the doors leading into the dining room. He'd be there soon.

❋

'Come on, baby, open your eyes,' Oakley said and hearing the worry in his voice Neve forced her eyes open and looked at him. His face flooded with relief. He was holding her hand and they were in a strange room and she wasn't really sure of anything else. She had a vague recollection of being loaded onto the air ambulance and watching the sky whizz past as Oakley sat next to her, clutching her hand. But she didn't remember much else.

She realised she was lying in a hospital bed, hooked up to a heart monitor which was beeping softly. Her arm and hand ached and as she became more awake the pain increased significantly.

'Hey, Freckle, you're awake. Does it hurt? Are you in a lot of pain?' he said, softly, the anger he had felt before clearly gone, at least for now.

Suddenly, everything came back. Her falling down the stairs and her hand went to her belly in horror. She had fallen so hard, her poor baby didn't stand a chance.

Sobs wracked through her body and Oakley squeezed her hand.

'The baby, is the baby OK?'

'I don't know. They want to do an ultrasound and check for the baby's heartbeat but they wanted you to be awake and they were waiting on some special baby doctor person to be available. Apparently she's on her way down here now. God, you gave me such a fright. I tried to get to you to stop you from falling but I wasn't close enough. I'm so sorry.'

Tears filled her eyes. 'I'm sorry too, about everything. I just. . .'

'Don't worry about any of that now. The important thing is that you and the baby are OK.'

She nodded and lifted the hand Oakley wasn't holding to wipe her tears before realising that it was really heavy. As she glanced at it, she saw that it was set in a thick white cast.

'Sadly your wrist didn't quite survive the fall. It's not a bad break though, but they think you'll have to wear that thing for about six weeks. Are you in a lot of pain with it?'

She waggled her fingers slightly. It hurt a lot, but she couldn't find it in her to care. All she wanted to know was whether their baby was OK.

'It's fine,' Neve said.

'They can't give you any painkillers unfortunately, it might hurt the baby,' Oakley explained.

Neve nodded and looked around again. 'Where are we?'

'We're in Lerwick. The air ambulance brought you here. They would only allow one person to come with you on the helicopter so Gabe, Luke and your mum and dad are coming over on the hotel plane. They should be here soon.'

Neve smiled slightly, wondering how Oakley had been the one to get a seat on the helicopter, rather than a member of her family, though knowing Oakley he wouldn't have taken no for an answer.

The door to the room opened and a blonde woman in her early forties walked in, followed by one of the hotel porters, pushing a wheelchair.

'Hello, Miss Whitaker. Good to see you awake. I'm Simona, I'm the obstetrician here. How are you feeling? Any nausea, dizziness?'

'I'm fine. I just want to know that the baby is OK.'

'I understand and we'll get to that in just a moment. I accessed your medical records and there's nothing on there about you being pregnant.'

'I only found out myself about two weeks ago. I was going to make an appointment with the doctor after Christmas. I work at a hotel and it's been so busy.'

'That's fine, do you know the date of your last period?'

Neve blushed, hating that they were talking about this in front of Oakley.

'Um, my periods have never been regular. Sometimes I don't get them at all. Maybe three months ago.'

Simona nodded. 'OK, well, we can have a look at the baby on the ultrasound and that will give us a good indication of how far along you are. Let me get you unhooked from the monitor and we can take you down there.'

Simona removed the pads and cables and Neve gingerly sat up. She ached everywhere. But before she could climb down off the bed, Oakley very gently scooped her up and placed her in the wheelchair. After making sure she was comfortable, he stepped back. 'I'll wait here for you, Freckle.'

'Mr Rey, you should come too. If everything is OK with the foetus, then you'll probably be able to see your baby for the first time on the ultrasound.'

Oakley brushed his hand through his hair, awkwardly.

'Please come,' Neve said, softly.

He hesitated for a second and then nodded.

The porter wheeled her down the corridor and Oakley held her hand but he didn't say anything. When they got to the scan room, Oakley repeated the process and lifted her gently onto the bed, sitting down next to her and taking her hand again.

Simona closed the door and dimmed the lights. She rolled up Neve's gown and sat down on her other side as she fiddled around with the ultrasound machine.

'This will be cold,' Simona warned as she squirted icy-cold jelly onto Neve's stomach.

Simona switched on the TV screen on the wall and it flickered white and black for a moment. She picked up the ultrasound scanner and moved it over Neve's stomach. Neve closed her eyes, suddenly not wanting to see if the baby was dead. Tears filled her eyes again.

After a moment, she felt Oakley kiss her forehead. 'Neve,' he whispered. 'Open your eyes.'

Neve did and stared at the screen in front of her. It was filled with grey, but in the middle was a black hole the shape of a large kidney bean and inside that hole something moved. As the camera moved around and then zoomed in, she could clearly see the shape of a head, and legs bent at the knees. Its little arms were bent behind its head as if it was lying back and taking things easy. It had a little fat belly and as it rolled over away from the camera, Neve could clearly see a spine. Right in the middle of the baby's chest something flickered and moved at a frantic pace and Neve smiled through her tears as she realised this was the heartbeat.

'Your baby seems perfectly healthy,' Simona said. 'I'll take some measurements and we'll have a good look around, but I can't see any problems at the moment.'

'It's alive, it's OK?' Neve said, hardly daring to believe it. She couldn't take her eyes off the screen.

'Yes, babies are often tougher than we give them credit for.'

'Thank God,' Oakley muttered next to her, visibly exhaling with relief.

She dragged her eyes from the screen to look at him and was surprised to see tears in his eyes too.

'Do you want to know the sex?' Simona said.

Neve whirled back to look at her and the screen. 'You can tell this early?'

'Yes, at this stage in the pregnancy we can have a really good guess, if we get a good angle. Fortunately your baby has just given us a great angle.'

Neve looked back to Oakley. 'Do we want to know?'

'I don't know, Freckle,' he said, gently. 'Do *you* want to know? It's your baby.'

Guilt and pain slammed into her chest. He couldn't even get excited about seeing this baby because, as far as he was concerned, it wasn't his.

'I want to know,' Neve said, gripping Oakley's hand. She was gratified when he squeezed her hand in return.

'It's a boy. You're going to have a son. A big, strong, healthy boy, by the looks of things. I would estimate a due date of the very end of June. I'll know more when I've done some more measurements.'

Simona continued to move the scanner over her belly, zooming in on some areas and taking measurements of other parts, while Neve sat mesmerised by the whole thing. She was going to be a mum.

When she had found out nearly two weeks before, it hadn't seemed real. She had stared at that tiny line on the pregnancy test and just couldn't imagine that nine months down the road the little line would turn into a little baby that would depend on her for every single thing. She had wanted this with Oakley, to get married and raise a family together, she had wanted it more than anything but before they had broken up he had made it clear that marriage wasn't really on his agenda and babies were very far down on his list of priorities. That, in part, had been one of the reasons she had ended it between them: though he had told her he loved her, he just didn't seem serious about a future together.

And now he had come back, proposed and she was pregnant with his child. It was everything she dreamed about and she had pushed it away. It might have been everything she wanted but it wasn't what he wanted and, though there was a huge part of her that regretted lying to him, there was a small part that did think maybe she had done the right thing. She never wanted to hold him back.

❇

Adam ran back towards the main hotel and the dining room. It was approaching two o'clock and he just hoped that Ivy had waited for him. After playing with Chester for half an hour with a bowlful of cold spaghetti, he had gone over to see if Pip was OK with Wren, knowing she hadn't been in the motherly role too long, fended off another journalist and dealt with three complaints about the noise of the helicopters over the last two days before he was finally free to go and have his lunch. He was starving but the fact that he was late for Ivy bothered him more than anything else. If there was ever a reason not to get involved with him it was because his job meant long and unpredictable hours.

He pushed open the dining room doors and his eyes found the table he and Ivy were supposed to share their lunch at. It was empty and she had clearly been and gone, if the empty wine glass and dirty napkin was anything to go by.

He sighed just as Cora, the head receptionist, and Heather, the banqueting manager, came over. The dining room was over half-empty now, but there were several guests still enjoying the festivities.

'How did lunch go, any problems?' Adam asked, switching back into managerial mode.

Cora shook her head. 'A few little problems but nothing that Heather didn't handle with her impeccable efficiency.'

Adam looked at Heather.

'One woman who ordered soup and then complained because the salmon looked so much better and she wanted that instead. One man complained that one of the waitresses knocked over the wine when she wasn't anywhere near the table, but we dealt with it professionally, of course.'

Adam smiled; the customer was always right, even if they were complete assholes.

'How's Neve, is there any news?' Heather asked.

Adam shook his head. 'Not that I've heard. I would have thought Gabe would have phoned us by now to let us know but maybe he's preoccupied.'

'Well, let me know as soon as you hear anything.'

'I will.'

Heather hurried off again to attend to the guests and Adam surveyed the dining room to make sure everything was still running smoothly.

'There was a girl who kept asking about you. I'm not sure if she was a guest or. . .' Cora trailed off.

'She's a friend.'

'Oh.'

They both had arrived from the London hotel only a few days before so it was fast work to be involved with someone already, especially by his standards.

'Did anyone tell her the reason I was late?'

'I don't think so. We didn't really want to tell the guests what was happening though some of them saw the air ambulance arrive and as I wasn't sure whether she wanted you specifically to complain about something, I kept fobbing her off and telling her you were busy. Sorry, if I'd realised she was waiting for you for a date, I would have explained to her.'

'It wasn't a date,' Adam said, knowing that he couldn't honestly call it anything else. 'We're friends.'

'Well, I'm sure your *friend* will understand.'

Adam cringed because knowing Ivy's prickly armour, understanding would probably be the last thing that she would be. Maybe it was for the best. He didn't want to get involved in a relationship, not when he was leaving in a few months, and trying to pursue one with Ivy would only lead to her getting hurt when he left, which was the last thing he wanted.

He would find her and apologise but he would leave it at that, though he couldn't shake off the sense of immense disappointment at that thought.

❊

Neve had just got back from having her ultrasound when her family arrived. Her mum, Lizzie, was the first to burst into the room, descending on her with a huge hug and lots of tears.

'Oh my darling, are you OK?' Lizzie said.

Neve could see Gabe, Luke and her dad, David, squeezing into the room behind her mum.

'I'm fine, a bit sore but fine,' Neve said, hugging her back with her one good hand.

Lizzie's eyes fell to Neve's belly, tears filling her eyes as she quickly looked away. Obviously her mum had heard she was pregnant.

'The baby is fine too, Mum. You're going to be a nanny again, this time to a little boy.'

There was so much noise and joy in the room then, with everyone passing on their congratulations and hugs to both Neve and Oakley. Oakley barely said a word though he didn't deny the baby was his either. As they all sat down around the bed, her dad spotted the engagement ring still shining brightly on her left hand.

'You're engaged? Congratulations! I'm so pleased you two have sorted out your problems. We've been so worried about Neve since the two of you broke up, but I'm glad you're back together again. You always made her so happy.'

Neve glanced down at the beautiful ring. Were they engaged? She hadn't even said yes. Instead she had thrown up all the possible reasons why they couldn't get married. Why was she so intent on pushing away the man she loved? She looked over at Oakley, wondering if he would simply snatch the ring back and walk out, but he just sat there, numbly accepting the second lot of congratulations. She had ruined everything and she felt awful.

But as she let her left hand fall back to the bed, Oakley took it, automatically entwining his fingers with hers. He was still here and seemingly not planning on leaving any time soon. It filled her heart with hope.

Not wanting to focus on what an idiot she had been in pushing him away, she turned back to her mum.

'I'm so sorry, I've ruined Christmas for you guys. I was so looking forward to spending it with you.'

'Don't you worry about that, we can always celebrate it when you come back home. You just need to rest and look after your little son.'

Neve smiled and turned her attention to Gabe. 'I'm sorry I ruined your day too. I bet Wren was so disappointed that Christmas was cut short.'

'No, she was just worried about you. Besides, before I left, I explained we would do Christmas Day when we got back. She really liked the idea of having two Christmas Days. She wanted to come here but I thought it might be best if she stayed at home. Pip is looking after her, so I imagine they are busy re-enacting the entire *Frozen* film by now.'

Neve laughed. 'She's so good with Wren.'

'They adore each other,' Gabe said. 'I feel so incredibly lucky to have Pip in my life. We had a second chance at love and now you two have that too.'

Neve looked back over at Oakley again and he smiled sadly at her. They'd had a second chance and she had thrown it away. It was very unlikely she would get a third.

CHAPTER 9

Ivy sat down at her computer and fired up Skype, ready to call her little sister. She adored Rose, and she missed her so much since she had emigrated to New York two years before, but the phone calls and Skype calls were always hard.

She checked the time – they were five hours behind so it should be around half nine in the morning there – but she knew her sister and brother-in-law would have been up for hours.

She took a deep breath and pressed the call button on the computer. It rang only once before Imogen suddenly appeared on the screen. Three years old, brown curly hair, the biggest eyes Ivy had ever seen. She was utterly adorable. The worst thing about watching Rose's children grow up was they all looked exactly like Rose and as Rose looked like a slightly younger version of Ivy, it was like getting a glimpse of what her own children would have looked like, had she been lucky enough to have any. Rose hadn't stopped at one child, however; they'd had five so far, whereas Ivy hadn't even been blessed with one.

'Hey, beautiful,' Ivy crooned. 'Imogen, can you hear me?'

Imogen blinked and then her whole face lit up in a toothy smile before she dropped the iPad and Ivy watched the chubby little legs run out of the room.

A few seconds later, the iPad was picked up again and this time Ivy was looking at her seven-year-old niece, Quinn. Ivy's heart filled with love for her.

'Hey, Ivy,' Quinn said.

Ivy smiled as she realised this time her niece was dressed up as a knight with a silver helmet, chainmail and a sword in one hand. The only nod to her femininity was the sparkly eyeshadow she had on and the bright pink lipstick.

'Hey, Quinn, happy Christmas.'

'Happy holidays,' Quinn said and Ivy laughed.

'Are you going all American on me?'

'Sadly I think I am, we're not even having turkey for Christmas lunch today. We're having ham served with sweet potatoes, which are not really sweet and not really potatoes either. We have pumpkin pie for dessert and we've been drinking eggnog all morning, not the stuff with alcohol in it, though. And did you know that over here they don't call Father Christmas, Father Christmas, they call him Santa Claus.'

'Wow, sounds like you're embracing the American way of life.'

'Yes, but Daddy has had some crackers sent over from the UK because we have to have the paper hats and the naff little toys and they don't sell them over here. Daddy says we can introduce them to the Americans and maybe one day they will all want them.'

'You definitely can't have Christmas without crackers,' Ivy said, thinking of the cracker that had remained unpulled, still lying on her table in the restaurant. There was something that was very sad about pulling a cracker by yourself.

She saw Archie, the oldest of the children, peer round the iPad to see who Quinn was talking to and he grinned when he saw it was Ivy. 'Hi Ivy, happy Christmas.'

'Is that Ivy?' Rose said from somewhere in the room and the next second her smiling face loomed into the picture as well in between Archie and Quinn.

'Hey, Rosy Posy,' Ivy smiled with affection for her little sister. 'Quinn's been telling me how you're betraying your homeland with the lack of turkey.'

Rose laughed. 'We did have turkey over Thanksgiving, so, yes, we are trying ham for a change.'

'Are you coming over soon?' Archie asked.

'Yes, I am, end of January for a whole week. As soon as the fire and ice festival is over, I'll be flying out. You guys are supposed to be coming over in the summer, aren't you?'

Rose blushed. 'I don't think it's going to happen this year.'

Ivy's heart sank a little. They didn't see each other as often as she would like. She understood that funding the flights for the seven of them worked out really expensive but she had been looking forward to showing them the beauty of Juniper Island. Her heart fell even more when Rose stroked her stomach. No, surely not again. She made sure the smile was fixed on her face as Rose spoke.

'I'll be in my third trimester by then. We're pregnant again.'

'Congratulations,' Ivy said, feeling her heart shatter into a thousand pieces.

❄

Adam put the phone down from another newspaper wanting a quote about Oakley. The story of his impending fatherhood seemed to have hit the media and spread faster than wildfire. He had fobbed them off but they were quite happy to run the story without any corresponding facts or information to back it up.

The unmistakable Skype ringtone suddenly sounded through his computer and he smiled, knowing it would be Taylor, his sister. He quickly clicked on the button to answer and a few seconds later her smiling face appeared on the screen, wearing a pink paper crown at a squiffy angle. She was obviously enjoying the celebrations. In the background he could see his niece and nephew playing with a video game against their dad while his mum dozed in a chair. It was the same scene every Christmas – they'd eat until their bellies were fit to burst and then play games all afternoon while his parents fell asleep on the sofa. He missed them and all their craziness and predictability. Although he had worked throughout Christmas in the past, he always managed to spend either Christmas Eve or Boxing Day with his family and sometimes even Christmas Day afternoon and evening. And although his temporary assignment had taken him away from that this year, he hadn't really minded. It felt good, in a way, to be out of that rut, doing something different and Taylor had promised him they would somehow play their annual game of Cluedo over Skype.

'Happy Christmas,' Taylor said, holding a glass of wine up to the screen.

Adam looked around for something to toast her with in return and offered up an empty coffee mug.

'Happy Christmas, sis.'

She frowned slightly. 'Are you working?'

'Yeah, you know how it is. There's been a bit of an emergency actually. Remember Neve? She fell down the stairs and she's been rushed to hospital.'

'Oh no, is she OK?'

'Her brother has just sent me a text to say she's fine and that he'd call me later so I'm presuming everything is OK. It's left things here in a bit of chaos though.'

'Is that your way of saying you haven't got time for Cluedo?'

'I've always got time for Cluedo, especially when it's with you,' Adam said, knowing he barely had the time for this phone call, let alone a very bizarre Skype game of Cluedo.

'We miss you, it's just not the same without you.'

He smiled, sadly. 'I miss you too.'

'Tell me you at least had time to eat some turkey with all the trimmings?'

'No, but I did have a rather nice turkey and stuffing sandwich.'

'How nice?' Taylor narrowed her eyes, suspiciously.

'Not as good as your turkey leftover sandwiches obviously.'

Taylor laughed. 'Good answer. How is it up there, is it really barren and remote?'

Adam looked out the window at the snow-covered lodges and the fairy lights strewn from the roofs, gently swaying in the wind. 'It's actually really beautiful. I saw the Northern Lights last night.'

'Oh wow, I've always wanted to see them! What were they like?'

'Incredible, watching them dance in the sky was not like anything I've ever seen. They were red and pink, which apparently, according to the locals, is a foretelling of love.'

Taylor studied him for a moment, then she leaned forward with a huge smile on her face. 'You've met someone.'

'I have not.'

'Yes, you have. I can see it on your face.'

'No, there's. . .' He sighed. There was no point lying to his sister, she could see right through him. 'There's a girl called Ivy, she seems really nice.'

Taylor squealed with excitement. 'Tell me everything.'

'There's not a lot to tell at the moment. We were supposed to meet for lunch today and after everything that happened with Neve, I ended up standing her up. It's not exactly a good start.'

'Yes, but surely you've apologised and explained to her what happened,' Taylor said, simply, even though Adam knew it would probably be a lot harder than she made it sound.

'Not yet.'

'Why not? Why are you sat here talking to me when you could be spending Christmas with your new girlfriend?'

'She's not my girlfriend.'

'But you're hoping she wants the position.'

He really did. 'I leave in three months.'

'So what? If you have something special, you'll make the distance work somehow. Go and talk to her.'

Adam smirked at how pushy his sister was. She had always been the same. But she was right. It didn't have to be over in three months. He didn't have to hold himself back from getting too attached. If they still wanted to see each other after the three months were up, they could work something out. Scotland was only a few hours away by plane from London. It wasn't the other side of the world.

'I'll talk to her. I will, I promise, but first we need to figure out how to play Cluedo over Skype.'

Taylor sighed. 'OK, but I want a full report tomorrow.'

'I promise, I'll give you the full details.'

'I've already dealt the cards and yours are here.' Taylor held up a small pile. 'So I figured I would just show you what you have and then put them under the board so no one else can see them.'

'And I can trust you that you haven't already cheated and had a peek,' Adam said.

Taylor gave a feigned look of outrage when they both knew she was a big cheater whenever it came to Cluedo. He smiled.

Oliver and Megan, his niece and nephew, suddenly came running over and waved at him inanely as they picked up their cards to inspect what they had, as if playing Cluedo over Skype was completely the norm. Maybe Christmas wouldn't be a complete washout after all. And if he could only sort things out with Ivy then Christmas could actually turn out to be quite wonderful.

❄

Oakley stared out of the hospital window at the dark sky filled with a thousand stars. Christmas Day was coming to an end and nowhere in his wildest dreams had he imagined it would turn out like this.

He had envisaged many possible scenarios and although him proposing and Neve throwing herself into his arms, crying tears of joy that they were going to be husband and wife was a nice dream, knowing Neve it was unlikely to be a reality. He had imagined that he would have to work at persuading her to say yes, that he would have to spend the whole week showing her how much he loved her and how important she was to him. He predicted that she would throw up a load of possible reasons why she couldn't marry him and he had believed that he had an answer for every possible excuse. He had never envisaged that one of those reasons would be her being pregnant with another man's child.

He focussed his attention on the woman he loved, fast asleep in the hospital bed. She had slept for most of the day which, in his mind, wasn't good. The hospital, however, had assured him that everything was fine. They had done so many scans and tests – taking her blood, taking a urine sample, poked, prodded, measured, listened to her heartbeat, listened to the baby's heartbeat, took more scans of her head, checked her for other possible breakages – and they were more than happy that Neve and the little baby boy were doing fine. As she had been sleepy, the hospital had wanted to keep her in overnight to be on the safe side and, though Neve had protested, Oakley had insisted she listen to them.

He hadn't let go of her hand all day. When her family had arrived they'd had to squeeze in around the other side of the bed as he had quite simply refused to leave her side. They'd all congratulated them on their engagement and the upcoming baby's arrival, assuming, of course, that he was the father. Neve hadn't told them otherwise and he hadn't found it in him to correct them either. In fact he had barely spoken since he had seen the baby on the scan. The little boy that wasn't his, growing strongly inside the woman he loved with everything he had.

He had been beyond relieved that the tiny baby was OK, he couldn't bear the heartbreak that Neve would go through if she lost the child she wanted so much. The child that he hadn't wanted to have when they were together. He did want children, one day, but with his career just taking off and his busy filming schedule shooting in several different locations, it would have been impractical to think about raising a child at that time.

Had that been why she had finished with him? Neve adored her niece, Wren, and he knew she ached for a child of her own and he kept putting her off.

Had she deliberately slept with someone just so she could get pregnant? Or had it been like she said, she'd just got drunk one night and the child had been the result of a drunken accident? The thought of Adam taking advantage of Neve when she was drunk and upset filled him with so much anger. And where had Adam been when her whole family had rushed to the hospital to be at her side? Clearly he didn't care about Neve or the baby and for him it had just been about sex, which meant Neve would be left to raise the baby on her own.

June twenty-eighth. That was the date when everything would change. Hell, everything had already changed. That was just over six months from now, which meant that Neve was already nearly three months pregnant. When had he flown out of

London? It was October, in the middle some time, he was sure it was the fifteenth or was it the tenth? He tried to do the maths but he was so unbelievably tired that he couldn't work it out. So it had been about nine or ten weeks since he left Neve. Had she slept with someone the day after he'd gone, when the scent of him was still on her skin? The thought made him sick, that she could move on so quickly was not good.

Yet he still had feelings for her, he couldn't just switch them off. He cared about her being in pain, he cared about the baby that wasn't his.

He lifted her hand and kissed her knuckles, then let his mouth kiss on top of her engagement ring, the ring that marked her as his responsibility, through good times and the bad.

Just then the door to the room was pushed open and a nurse he hadn't met before jumped at seeing him there.

'Visiting hours finished hours ago,' the nurse said, walking to the other side of Neve's bed and checking the monitor she was hooked up to.

Gabe and his family had been ushered out a few hours before and he knew they were all staying in a nearby hotel for the night. There was no question of him leaving though.

'I can't leave her,' Oakley said, his voice coarse and croaky.

The nurse sighed. 'Can I get you a drink or something to eat?'

'Some of that horrible black stuff the machine calls coffee would be great,' Oakley said.

She smiled. 'I'll see what I can do. There's, um. . . been a few journalists hanging around, asking questions.'

Oakley blinked, wondering how this could possibly be newsworthy, but everything he did was considered a matter of public interest so the possibility of him being about to become a dad for the first time would have been very interesting – well, at least to the paparazzi that hounded him everywhere he went. How they had found out he was here was a different matter entirely.

'What did you tell them?'

'That you weren't here and that they were obviously mistaken.'

Oakley smiled with gratitude. It wouldn't throw them off the scent, but it might buy them some time while he worked out how he could protect Neve from the fall-out of this too.

❄

Adam walked into the village, the sound of snow crunching under his boots the only noise he could hear, beyond the distant waves crashing onto the rocks.

It really was quite beautiful here, a tranquil haven away from it all. The noise of London never stopped, no matter what time of day it was, but here it was almost silent and he liked it. He had liked the noise, the hustle and bustle, the constant busyness of the city, it helped to distract him from the heartbreak he felt after his last relationship ended. But now it was quiet here and he could listen to his head and his heart again. The pain was no longer there and maybe it was time to stop hiding and move on with his life. And maybe, just maybe, Juniper Island would be the place to do it.

He looked around him and smiled. Most of the houses lay in darkness, though there were a few that emitted golden pools of light and he was gratified that Ivy's was one of them.

It had been a long day. He had stayed to help with the clearing-up of the dining room and setting up for breakfast the next day, keen for the staff to be able to have a few hours off to enjoy the remains of Christmas Day. He had talked with Gabe at length and was relieved to hear that Neve and the baby were doing fine and would most likely be able to return home the next day. Gabe also explained how they needed to start taking down the ice-carving display in the ice palace ready for the New Year's Eve ball and Adam reassured him that he would take care of it first thing on Boxing Day morning.

Annoyingly the journalists had been sniffing round, asking questions all day but thankfully, because Neve had never told anyone about being pregnant, the staff, when asked, could quite honestly deny all knowledge of it.

He'd sat in his office and replied to numerous emails that had come in for Neve and Gabe's attention. Now he just wanted to climb into bed and fall asleep, but he knew he had to apologise to Ivy first, though his plan of leaving her to calm down for a few hours had backfired when he realised just how much work he needed to do in Neve's absence. It looked like he didn't care about letting her down, when nothing could be further from the truth.

He hovered outside the door to her shop for a moment, wondering whether to knock or just let himself in. He suspected the door would be unlocked as she didn't seem to have any regard for her safety. The shop and the workshop beyond looked empty and Ivy was probably upstairs in the main living area of the house.

He turned the handle and sure enough the door opened and he sighed. He closed it behind him and, not wanting to scare her, he thought he should make his presence known.

'Ivy!'

He walked to the bottom of the stairs, just as she peered over the top to see who it was. She didn't say anything as she walked away but she didn't yell at him to get out of her house either, which he took to be a good sign.

Adam walked up the stairs and watched her as she moved around the kitchen, making a sandwich. She knew he was there but she didn't acknowledge his presence. But what was utterly adorable was the fact that she was wearing a fluffy penguin onesie.

'I bought you these,' he said, feebly, proffering the bouquet.

She glanced over at them and then back at the sandwich she was making that seemed to be as much of a work of art as her paintings were.

'Stole one of the table decorations you mean.'

Adam smiled, slightly. 'Actually no, I did this myself on the way down here. Admittedly the poinsettias were stolen from the vase on reception, but the holly leaves, berries and fir branches were all picked fresh a few minutes ago.'

'Flower arranging one of the many skills of a busy hotel manager then?'

'My skills stretch from flower arranging, napkin folding, making a bed, how to unblock a toilet, and how to make a great cup of coffee. I wish I could say that after many years working as a deputy manager I would be more skilled at delegating but I often find that when things go wrong, it's just better to roll up my sleeves and do the jobs that need doing.'

'Very noble,' Ivy said, slamming the top piece of bread on top of her sandwich and cutting into it with a large knife so angrily that he almost took a step back.

'I am very sorry I wasn't able to join you for lunch today. I was really looking forward to spending time with you.'

She slammed the knife down, which he was thankful for as she spun around to face him.

'I sat there alone at that table for over an hour and a half, pathetically waiting for you to turn up. I didn't want a relationship, I didn't want to get involved with anyone because being involved means putting your trust in someone, and that always means getting hurt. I should have listened to my head, not my heart, but foolishly, I thought you might be different.'

Adam watched her, her hands gesticulating wildly as she spoke, the beak of the penguin hood wobbling almost comically and he wanted nothing more than to kiss her right then. He loved her passion and the fact that her anger was directed at him didn't put him off at all.

'So many times I waited for my husband like that, in fancy restaurants, or at home after I had spent hours cooking for him, and so many times he let me down. Turned out he was sleeping with Lucy the whole time because what I was offering him at home wasn't good enough. And now I find out that unblocking toilets and folding napkins was much more preferable to spending time with me.'

He stepped closer. 'That isn't the case at all. Believe me when I say it would only have been an emergency that would have kept me away from you.'

'So what happened?'

'Neve fell down the stairs and knocked herself unconscious. I had to tell her family. We had to call the air ambulance to take her to hospital and then I had to get someone to fly her family out to the hospital too. At the time I should have been having lunch with you, I was babysitting Chester and playing with a bowl of cold spaghetti as his dads were ferrying Gabe and his family to the hospital.'

The fight went out of her almost immediately. 'Oh God, is she OK?'

'Yes, she's fine and the baby is fine too.'

'She's *pregnant*?' Ivy almost whispered.

'Yes, but they're both OK and she'll be back tomorrow.'

'Why did no one tell me this when I kept asking where you were?'

'I don't know. I don't think the staff realised you were my date and they were trying to keep what had happened under wraps, rather than alarming the guests. I'm so sorry.'

'Now I feel like a complete bitch again.'

Adam smiled and rested the bouquet on the table as he approached her, caging her in with his hands either side of her. 'You're not a complete bitch.'

She grinned. 'Just half of one?'

He pulled a face slightly. 'Maybe a quarter of one.'

Ivy laughed and he wanted to keep that smile on her face.

He reached round her, under the pretext of hugging her, but grabbed one half of her sandwich instead and as she leaned in to kiss him, he took a big bite of the sandwich.

'Hey, that's my sandwich!' Ivy said as Adam danced away from her, mocking her by holding the sandwich just out of reach.

'I'm starving. If you want your sandwich then you're going to have to come and get it.'

As he darted into the lounge, she quickly ran after him. He sat down on the sofa and as she came for him, he tugged her down onto his lap. She giggled as he offered her a bite. She took one and he took another for himself before putting the half-eaten sandwich on the corner of the coffee table next to him. He brushed the dark, curly hair off her shoulders as he quickly chewed and swallowed and she played with his fingers as she swallowed her bite.

'I'm sorry,' she said.

'I'm sorry too.'

He cupped his hand round the back of her neck and kissed her, softly at first but as she let out a little sigh of need, he slipped his tongue inside her, tasting her. God, she tasted so good. He could easily forget the rest of the sandwich and just spend the rest of the night kissing her.

Adam pulled back slightly. 'I've had a lousy Christmas Day, but this, right here, makes up for every bad thing that has happened today.'

'Kissing me?'

'Being here with you.'

She smiled and kissed him again and he knew he was getting in way above his head here. It was supposed to be lunch, simple as that. This morning, he'd had no intention of kissing her again and making things complicated between them. But this, right now, felt more right than anything had for a long time. It was as if something huge and integral had been missing from his life all these years. And as she stroked his face, he realised it wasn't just intimacy with a woman that had been missing, it was Ivy. The connection between them was too tangible to deny. Something told him they were supposed to be together and that scared him to death.

❅

Ivy lay on the sofa as Adam stretched out half on top of her, kissing her. They simply hadn't stopped since he'd arrived. As Christmas Days went, this was one of the best she'd had in a very long time. He hadn't tried to take it any further though and she liked that he was being gentle and really careful with her, though part of her was tempted to throw caution to the wind and take it to the next level. If he made love half as well as he kissed then she knew the next stage in their relationship was going to be amazing.

Knowing he would be leaving in three months somehow made it easier to do this with him. She could have fun with Adam without any of the emotional attachments, she didn't have to worry about letting him down or not being good enough. She didn't have to think about how that conversation would go when she told him she couldn't have children and then seeing the disappointment in his face. And she wouldn't have to put her trust in a relationship again, knowing at some point down the line, he would probably grow bored of her. This way was much better, they could have fun, they could spend time together and then he'd leave. She would just ignore the voice in her head that said if her feelings for him were that strong now, they would be even stronger in three months' time and it would be even harder to say goodbye.

He pulled back slightly to look at her and the softness in his eyes was like a punch to the stomach. He liked her too, she could see that.

'I better go,' he said, kissing her fondly on the forehead and that simple, affectionate gesture was her undoing. 'I'm knackered and I have to be up early tomorrow.'

The thought of him leaving made her suddenly feel sad. She reached up to stroke his face. 'You could stay.'

He arched an eyebrow at her.

'To sleep,' Ivy added quickly, suddenly fearful of bridging the gap between them and forging that connection she didn't want, the connection that could lead to her getting hurt again.

He smiled. 'OK, but I will have to be up and out early.'

'I'm always up early anyway as I go for a walk every day.'

'Yes, please stay away from ponies and ditches tomorrow.'

'I will, I promise. Or you could come with me, make sure that I don't befall any other disasters.'

His smile grew. 'I'd really like that. I need to be back at the hotel by eight, so maybe we could leave a little earlier.'

'We can do that.'

He stood up and offered out his hand to her and when she took it, she led him to the bedroom, a burst of excitement bubbling through her at having him in her bed.

Ivy watched him unashamedly getting undressed, and quite rightly too. This was a man who had nothing to be embarrassed about. From his muscular broad shoulders and arms, to his toned stomach, tight, cute bum and those huge, strong thighs, he was a delicious Christmas present that was unwrapping itself right before her eyes. He left his tight black boxers on and climbed straight into bed.

She looked down at herself and the penguin onesie she was wearing. Surely, if she was going to spend the night in bed with Adam, she should wear something sexier than this, even if they weren't going to do anything. He would be secretly disappointed too, but it seemed strange to change now.

Ivy looked up at him and her heart leapt when he held up the duvet for her to join him. The look on his face showed that he was as excited about sharing a bed with her dressed like this as she was about sharing a bed with him when he was almost naked. He not only accepted her for what she was wearing, he wanted her.

She quickly clambered under the duvet and Adam lay down and pulled her into his chest, his arms tight around her. Her breath caught in her throat, her heart hammering against her chest. This was so alien to her. Callum, her ex-husband, had never wanted to cuddle, in bed, out of bed or at all. The only act of intimacy they had was sex. Kissing always led to sex, he had rarely kissed her just because he wanted to kiss her. Looking back at the complete lack of love in their marriage, she had no idea why she had stayed as long as she did. But it was hard to miss something she'd never had and she had long assumed that what she and Callum had was the norm.

She closed her eyes and snuggled in closer to Adam, breathing in his wonderful scent and when he held her tighter, kissing her head, she knew she was falling for him, which was why it was more important than ever to keep him at arm's length.

But right then, there wasn't a single bone in her body that could do anything about it.

CHAPTER 10

Ivy looked up at the sky as snowflakes peppered her face. She needed some kind of distraction from how wonderful it felt to be walking through the hills and trees, hand in hand with Adam. That morning she had woken from one of the best night's sleep she had ever had, with Adam's arms tightly around her. It felt so good and so right that she was having trouble keeping the promise to herself that she wouldn't let herself get emotionally attached.

'It's beautiful out here,' Adam said. 'The snow makes everything look so bright and clean. It's like a new beginning every day.'

'I love it here, it's so peaceful and quiet. I like to walk out here every day because I know I've only got a year here and I want to make the most of it.'

'A year? You can't stay here forever?'

'Like many of the artists that Gabe brought in to sell their crafts, we all signed a contract for a year. After that, it'll be up to Gabe to decide whether to keep us on for another year. If our sales are good I'm sure that will play a part in his decision, but he might want to update the village by having different crafts and shop owners every year.'

'Would you want to stay here if Gabe asked you to?'

'Yes,' Ivy said, without hesitation. 'I've been truly happy here, more so than any other place I've lived. The villagers are so friendly and welcoming, the island is utterly beautiful. I will be gutted to leave.'

'Where would you go?'

'No idea. My parents moved around a lot while I was growing up so I never really put down roots or made lasting relationships. I went to university in Edinburgh and I fell in love with Scotland but then I met Callum and I moved to London with him. We married very quickly. All his friends became my friends. After the divorce it's funny how many of them went straight back to being his friends again. One or two of the girlfriends and wives tried to stay in touch for a while but it was awkward to maintain any kind of friendship when their husbands were such good friends with my ex. I don't really have any ties to anywhere now. My parents sadly died many years ago and my little sister is in New York. Maybe I'd move there. Maybe I'd move to somewhere else in Scotland, I'm not sure.

'I didn't come out of the divorce with a very good settlement. I moved into Callum's house when we got married, and although I contributed to the mortgage and bills over the years, because the house was in his name he was able to keep it and I got a few thousand pounds in the divorce. Wherever I go, the rent will have to be cheap.'

'So you wouldn't go back to London?'

Ivy shook her head. 'No, it's lost its charm for me now. After the divorce it felt tainted. I don't think I'd ever want to go back there.'

Adam sighed softly next to her and she knew that she had inadvertently taken off the table any chance of making the relationship permanent. If he was in London and she didn't want to live there then what future did they have? Maybe London wouldn't have to remind her of her relationship with her ex-husband. Perhaps she could make some new memories there with Adam instead of holding onto the bitterness of her past. But it was jumping too far ahead to think of things like that. Adam was getting involved with her knowing he was leaving; for him this was probably no more than a bit of fun. There was no point thinking about their future. But the way he was holding her hand, the way he held her in bed, it felt like something much deeper than casual and fun.

She sighed. If things were still going well between her and Adam when he left in three months it was something they could discuss then. Maybe he would want to stay here.

'What about you? Did you always want to be a hotel manager, do you ever crave for something new, something different?' she asked, wondering if she could tempt him away from the bright lights of London.

He shook his head. 'When I was a child I wanted to be a fighter pilot. Too many years watching *Star Wars*, *Top Gun* and any other film that had big dramatic flying scenes led to that dream going on far longer than most childhood dreams last. I studied Aviation at university, which gave me a lot of the basic skills I needed to become a pilot. I even got my private pilot's licence.'

'What happened? Why didn't you pursue it?'

'A life in the forces was never something I wanted. I'm too stubborn and pig-headed to be told to shine my shoes and run around the parade square twenty times every morning. Besides, the reality of being a fighter pilot and the thought that actually I might have to kill people never really struck home until I was older. I thought perhaps I might be a commercial pilot instead but. . . I don't know, do you ever just find yourself stuck in a rut?'

'I was married for five years to a man who never loved me, my rut was pretty deep. When he asked for a divorce it was something of a relief.'

He stared at her for a moment, the compassion in his eyes evident. She looked away, hoping he wouldn't pursue it, and he must have picked up on her desire not to talk about it as he squeezed her hand and carried on where he'd left off.

'Exactly, it's so easy just to plod along in the life you have, never rocking the boat or being brave enough to change. I was eighteen when I started working as a porter in a hotel in London. I worked there all through my university years. The money was good, the job was fun and interesting, and I enjoyed it. I was made team leader and then front-of-house manager before I even finished my studies. The money was even better and I suddenly had no real desire to leave. I still loved to fly but it became more of a hobby than a possible job. Gabe bought out the hotel not long after I finished university. He fired a ton of people but he kept me on. He told me I had a load of potential and that he could see me being manager one day. It was the first time that someone actually believed in me – he had faith in me when I didn't have any in myself. He's only a few years older than me and he had this clear vision, this big plan for his life, and he was just a big inspiration to me.'

'He's wonderful. I love what he's done here, he's very clever,' Ivy said.

Adam nodded. 'A few years later he made me deputy manager and it was this massive role that I absolutely thrived on. It came at just the right time too. Things ended badly with my girlfriend and I needed the distraction of the long hours and the constant challenges to throw myself into. Every day is different and I love it. Being a hotel manager or deputy manager was never my end goal when I started working at the hotel all those years ago and sometimes I regret that I never pursued the pilot thing more, but life takes you on weird twists and turns and sometimes where you end up is where you're actually supposed to be.'

She smiled at that philosophy. 'Our lives change and we adapt and make new dreams but it doesn't mean we have to give up on our old dreams entirely. It's not too late to pursue the pilot thing. You could carry on being a hotel manager but you could still do some pilot training in your spare time.'

'I don't get a lot of that.'

'You can't work seven days a week, that's not realistic. There's a place on one of the other islands, might be Lerwick, I can't remember, but there's somewhere nearby that offers some kind of commercial pilot training. They need planes to fly people between the islands and pilots are apparently in short supply up here. You could do that. Do the training while you're a manager here, then at least if in the future you get tired of this job you still have the option of being a pilot. Or you could offer sightseeing tours over the islands as part of one of the added extras for the hotel. I know they plan to offer helicopter tours in the summer but maybe you could approach Gabe about doing small plane tours instead. It's something you could do once a week so it didn't interfere with your other duties.'

He walked in silence next to her for a minute or two and she wondered if she had pushed him too far. She barely knew him and she was interfering in his life already.

'That's not a bad idea. I haven't flown half as much as I would have liked over the last few years. So if anything it would be good to get my private pilot's licence topped up and get some more flying hours logged. Sightseeing flights would be fun, even if I only did them now and again. On the rare occasions I've taken passengers up with me, I've always enjoyed seeing their reactions to flying and the views the most. I'll look into it, at least see what it would take to make that transition from private flying to commercial or a light aircraft licence. Thank you.'

She smiled at him, feeling happy that she had made a small difference for him.

'What about you?' Adam asked. 'Was painting always what you wanted to do?'

'I've always loved painting, and I've tried different mediums but I love the feeling of creating something with my bare hands. The fact that I'm now making money from it is fantastic, even though it isn't very much.'

'You're living your dream, that's wonderful. Not many people can say that.'

'I'm living most of my dream. I always imagined by the time I was twenty-five, I'd be in a big white wooden house overlooking the sea, with a dog, an adoring husband and four kids, painting in my little studio every day. I'm thirty next month and while my house isn't white, it is made from wood, I do live near the sea and I paint for a living, which is what I always wanted to do. I didn't get the rest but I'm very happy with what I have got.'

Ivy looked away from him as the pain of the lie sliced through her chest. She was happy with her life. She counted herself lucky every day that she was here on this beautiful island, that she got to paint instead of going to work in a job she hated. But the pain of not being able to have children was something that would simply not go away.

'There's still plenty of time for the rest of your dream to fall into place,' Adam said, encouragingly. 'Or you make new dreams, you adapt.'

She smiled as he used her own words against her.

Ivy looked up and realised they were approaching the hotel. Adam suddenly realised that too and she was gratified when he looked as disappointed as she felt that their walk was over.

He turned to face her, his hands going to her waist as he dropped a kiss on her forehead.

'I've really enjoyed our walk this morning, maybe we could make it a regular thing,' he said.

'Maybe that can be arranged,' Ivy said.

He smiled. 'I better go, I've got a busy day ahead and I doubt I'll even have time for any lunch but I could come round again tonight, if you're free.'

'I'm most definitely free.'

Adam pulled her gently against him, kissing her lips just briefly. His eyes were filled with affection as he gazed at her.

'I'll see you tonight then, Ivy Storm.'

'I'm looking forward to it.'

He smiled and she waved him off, her heart filling for him as she watched him go. Maybe he could be part of her new dream.

✲

Neve stared at the array of breakfast treats that Oakley had brought from the hospital restaurant for her. He had literally bought one of everything: pancakes, waffles, Danish pastries, croissants, porridge, lots of bowls of different cereals, bacon sandwiches, sausage sandwiches and toast with several different spreads to choose from. He hadn't said a lot when he had unloaded everything onto the bedside table, just muttered about her eating for two now. She had forced down a slice of toast and it lay heavy in her stomach along with the lie that she somehow had to salvage. They had barely spoken all morning, though she had been beyond happy to see him there when she had woken up, evidently having spent the night with her. She was grateful when her family had arrived to break the awkward silence between them and to help eat the huge breakfast supplies.

'This bacon sandwich is amazing,' Gabe said, devouring his third. 'Much better than the ones they served in the hotel this morning.'

'We've all been so spoilt with the food you serve at the Stardust Lake Hotel then when we are forced to stay elsewhere, we have to come back down to earth again,' Lizzie said, digging into the waffles.

'You guys didn't have to stay over in Lerwick, you could have gone back to Juniper Island last night,' Neve said. 'I think they're going to let me go home tonight anyway.'

'Of course we wanted to stay here, we've all been so worried,' David said, making Neve feel even worse.

'Did you guys at least sleep OK?'

'The beds were very comfortable,' Lizzie reassured her. 'Which is more than I can say for that chair. Did you sleep at all, Oakley dear?'

'A little.'

'Now, tell me, when are you two planning on getting married?' Lizzie blundered on, making an awkward situation even worse.

'Lizzie, they've only just got engaged,' David protested, smiling at Neve apologetically.

'Oh, but we need to make sure we're here for it. We have three cruises booked for next year. We could change things around so we're here, that China cruise isn't finalised yet. I presume you'll be having the wedding here. Or do you plan to get married in America?'

Neve swallowed, the ache in her heart increasing significantly. There would be no wedding but she had no idea how to explain that. 'We've not had much chance to discuss the specifics. He proposed and. . . I fell down the stairs.'

Oakley looked at her and she felt herself blush with shame, knowing she had left out the worst part.

The bedroom door was pushed open and Neve felt a huge smile spread across her face as Wren came running in, followed by Pip. Neve watched as Gabe's whole face lit up at Pip's arrival. They couldn't have come at a better time to diffuse the situation and Neve had really missed her niece.

'Neve!' Wren ran towards her and Luke managed to catch her before the little girl launched herself onto the bed.

'Aunty Neve is feeling a bit sore so give her a soft hug,' Luke said, releasing her.

Wren wrapped her arms around her gently and Neve was touched with the tenderness the four-year-old was showing her.

'I hope you don't mind us coming,' Pip said. 'She wanted to see you. Well, we both did.'

Gabe stood and approached his girlfriend, leaning his forehead against hers. The look they shared was one of complete and utter love and it filled Neve's heart to see it. She turned her attention back to Wren, feeling somehow that she was intruding on this private moment between Gabe and Pip just by watching them.

'Hey, sweetheart, I'm sorry that I missed Christmas with you.'

'That's OK, Daddy says we can have a second Christmas Day when you come home.'

'I'd like that very much,' Neve said.

'I drew you a picture,' Wren said, reaching into her coat pocket and pulling out the crumpled sheet of paper.

'Oh thank you.' Neve spread it out on the bed and smiled at the two figures. They had rounded bodies and stick arms and legs and big bulbous heads, but one figure was a lot bigger than the other and was wearing a superhero eye mask. They were holding hands.

'It's you and Oakley,' Wren explained though Neve had already gathered that. 'And you're holding hands because Oakley loves you forever and ever.'

She glanced over at Oakley and passed him the picture.

He stared at it for the longest time. When he spoke his voice was thick with emotion. 'Thanks, Wren, this is lovely.'

Gabe and Pip came to sit back down, Pip sitting on Gabe's lap as they were short on seats and Wren climbing up on Oakley's lap to explain more things about the picture. He listened intently and asked her questions quietly, somehow knowing the exact things to say to a four-year-old girl.

'How are you feeling?' Pip asked, meaningfully, and Neve knew she meant more than just the aches and pains. Pip wanted to know how things were with Oakley. She had clearly picked up the atmosphere in the room straight away.

'I'm fine,' Neve said, as it was the only thing she could say. 'The baby's fine too.'

Pip nodded, knowing that Neve couldn't say any more, but she reached out and squeezed Neve's arm in a sign of solidarity that meant much more now than the words they couldn't say.

'Thank you,' Neve whispered.

'We just hope you're feeling better soon,' Gabe said, deliberately.

Neve sighed. Her broken bones would heal, the bruises would fade away. There was no cure for stupidity and there was no getting over a broken heart.

❅

Adam quickly pressed 'send' on yet another email and sighed as he looked down his massive to do list. It was no wonder that Neve was finding it hard going, the list of things to do was seemingly endless. As it was Boxing Day, he had hoped for a slightly quieter day. Everyone and their dog was enjoying a nice Christmas break but in the hotel trade it never stopped. That morning he had already met with the team responsible for the changeover in the ice palace from Santa's Grotto to glamorous ballroom in preparation for the New Year's Eve ball. Lots of the guests, including most of the journalists, had left and later that afternoon the new guests would be arriving to spend the lead up to New Year's at the hotel. He would need to greet them and make sure they were all happy. The housekeeping crew were having to do a very fast turnaround, a fresh delivery of food had failed to arrive and Adam had had to make an emergency contingency plan. He was starving and he hadn't even had time to go down to the kitchen and make himself a cup of coffee yet.

When the phone rang for what felt like the hundredth time that morning, he nearly picked it up and threw it out of the window.

He opened up another email as he answered it.

'Hi Adam, it's Gabe.'

The tone in his voice made Adam stop what he was doing and give Gabe all of his attention.

'Hey, how's Neve?'

'She's fine, broken wrist which is now in a cast, she's a bit sore and very tired, but with all the tests they've run on her and checking on her all through the night, she's not getting much rest at the moment. The doctors are happy that both her and the baby are fine though and they are going to discharge her later today. How are we doing for flights, would the plane be able to come and collect us from Lerwick airport later?'

Adam quickly consulted the flight plan. 'Mikael is on his way to Edinburgh now to pick up some more guests, he also has a flight from Glasgow this afternoon and Aberdeen around six tonight. I could get him to come to Lerwick about eight, maybe nine. I'll call him now and ask him what's the earliest he could get to you. It's possible he could squeeze you in before the Aberdeen flight. Let me ask him and I'll come back to you.'

'OK. I need Neve to have some rest over the next few days.'

Adam laughed. 'She won't be happy about that.'

'Tough, she can be unhappy about it while she sits in her house with her feet up. Oakley is also worried about the attention from the press. Some journalists have been sniffing around here. Have you had any trouble there?'

'A few journalists asking questions but nothing we couldn't handle. Most of them have gone now, there's only one left.'

'Bad timing on our part with all the journalists there to cover the opening. Bet they think all their dreams have come true with a story this big. I think there'll be some coverage in the tabloids either today or tomorrow and both Oakley and I would prefer that Neve doesn't see it. Can you do something to lock her out of the computer?'

Adam quickly accessed the employee log-in list on the computer. As assistant manager he had the authority to create accounts for people and delete them if and when they left the employment of Stardust Lake Hotel. He clicked on Neve's account and locked it.

'It's done, she won't be able to log in now. I can unlock it for her when she comes back to work.'

Gabe laughed. 'Good job. Now, with her out the picture for the next few days, will you be OK to take over from her until the New Year?'

'Of course I can do that.'

Adam could hear the smile in Gabe's voice when he spoke. 'I know you thrive on being busy and I know you'll be brilliant as manager for a few days but I'll be back tonight and I can give you a hand too and we can spread some of the work to Cora as well.'

'You don't need to worry, I'm more than happy to step in.'

He had been itching for a chance at being manager for a few months now and this was the opportunity to show Gabe he was ready for this.

'Thank you, you have no idea what it means to know you're there taking care of everything for us. The hotel is in very safe hands.'

Adam could hear that Gabe was worried about something, though it didn't sound like it was leaving him in charge.

'Are you OK, Gabe?'

Gabe sighed. 'Something is going on between Neve and Oakley and I don't know what. I can't get Neve on her own to ask her as Oakley won't leave her side but they're barely speaking. He'll ask her if she wants something to eat and drink but other than that, they hardly say a word. Admittedly, Neve has been asleep for a lot of the time but even when she's awake they don't talk. Luke said that Oakley thinks the baby is yours.'

Good lord, the prospect of Gabe making him a manager in one of his hotels one day was suddenly slipping through his fingers like sand. If Gabe thought that Adam had been secretly screwing around with his sister behind his back that wouldn't look good.

'The baby isn't mine, I promise you I've never even laid a finger on her. You know we're friends and it has never been more than that.'

'I know that, but why does Oakley think that the baby is yours?'

'I have no idea. I wonder if Neve said something to him or whether he misunderstood. I was as surprised as you are when Oakley said that to me. Look, we'll get them both back here and we'll sort it out. Even if we need to lock them in a room together and refuse to let them out until they've talked it through. Oakley is crazy in love with her, she's carrying his baby. They're going to be OK. This is just a little bump in the road for them.'

'OK, thanks. You're right, this is too important to let them screw it up. We'll just have to intervene if we need to.'

'I'm good at that, I'm very good at poking my nose in other people's business when necessary.'

Gabe laughed. 'Thanks, mate.'

They ended the call and Adam had just started writing another email when there was a soft knock on his open door. As he looked up, he saw Ivy standing there. He couldn't help the huge smile that suddenly spread across his face.

'I thought you might be hungry so I brought lunch,' she said, coming into the room more fully and holding up what looked like a large picnic hamper. 'There's chocolate cake in there with three layers.'

He laughed and looked down for a moment at his huge list of things to do.

Her smile faltered. 'I know you're really busy. You don't have to stop work and talk to me or anything. I can leave it all here and you can eat it as you work. We can do dinner tonight as planned and we can catch up then.'

But he wasn't going to be that asshole who asked her to leave the food on his desk and leave, not after the amount of time she had clearly put into preparing it. He never normally had time for lunch in his job but today he would make time. Ivy was important and half an hour out of his day would make no difference to him, but it would make all the difference to her.

'Give me one second,' Adam said as he picked up the phone and dialled down to reception. A moment later, Iris answered. 'Iris, it's Adam. Is everything OK down there, any problems?'

'No, it's all a bit quiet really as we wait for the new guests.'

'OK, I have an important meeting I need to take. I'm going to divert all my calls to the answerphone for the next half hour. Can you make sure, if anyone comes looking for me, that I'm not disturbed?'

'Of course.'

He rang off and looked up into Ivy's smiling face. 'You didn't need to do that,' she said.

'Yes, I did.'

Adam stood up and closed the office door, locking it from the inside. He turned to face Ivy again, who was looking at him with surprise. 'I just want to make sure we're not disturbed.'

'And what do you plan to do now we're alone and not likely to be disturbed?'

He walked up to her and cupped her face. 'I'm going to start by kissing you.'

He bent his head down and kissed her and as she kissed him back every problem, every query, every stress that had occupied his head all morning, just melted away. Ivy filled every one of his senses, his every thought was only of her. As distractions went, it was one of the finest.

❊

It was late on Boxing Day night by the time the plane touched back down on Juniper Island. Oakley gazed down at Neve's hand in his and then back out the window as the plane came to a stop on the runway. She was fast asleep.

There had been no time to talk to Neve all day, with the doctors coming and going and all the further tests and checks they wanted to do. Her family had been there for a large part of the day and when they weren't there she had been asleep. Oakley had been quite thankful for the interruptions. He had no idea what he would say to her if he'd had the chance.

He felt numb.

Lizzie and David moved towards them.

'Will you guys be OK? I hate seeing her like this. She could stay in our house, we'd look after her,' Lizzie said.

'We'll be fine, Mrs Whitaker,' Oakley said, automatically. He had no idea if they would be.

The plane door was opened and a gust of snow blew in. He took his coat off and wrapped it around Neve and then scooped her up into his arms. She stirred slightly but didn't wake.

Lizzie smiled at them. 'I know she's in safe hands.'

He nodded and carried Neve down the steps to the waiting car. After settling her in the back, he got in next to her. Gabe got in the front, while Luke, Pip, Wren and Neve's mum and dad got in the other car waiting for them.

The car took off towards the hotel and Gabe turned round to talk to Oakley.

'I'm not sure what's going on between the two of you. You came here to win her back, you've got engaged, she's carrying your child, but the tension between the two of you today was almost palpable. Did you have a row?'

Oakley shrugged. They hadn't really. It had been over way too quickly for it to count as a row. 'Something like that.'

'She's going to need someone to look after her for the next few days at least. She'll need help washing so she doesn't get her cast wet and help getting dressed and she'll be in a lot of pain. If you can't help her, or don't want to, then let me know and we can look after her.'

'I'll take care of her,' Oakley said, wondering why he was volunteering for that.

'Are you sure?'

Oakley nodded as he looked down at Neve sitting next to him, asleep, fragile and incredibly vulnerable. He honestly didn't know where they stood in their relationship or whether they had any kind of future together but he cared about her and the very least he could do was look after her for the next few days.

The car pulled up outside Neve's home and, without another word to Gabe, Oakley got out and scooped her into his arms again. He carried her up the steps and Gabe ran on ahead to help him with the door. Oakley walked into the house and straight up the stairs to Neve's bedroom as he heard Gabe leave, closing the front door behind him.

Oakley laid her down gently on the bed and then very carefully, very slowly, pulled off her jeans. He undid the cuff of his shirt she was wearing so he could slide it over her cast. When she was naked, he tucked her into the duvet. She chose that time to wake up.

'Oakley?' she said, sleepily.

'I'm here. You're home, everything's OK,' he whispered, soothingly, brushing the hair from her face.

'Will you stay with me?'

Neve drifted back off to sleep, her breathing becoming heavier.

Oakley watched her for the longest moment, trying to decide what to do. He lifted her broken arm and rested it on a pillow and then made sure that was tucked under the duvet too. He stared at her, wanting to kiss her and shake her and wrap her in his arms and protect her all at once. But knowing the angry, upset part of his brain wouldn't let him sleep in the same bed with her as if nothing had happened, he left her alone and went downstairs to sleep on the sofa.

CHAPTER 11

Neve woke early the next day to the bright light of the fresh fallen snow. It was still snowing heavily outside, fat flakes dancing and swirling in the grey sky. And she was alone. There was no sign of Oakley. She wondered if he had got on the next plane out of there and left her. She couldn't help the stupid tears filling her eyes at that thought. She was so emotional lately and she knew it was the baby hormones. Up until when she had broken up with Oakley she hadn't cried for years but her grief over losing him had soon developed into emotional baby hormones even before she had recognised what they were, making her cry at the slightest thing. She put a hand over her belly and felt the sob burst from her throat. In trying to do something good for Oakley, she had hurt him, and ruined any chance of a proper future with the man she loved.

She heard the thunder of feet on the stairs and Oakley burst into her room. He was wearing just his tight black boxers and his hair was ruffled as if he'd just woken up. The tears stopped almost immediately at seeing he was still there. At least for now.

'What's wrong? Are you hurt?'

'No, I'm fine. I'm just. . .' she trailed off.

He smiled sympathetically. 'At least I know where all these tears have come from over the last few days. I should have guessed something was going on when you cried more in the first day I was back than the whole ten months we were together. In fact, I don't think I've ever seen you cry before now.'

'It's baby hormones.'

'I know,' he said, softly.

'You weren't here when I woke up,' Neve said, hating how needy and pathetic she sounded.

'Is that what made you cry?'

'I thought you'd left.'

'I. . . just didn't want to sleep in bed with you and risk hurting you.'

It was a terrible lie and they both knew it.

'You hate me,' Neve said, quietly.

'I'm angry at you. It's not possible for me to hate you.'

She stared at him. They needed to talk but she wasn't sure she had it in her right now.

She sat up gingerly, but her whole body protested. It hurt everywhere; her back, legs, arms, neck and her head. The doctors had warned that she would feel worse today than the day before, but she hadn't imagined it would be like this.

Oakley could see she was in pain and rushed to help her stand up.

'How about I run you a bath? That might help with the aches and pains. It will probably be easier to keep your cast dry in a bath than if you had a shower.'

'Thank you, but I can run my own bath. I'm pregnant, not dying.'

'You've had a bad fall, you knocked yourself out, let me look after you.'

After a moment, she nodded, reluctantly. 'Not too hot though. Pregnant women are not allowed to take hot baths.'

He blinked. 'There's a whole load of new rules with pregnancy, isn't there?'

'Sadly, yes. One of them being no cheesecake and I love cheesecake.'

Oakley looked shocked. 'No cheesecake?'

'I know, it's a travesty.'

He laughed and she couldn't help but smile. Maybe they would be OK. Maybe they couldn't be together and, despite being in love with him, that was probably for the best, but maybe they could be friends.

With one arm around her waist, he helped her into the bathroom, her legs and back protesting with every step.

He started running the bath and poured in some muscle-relaxing bubble bath which she had been bought but never used. When he was happy with the temperature, he lifted her and lowered her into the water.

She sat awkwardly, with her bandaged hand balanced on her shoulder. It was a corner bath and one that she had never used since she had got there. In fact she couldn't remember the last time she'd had a bath. In her job as hotel manager, working long hours, she barely had time to have a quick shower in the mornings before rushing off to work. She wasn't sure how long a relaxing bath was supposed to take and whether she was just supposed to sit there. She didn't do relaxing very well. For the last few months everything had been about the opening of the hotel and now that had been and gone, she'd forgotten what relaxing actually meant.

She started rubbing her legs a little with her good hand, not really feeling the benefits of a bath that everyone raved about, when she was distracted by Oakley undressing. She stared at him in shock and, despite the fact that she ached everywhere and their relationship was in tatters, she couldn't help but think about doing all kinds of wonderful and dirty things with him in the bath.

He stepped into the bath behind her and sat down, his legs either side of her hips. Oakley was so huge that even in the large corner bath, he seemed to fill it. With his hands on her shoulders, he encouraged her to lie back and lean against his chest. He wrapped an arm around her chest, just above her breasts.

'Here, rest your arm on top of my arm, then it won't get wet.'

Neve did as she was told and rested her head on his shoulder and, as the warm water enveloped her, wrapped in his arms, she felt all the stresses seep out of her, even if it was temporary.

A noise downstairs disturbed her and her eyes shot open. 'What was that?'

'What?' Oakley asked, as he gently lapped the warm water over her body.

'I heard a noise, it sounded like a door slamming.'

They both listened for a second but couldn't hear anything else, so she relaxed back into him.

'Neve!' came her mum's voice from the bedroom.

'Crap.' Neve hissed, as she tried to get out of the bath.

Oakley held her in place. 'You're the only thing that's protecting my modesty at the moment. I love your mum but I really don't want her to see my bits all wangling and a dangling.'

'I don't want her to see me naked either.'

Oakley moved his arm over her breasts and scooped bubbles over her in an attempt to hide the rest of her just as her mum walked straight into the bathroom.

'Oh my! Sorry, I didn't realise,' Lizzie said, her feet frozen to the ground. 'I just came to see if you needed any help getting washed and dressed. . .'

Neve suppressed a little giggle at the ridiculousness of the situation.

Oakley cleared his throat. 'We've got everything taken care of, Mrs Whitaker.'

'Oh, please, call me Lizzie.'

Of course they had to be on first name terms now her mum had practically seen Oakley stark naked. And still she wasn't leaving.

'Mum, thanks for coming round but Oakley is taking really good care of me. Why don't I pop round later and we can have a chat then?' Neve said, hoping the dismissal was nice but firm enough to get her to leave while they all had some dignity intact.

'Yes, of course. Well, if you need anything, you know where I am,' Lizzie said and with a little wave she left, closing the door behind her.

Neve waited a few seconds before she burst out laughing and she felt Oakley shake with laughter as he chuckled into her shoulder.

'Well, that went well,' Neve said.

'Why would you need help getting dressed when they know I'm here?' Oakley said, as he was still laughing.

'They know something is weird between us. I think they're all worried about us.'

She felt Oakley's laughter die and fade away as he grew serious.

They lay in silence for the longest while but eventually Neve spoke.

'What are you still doing here, Oakley?'

'Where would I go?'

'Back to California and your glamorous life of the rich and famous, find yourself a nice, plastic, beautiful girl to adorn your arm who has no complications or baggage. You don't need to be here with me.'

'I don't know why, but you don't think very much of me, do you? I have given you no reason to doubt me, even when we were on a break, and yet you still don't trust me. You say you love me yet you keep trying to push me away. What's the real reason you're afraid of being together?'

She sighed. How could she tell him that his mum had made her feel like she wasn't worthy enough to be with him? His mum had told her that she wasn't special enough to keep Oakley's interest over the long term and he would never want forever with her. She hated that his mum had made her doubt herself, she had never been a particularly confident person but she believed Oakley loved her in the beginning and that this thing between them was as special to him as it was to her. One visit from his mum had changed all that. And the subsequent visits had slowly chipped away her confidence in herself and what they had until there was nothing left.

And she knew his mum was right. She hadn't been enough for Zander. He needed someone far more glamorous and famous to complete him. A stable girl was not good enough for him. And eventually Oakley would feel the same. The beautiful girls he had been linked with while they had been apart were a brutal reminder of what he could have and what he would no doubt choose to have one day. But she didn't feel she could say any of that. He was close to his mum and coming between them would not end well for them. And he was so idealistic with his big plans for their future. He would never understand this doubt she had in herself, that it would never go away and she'd always be fearful of losing him. Maybe she could explain some of what she felt.

'Do you remember me asking you what you saw in our future?' Neve said.

Oakley sighed.

'We were heading towards the end of your time in London and I hoped we could have some kind of conversation about our relationship, whether it was worth fighting for after you had gone. I wasn't expecting a marriage proposal but just some kind of affirmation that we were heading that way eventually. You told me you saw lots of passionate sex in our future, that you wanted to try every sexual position known to man and then make up a few of our own. That didn't exactly give me a lot of hope for a serious future,' Neve said.

'I was joking. I didn't realise you wanted a proper conversation. We never did serious. We laughed and joked, we talked.'

'I know. I had so much fun with you, you made me smile so much. I wanted forever with you.'

'I wanted forever with you too,' Oakley said, wrapping his other arm around her belly and pulling her tightly against him.

'I asked you whether you wanted children and you laughed and said maybe, some day, in ten years from now.'

'I'm twenty-six.'

'I'm thirty-one, ten years from now would make me forty-one. Not many women can have babies at that age.'

'So you decided to just get pregnant anyway. I wouldn't give you a child so you'd find someone who would.'

'No, I would never do that. Believe me, I was as shocked as you were when I found out I was pregnant. Well, not as shocked as *you* were. I think if I'd come at you with an axe in one hand and a severed head in the other, you wouldn't have been more scared than when I told you I was pregnant. That's why I don't understand why you're still here. I thought you would be over the moon that the baby isn't yours. I thought you would be relieved that the responsibility has nothing to do with you. You can go back to your fabulous life and you don't have to worry about me.'

'I had a lot of time to reflect while we were apart. My fabulous life, as you call it, with the celebrity parties and ultra-glamorous people, seemed empty and dark without you. I love being an actor, I love going to work every day, donning my superhero suit and learning to fight and fly and use my superhero powers. It's been my dream come true. But everything else that comes with it – the parties, the drugs, the alcohol, the women, the casual sex – means nothing to me. Acting is my dream but you were my life and I just wanted to come home after a day's filming and curl up in your arms, make love to the woman I loved and talk to you about your day. I came here to ask you to be a part of my life because I wanted forever with you. Yes, I was shocked to find out you were pregnant but I felt no relief that the baby isn't mine. I was hurt and angry and disappointed but I definitely wasn't relieved.'

Neve swallowed down the pain she felt at how much she had hurt him.

'What are you saying, that if the baby had been yours, you would have still wanted to marry me? You never wanted this. Part of your filming schedule for this movie means going to Australia and Russia. I would be in California, on my own with the baby, instead of here with my family and friends. When you were at home, you'd resent the lack of sleep a small baby would bring and then you'd end up resenting me and your son.'

'I could never resent you or our son. It wouldn't have been ideal, but I'd have done the right thing by you. I wouldn't have left you alone. We would have made it work somehow.'

'I didn't want you to do the right thing for me, I didn't want that for you or for us. We shouldn't have to make our relationship work.'

'Of course we should. It's never going to be easy for us. Even without a baby to consider. We'd argue and get tired and ratty with each other but we would make it work because the alternative of not being together doesn't bear thinking about.'

Her heart suddenly ached. Had she been wrong to do what she had done? He had been right, they had loved each other, that was the only thing that mattered. Had she given up on her dream too easily? Shouldn't she have at least tried to make it work rather than giving up?

'So what happens now?' she asked.

He shifted his arm around her belly so his hand was directly over where their baby was growing inside her.

'I honestly don't know.'

She glanced down at the engagement ring on her finger. 'Do you want the ring back?'

'No, keep it. It will be a reminder for me of why I asked you in the first place. A reminder of when I loved you more than anything. I need to remember that.'

Loved not love. She closed her eyes.

'Is that love now gone?' Neve asked, her voice choked with emotion.

He didn't answer, clearly not knowing what words to say. Had he ever really loved her at all if he could turn it off so easily? Or had she just pushed him away one too many times and he'd finally given up?

She linked hands with him over her belly and he didn't pull away.

Was love really enough?

❄

Ivy woke with Adam's arms tightly around her after another glorious night's sleep. They had both slept much later than normal and the chance of another early morning walk was now off the cards. They had spent most of the night chatting and kissing, so she wasn't surprised that they had slept in so late.

As she swept her fingers across his bare chest, his long, dark eyelashes fluttered open and when he saw her, he broke into a huge smile.

'Morning, beautiful, are we going for a walk?'

'I'm afraid it's too late for that.'

Adam frowned and quickly checked his watch. 'Oh, wow, that *is* late. I'd better get to the hotel soon.'

'Isn't Neve back from the hospital now?'

'Yes, but she won't be back at work until the New Year, something that she won't be happy about. She's never been one for sitting still.'

'You like her?' Ivy said and then immediately regretted it.

He cocked an eyebrow at her and smiled. 'We've been friends for a very long time but I can assure you that nothing has ever happened between us.'

'I trust you, you have very trustworthy eyes,' Ivy said. 'It's one of your best features.'

'It *is*?'

'That and your gorgeous body,' Ivy laughed, running her hand over his chest. 'Can I paint you tonight? I think you'll make a superb model.'

Adam rolled her over, quickly pinning her to the bed with his weight. 'Provided that the painting is not going up for public sale.'

'No, just for me to perv over.'

He kissed her and she reached up to stroke his face. He pulled back slightly to look at her. The tenderness in his eyes completely unravelled her.

'What are we doing, Adam? For two people who don't want to get involved in a relationship, we're both doing a really bad job.'

He shrugged and kissed her nose. 'I don't know, but I'm having way too much fun to want to stop.'

'Me too, but I'm scared.'

'Scared of what?'

'Of us, of things going too far, of falling for you and then watching you leave in a few months' time.'

'What if I stayed?'

Her heart leapt. '*What?*'

'This place, it's so peaceful. I feel like I can finally breathe here. Neve needs help and I don't think a few months is going to cut it. The hotel in London had a manager and two deputy managers, where here there's only Neve. Admittedly the hotel there is bigger than here, but the workload is still the same. I was thinking I might talk to Gabe about making the move here more permanent.'

'You'd move here for me?' Panic settled into her gut. 'What if things went wrong? What if we broke up?'

'I'm up in the hotel, you're down here, it would be very easy to avoid each other if we had to. If I moved here, you would be part of the reason, but not the only reason. I told you before that I felt I was stuck in a rut down in the hotel in London. I've been deputy manager at that hotel for the last five years with no chance of becoming manager unless our current manager leaves and he loves his job. This could be a welcome change for me, a new challenge to get my teeth into. I've been thinking about this and I'm going to ask Gabe to make me joint manager here with Neve. She needs the help and she won't be coming back to work straight away when the baby comes. I can help out here until she does.'

'So I guess that means this wouldn't be something casual any more?'

'I don't think it ever was.'

She ran her fingers over his cheeks, and down to the stubble on his jaw and neck. 'You said that when you became deputy manager things had just ended badly with your ex-girlfriend. Has there been no one for you since?'

'No, but I'm ready to move on in my personal life too.'

Something serious scared her to death, because what if something serious turned into marriage and then the question of children came up? No, she would have to tell him that she couldn't have children before it got too far and then risk losing him for good. But that was an awkward conversation to have when they hadn't even slept together yet. They might not even be together in a week's time. When was a good time to ask the 'Do you want children?' question? A few weeks down the line? A few months' time when they would be too deeply involved to get out without getting hurt? She'd have to tell him soon, it was only fair. But it was so hard to bring that up without sending him running for the hills, thinking she wanted marriage and babies already.

But as he kissed her, his hot mouth travelling down her throat to her collarbone, she knew it was a conversation that could definitely wait a few days at least.

CHAPTER 12

Neve took a swig of her tea as she looked out on the view from the dining room window. The dining room was a huge glass conservatory that had one of the best views of Juniper Island, though she'd barely had time to look at it since her arrival.

It was the day after Boxing Day and the families that had made it down for breakfast all looked a little worse for wear from their celebrations over the last few days.

Neve had been so looking forward to spending Christmas with her family this year, especially her niece Wren, who had been beyond excited about the big day for weeks. Instead she had spent the last two days in hospital. She still had all her family's presents to give them, she'd have to make sure they got them, but right now she needed to get to work.

Oakley had refused to let her go to work when she had mentioned it earlier, saying she needed to rest. She had ignored his protests and come over to the main building anyway, leaving him muttering to himself words that sounded like, 'We'll see about this.'

She stepped out of the dining room, taking her mug of tea with her, and bumped into Pip.

'Neve, I can't stop, I'm following a couple around the island this morning. I think he's going to propose so he has hired me to follow them and take lots of photos. But listen, are you OK? Me and Gabe have been so worried about you. What's going on with you and Oakley?'

'I. . .' Neve trailed off. How could she even begin to explain how stupid she had been? She had no idea where she and Oakley stood either. He hadn't left, but it didn't seem like they were together any more. 'I have no idea but maybe we can catch up later this afternoon when you have more time and I can tell you all about it.'

'I'd like that,' Pip said. She gave Neve a quick hug and ran out the door.

Neve walked past the reception area and up to the first floor, where all the offices were. She walked into her office, switched on her computer and tried to log in. The computer beeped plaintively, informing her the password she had typed in was incorrect.

Neve sighed, rubbing her head, which was starting to ache already. She had changed the password just recently and she tried to remember what she had changed it to. She tried the computer again but still couldn't log in.

There was a soft knock on the door and Adam walked in. She smiled when she saw him – he always made her feel better.

'Hey, how you feeling?'

'I'm fine, a bit sore, but fine, I promise.'

'That's good and I hear you're pregnant, is that true?'

'Yes. A little boy.' Neve took a swig of her tea.

He smiled. 'Congratulations. Is he mine?'

She nearly choked on her mouthful of tea and then burst out laughing. She had known Adam for over eight years. They had become really good friends over the years but never in the whole time since they had known each other had they shown any interest in each other. She didn't fancy him in the slightest and they'd never even kissed so for him to ask that question was completely out of the blue.

'Yeah, I didn't think so,' Adam said. 'I felt sure that I would have remembered if we had slept together. But I saw Oakley shortly after your fall and he seemed to think the baby was mine. Now where would he get that idea from?'

The smile fell from her face. She'd forgotten that with the lie she had told she had inadvertently implicated Adam. Fortunately, he didn't seem too bothered by it.

'Oh God, was he mad at you?'

'Well, let's see… He pinned me to the wall and threatened to kill me. Then he proceeded to ask me if I intended to do the right thing by you and marry you.'

'I'm so sorry. It's all been a horrible misunderstanding. What did you tell him?'

'I said that this was the first I knew about a baby and that I needed to speak to you. Want to tell me what's going on? Why does he think the baby is mine?'

'Because I told him it isn't his and he assumed that the baby must be yours. He's always been convinced that something is going on between us. He says men and women can't be friends,' Neve said.

'We've done OK so far but that aside, why on earth would you tell him the baby isn't his? Wait, it *is* his, isn't it? You haven't been with someone else up here, have you?'

'Of course it's his. There has been no one else. He had been telling me how much he loved his new job, how wonderful it was, and when I told him I was pregnant you should have seen his face. I've never seen anyone look so scared before. He didn't want our baby and I couldn't bear our son growing up with a dad who hated him. I didn't want to do anything that might ruin his career and his dreams so I told him the baby wasn't his so he wouldn't feel obligated to stay with me and end up resenting me.'

Adam stared at her in shock and didn't say anything for the longest while. Eventually he sighed.

'When my sister was pregnant, she completely lost her marbles. Before Oliver was born Taylor used to be a lecturer at university, teaching biology; she is one of the cleverest people I know. But when she was pregnant she lost all ability to make any kind of decision. I remember sitting with her in a restaurant once and she cried for a full fifteen minutes because she couldn't decide what to order and there was too much choice. And that was after she had turned up late because she had cried over trying to decide what to wear. When Taylor did make decisions, she made bad ones. Like giving her credit card details to some guy on the street because he was supposedly raising money to build an animal sanctuary in Talakstan.'

'Talakstan?'

'Yes, you don't need to look it up, it doesn't exist. And then there was the time she agreed to look after a colleague's pet while they were on holiday without checking what kind of pet it was first and ended up babysitting an eight-foot python for a week when she hates snakes. Taylor lost all her common sense and rationality, she forgot dates, meetings, which drawer of the freezer she kept the bread in. She went to work once with odd shoes, one purple, one green. Quite simply, she went doolally. So I understand that you weren't perhaps thinking straight when you made the decision to lie to the man you love about his paternity to your unborn child.'

'I did it for him,' Neve protested. 'This wasn't selfish or malicious. He didn't want a baby so I let him go.'

'And that's very noble. But he has a right to know he is going to be a father and he has a right to choose for himself whether he wants to be part of that kid's life. Even if that means that Oakley only pops over here once a year with exorbitantly expensive presents.'

'He said if the baby was his he would have stood by me and married me. But I didn't want a relationship based on loyalty, I want one based on love. I wanted him to *want* to stay with me and the baby.'

'And you think he doesn't love you?'

Neve stared down at the engagement ring that proved that he did.

'OK,' Adam said slowly when her silence answered the question for him. 'You tell him you don't need to be married to him for this to work. That he can see the child whenever he wants. You're a strong person, Neve. You can raise a baby on your own. If you stayed here your brothers would help you, Pip too, your mum and dad whenever they came to visit. I'd help you and I expect everyone in the village would help as well. Or if you wanted to move closer to Oakley, not with him but close to him, then Oakley could see his son any time he wanted to and maybe in time he would realise how much he is missing out by not being in the boy's life full-time and he would choose that life with you instead of feeling like he was forced into it. Oakley asked you to marry him, he obviously loves you. He probably just needs a little time to get used to the idea that marrying you means being a dad too. But let him have that choice.'

'What can I do? Tell him I lied to him? He'd be furious.'

'And how furious do you think he'll be when your son asks about his dad in a few years' time, says he'd like to meet him, and you give Oakley a call and tell him the truth. How mad do you think Oakley will be then when he has already missed out on so much of his son's life? You're not thinking about this logically. Do you want my advice?'

'Not if it involves sex. Your solutions to most problems involve sex. This is how we ended up in this situation in the first place – because you told me to sleep with Oakley and see if we had any real spark beyond sex.'

'And did you?'

'Yes, of course we did. I fell completely and utterly in love with him, but we'd never have known that if I hadn't slept with him in the first place.'

Adam chuckled and shook his head at Neve's logic and even with her pregnancy hormone-addled brain she could see her argument was flawed.

'Well, you're not going to like this advice any more but I think you should get naked, make love to him and while you're in the throes of passion, just slip it into the conversation then. Men can rarely get angry during sex.'

Neve laughed.

'Look, in all seriousness, yes, he'll be angry but he'll appreciate the sentiments behind the reason you did it and then at least he can choose for himself rather than having the decision made for him.'

Neve let her head fall into her hands. It was such a mess.

'What a tangled web we weave,' Adam said, picking up the phone and dialling out. He spoke to whoever was on the other end. 'Yeah, she's here.' He put the phone down and she looked at him in confusion.

'Who was that?'

'It doesn't matter.'

Neve sighed, and joggled the mouse on the computer, needing the distraction of work so she wouldn't have to think about how stupid she had been. 'I can't log in to my computer, has something happened to the system?'

'No, your password has been locked out. Gabe doesn't want you to work until the New Year. You have the week off so go and enjoy yourself with your lovely man and have lots of hot sex.'

'What? That's ridiculous.'

'Not really. You've had a bad fall, you were rushed to hospital unconscious, you've broken your wrist. You probably have concussion. Your little son probably had the shock of his life so you need to comfort him by eating lots of cake and chocolate and putting your feet up.'

'I do not have concussion – if that was the case the hospital would have kept me in. And you can't just kick me out of my job for a week. If I think I'm fit enough to return to work then that's down to me.'

'Judging on what you've told me this morning, I don't think much of your decision-making skills at the moment. You're no good to me like this.'

'I'm the manager, you're the assistant manager,' Neve said, marvelling how everything was unravelling beyond her control.

'Yeah, pulling rank doesn't work on me.'

'Adam, there's loads that needs to be done before the New Year's Eve ball. I can't leave you with all that.'

'Not really. The great thing about taking over from you is that you're so bloody efficient and organised, everything was planned months ago. The boys are down at the ice palace now, taking down Santa's Grotto and rearranging everything ready for the ball. The kitchens are all prepared with food and drink. There really isn't a lot for me to do.'

'I'm not leaving,' Neve said, folding her arms across her chest.

'Yes, I figured you'd say that, that's why I just called security to have you removed.'

This was getting sillier by the minute. 'We don't have security here. We're a tiny hotel on the tiniest northernmost island in Scotland, we don't have problems that require a security guard.'

'Gabe hired one this morning.'

Just then there was a knock on the door and Luke walked in, dressed all in black and wearing the obligatory security sunglasses. He was the biggest man Neve had ever known, almost as broad as he was wide, and at nearly seven foot tall that was saying something.

'Miss Whitaker, if you'd like to come with me, I'll escort you off the premises,' Luke said, without raising a smile.

'No, this is stupid. If you want me to leave my office, you're going to have to make me.'

Luke didn't hesitate as he moved round the desk and lifted Neve in her chair and carried her and the chair out of the office. Adam stood and waved at her as she was forcibly removed, a huge grin on his face.

'Put me down this instant,' Neve protested, though fighting against Luke was quite clearly a waste of time. As they approached the top of the stairs, she stopped struggling and shouting in case any of the guests heard her.

When they reached the bottom of the stairs, Oakley was waiting for her and he suppressed a grin as Luke approached him.

'I believe this belongs to you,' Luke said, passing the chair and Neve straight into Oakley's arms. 'Please make sure she doesn't escape again.'

'I will.'

'Tie her up, if need be.'

'Hey. I am here! Don't talk about me over my head like I can't hear you,' Neve said.

Luke shrugged and moved to stand as a blockade across the front of the stairs in case she tried to make a run for the offices again.

Oakley put her down and offered a hand to help her up.

'Is this your doing?' She scowled at him, refusing to get off the chair.

'I might have had something to do with it.' He offered out her coat and she took it. 'Come on, let's go for a walk.'

She continued to scowl at him.

'Come on, I'll buy you some chocolate truffles. I know you love them and apparently the chocolate shop in the village makes a wicked version. Have you tried any yet?'

She shook her head as she stood up and slipped on her coat. 'I haven't had time.'

'Then I'll treat you. Look, you take a few days off, take it easy and once Gabe is happy you're OK, I'm sure he'll let you go back to work then.'

Neve walked out the door, reluctantly conceding that it would be nice to have a day or two off work. She still ached a lot and sitting at her desk all day was going to aggravate that. She also couldn't remember the last time she'd had any time off at all, so maybe she'd make the most of it. But she wouldn't tell Oakley that she was happy with this arrangement.

As she reached the top of the steps down from the front entrance, Oakley took her arm and guided her down.

'Your track history with stairs isn't great.'

She flashed him another scowl but his huge smile showed he was completely impervious to it.

'I need to go and check on Shadow and Knight before we go to the village. I haven't seen them for a few days, though I know Luke would have made sure they were OK.'

'Sure, no problem. It'll be good to see the boys again, just show me the way.'

Snow was still falling thick and fast and silence fell over them as they walked down the track towards the stables, the only sound the gentle patter of snowflakes against the wet, cold ground.

Neve didn't know what to say to him. She was still half expecting him to get on the next plane and leave her alone. Why would he stay if he didn't see a future together any more?

Eventually, when the stables were in sight, she spoke. 'Why are you being so nice to me?'

Oakley didn't say anything for a while.

'I loved you, Freckle, I probably still do. I'm having a hard time forgiving you at the moment. Judging by how far along you are, you must have got pregnant seconds after I left and that thought just makes my blood go cold. Maybe you didn't love me at all if I meant that little to you that you would jump into bed with Adam so quickly. I don't know if I can get past that. But I feel guilty that I shouted at you seconds after you told me you were pregnant, I feel guilty that it was partly my fault you fell down the stairs. And. . . I still care about you. I want to look after you. I'm only here for a few more days and then. . .'

'And then?' Neve prompted. She wanted to know if they had any future at all.

'I go back to California and. . .' he trailed off again.

He left the words he clearly wanted to say unspoken. She would stay here and they'd probably never see each other again. Pain seared through her chest at the thought. She needed to tell him the truth but that wasn't going to be an easy conversation to have.

'I didn't sleep with Adam,' she said quietly.

He stopped walking. '*What?* Who did you sleep with?'

'No one, I—'

'No one? Christ! At least when I thought you'd slept with Adam, I could sort of understand that you were looking for comfort from a friend. I think that makes it even worse that you got drunk in a bar and just slept with some completely random man. Did you even catch his name before you let him put his hands on you?'

Neve stared at him in shock. 'Hang on, that's a bit judgemental. Before we met you used to meet girls in bars all the time and sleep with a different one each night.'

'Yes, before I met you, before I fell in love with you. You were supposed to be in love with me too and you just jumped into bed with a complete stranger.' He looked down at her as if he didn't know her at all before he strode off.

She stared after him and then ran to catch him up. 'Wait, you've misunderstood—'

'Does the baby's father know he's about to become a dad?'

'No,' Neve said truthfully, cursing herself.

'Are you going to tell him?'

'I'm *trying*. I made a terrible mistake and I'm trying to put it right. Will you stop walking and listen to me?'

He stopped and looked at her but over his shoulder Neve suddenly spotted one of the guests outside the stables.

The young girl Neve knew was called Poppy was in a wheelchair and Neve thought she was about twelve years old. She'd seen her about the place always with a big smile on her face and, as she watched, Poppy leant up to stroke Shadow, her beautiful black stallion.

Neve left Oakley's side and ran down the track towards the stables. Although Shadow had never bitten anyone before, Neve didn't totally trust him around people. He was grumpy, temperamental, easily spooked too. If he had been human, he would have been a stroppy teenage boy with an attitude problem. He responded to her, listened to her every command, but she'd never let anyone else ride him until earlier that summer when Oakley had ridden him. Oakley had a complete affinity with horses and Shadow had responded to him like a puppy responding to his master. If Shadow could have rolled over so Oakley could stroke his belly, he probably would have. Where Shadow tolerated Neve, he adored Oakley.

With his long-legged stride, Oakley ran past Neve towards the stables, clearly recognising the potential threat too.

'Hey there.' Oakley called and Neve saw Poppy and her mother turn towards him and then both their eyes widen in surprise at the Hollywood star fast approaching them.

Oakley took Shadow by the head, stroking him, and by the time Neve arrived, Shadow was nuzzling into his arms. Neve rolled her eyes at the transformation.

'Shadow can be a bit unpredictable,' Neve explained, as she tried to catch her breath. She had always been quite fit but the aches from the fall were still hurting her and with her kiwi-sized baby growing inside her, she suddenly found herself more unfit than she realised.

'He's so beautiful,' Poppy said, her eyes resting on Shadow for a moment before casting back to Oakley in shock.

'He is, but he's like a stroppy child sometimes,' Neve said.

Shadow snorted as if in disagreement.

'Is he a Friesian?' Poppy asked as Oakley whispered words of encouragement into Shadow's ear.

'He is. You like horses?'

'I love them.'

'Have you met Knight? He is much more friendly,' Neve said, tapping on the door of the adjoining stable and right on cue her wonderful dappled grey Andalusian poked his head over the door.

'Oh, he's gorgeous,' Poppy laughed as Knight chewed on a piece of hay and then accidentally dropped it.

'Poppy used to love riding,' her mum said, coming out of her starstruck reverie.

'Before a car accident stole the use of my legs,' Poppy added, practically.

'I'm sorry to hear that,' Neve said, not entirely sure what the right words were to convey her sympathy for such a tragedy.

'Hey, I'm still alive,' Poppy shrugged.

Her mum smiled. 'Fortunately Poppy is still able to do most of the things she enjoyed before. She swims, and she's just joined a basketball team. We were just about to go snow-mobiling actually.'

Neve noticed for the first time that they were both dressed in thermal snow suits. She really wasn't very observant.

'There's no reason you can't horse ride as well,' Neve said.

'I don't have the use of my legs, so I can't control the horse.'

'Knight has been trained with paraplegics. He responds to voice and hand commands. He is so gentle, he would be perfect for your first foray into riding again. I used to work at the stables the British Olympic show jumping team trained from and we had a number of paraplegic and quadriplegic riders there. It was something I always wanted to get more involved with, so I trained Knight to respond to voice commands. I have a special saddle too. It has a back that we can strap you into if you don't feel safe and we can strap your legs in too so they are in the right position. He is the most wonderful, calm horse. I can assure you it would be very safe. We can do it tomorrow if you want. I can ride with you. I'll take Shadow out, I'm sure he would appreciate the chance to stretch his legs.'

Poppy's eyes lit up. 'Can I, Mum?'

'We have the boat trip tomorrow.'

Poppy's face fell.

'But we could do it the day after tomorrow if that suits you?' Poppy's mum said to Neve.

'That's fine, shall we say eleven o'clock?'

Poppy nodded gleefully but when Neve glanced up at Oakley, he was scowling.

'Should you be riding in your condition?'

'What? I'm pregnant. I do not need to be wrapped in bubble wrap and. . .' she trailed off. Was horse riding another one of the things she shouldn't do, along with not eating runny eggs, pâté and certain types of fish? The thought of not riding for the next six months was a depressing one, but it was something she would have to ask her doctor before she risked it. And with a broken arm it wouldn't be particularly practical. Maybe Oakley was right.

'I'll take her out,' Oakley said. 'You know Shadow likes me.'

Poppy let out a little squeal of excitement at the prospect of going riding with a huge star and Neve didn't have the heart to deny her that joy; besides she didn't have any alternatives.

'OK,' Neve nodded reluctantly. She had been looking forward to getting on Shadow again, but of all the horses to ride when pregnant, Shadow was not the ideal choice.

Just then Boris, the snowmobile instructor, came out of the shed opposite with his husband Mikael and their five-year-old son Chester. Boris was effortlessly dragging one of the snowmobiles with him while Mikael was dragging a second one. Poppy's mum eyed them both appreciatively. Neve smiled; with their gorgeous model looks, they must turn heads everywhere they went.

'Here you go,' Boris said as he looked up, his eyes bulging as he spotted Oakley. 'Oh my God, Oakley Rey!' he squeaked, like an over-excited teenage girl. 'I'm your biggest fan, we both are. We knew you were on the island but I didn't expect to see you here.'

Neve watched in amusement as Boris ran over and shook Oakley's hand. She had forgotten that being with Oakley, this kind of thing happened all the time. The staff in the London hotel had quickly got used to his presence as he was there for so long and most of the time she spent with him was either in her bedroom or his so she didn't see a lot of his fans fawning over him.

Chester came running over too and he pulled on Oakley's free hand. 'Are you Obsidian?'

Oakley kneeled down to talk to him. 'Yes, I am.'

Chester stared at him for a brief moment and then threw his arms round Oakley's neck and hugged him tight. Oakley laughed but when Chester showed no signs of letting him go, Oakley stood up with Chester in his arms.

Boris continued to stare at Oakley in amazement.

Neve cleared her throat. 'Boris, our guests.' She indicated Poppy and her mum.

Boris quickly hurried back over to the snowmobiles.

'OK, if you two climb on, I can explain the controls and oh. . . erm, do you need help getting on?' he asked Poppy.

'No, I can do it,' Poppy said, as she rolled her wheelchair to the side of the snowmobile, applied the brakes and then pulled herself out of the chair and manoeuvred herself onto the back of the snowmobile as if she had been doing such things all her life.

Neve smiled.

Boris talked them through the controls and how to do certain things and Neve turned back to Oakley to see him and Chester deep in conversation about Obsidian and his powers. Something unfurled inside her. In a few years' time this could be Oakley holding his son, playing with him and talking to him. Adam was right, she couldn't deny him that chance. As soon as they were alone, she would tell him the truth.

Boris dragged another snowmobile out of the shed and passed Poppy and her mum a helmet each. He climbed on his snowmobile and encouraged Poppy to take the lead. She gunned the snowmobile into life and took off down the track. Boris took off after her and Poppy's mum followed close behind, leaving them alone with Mikael and Chester. Chester was still gabbling away happily to Oakley and Neve had to smile as she had never heard Chester talk so much.

'Well, we must leave Miss Whitaker and Mr Rey to their business now, Chester,' Mikael said, when Chester showed no sign of stopping.

'That's OK. We were just going down to the village, we're not in any rush,' Oakley said.

'Can we go to the village with them, Daddy, *can* we?'

'If they do not mind us tagging along,' Mikael said, in his stilted English.

'Of course not,' Oakley said and Neve wondered if he'd said that deliberately so he wouldn't have to be alone with her.

Neve spent a few moments giving Shadow and Knight some fuss, and checking they had enough food, but, as she already suspected, Luke had been down there earlier that morning to check they were OK and to feed them.

When she was ready to leave, Oakley strode off down the path with Chester still chatting to him, leaving her alone with Mikael. So much for telling Oakley the truth.

'I heard you were pregnant, Miss Whitaker, congratulations,' Mikael said.

'Thank you. I want this baby so much, but I find the whole thing terrifying, if I'm honest.'

'It is scary, yes. When you hold your baby for the first time, there is nothing more frightening than this little person relying on you for their every whim and need. But the love you feel for your child is not like anything else you have ever felt before and that love is enough to make sure your baby is happy and healthy.

And I think Oakley will make a wonderful father. He will help you with this.'

'What if he isn't ready?'

'None of us are ever ready to be a parent. No book can prepare you, no baby classes can teach you, but you and Oakley will do your best for your baby. I know this and your child could never ask for anything more than that.'

Neve stared down at the snow as they walked. Mikael was right. As long as they loved each other and loved the baby, that was the only thing that mattered. There was never going to be any right time to have a child and it wasn't fair to judge Oakley on his immediate reaction to the news of her pregnancy. She would tell him the truth and let him have time to digest it properly. Then he could choose for himself.

CHAPTER 13

Adam was just reading through some of the reviews that had started to appear about the hotel when there was a knock at his door. He looked up, half hoping it would be Ivy who had come to distract him again, so he was slightly disappointed to see it was Gabe.

Gabe came in, closing the door behind him and sitting down in the chair opposite Adam's.

'How's things?'

'Good, busy but good,' Adam said.

'Do you need any help with anything? I know you've only been here a few days and you've been thrust into the thick of it already.'

'No, everything's fine. You've got a great team here and Neve is so efficient that it's a dream taking over from her for a short while.'

Gabe nodded. 'I haven't seen Neve since we got back last night. Did she try to come to work this morning?'

'Of course she did! I had her removed.'

Gabe laughed. 'Are you any wiser to the whole baby daddy saga?'

'Yes, actually. Neve told Oakley the baby wasn't his because she didn't want to land him with the burden of a baby he didn't want. The natural assumption that Oakley leapt to was the baby must be mine,' Adam said, dryly.

Gabe sighed. 'I can't believe she did that.'

'Don't be too hard on her, she did it for the right reasons. I've convinced her to tell him the truth so hopefully it won't be too long before the situation is resolved.'

'Well, that's kind of what I wanted to talk to you about.'

'Oh?'

'They're engaged, she's pregnant with his child. At some point they will sort out their issues and if they don't I'm not letting Oakley leave here until they do. He's an actor in California, he can't exactly relocate here. It makes sense that she'll eventually end up moving over there and I wondered if you'd be interested in taking over from her when that happens.'

'As manager?' Adam clarified.

'Yes.'

Adam wanted to leap up from his chair onto the desk and do a dance of joy. It was everything he wanted. OK, it wasn't in London but, as he'd said to Ivy the day before, over the years his dreams had changed and this change was one that he liked.

Gabe misread his silence.

'I know you're happy in London but I doubt a managerial role will come up there, not with Franco showing no sign of moving on any time soon. If he ever leaves you'll be the first person I'll ask to take over from him, I guarantee you that. I know this place is remote and barren, I know it's very different to what you're used to, but it doesn't have to be forever. But I need someone I can trust to take over from Neve if she leaves.'

Adam looked out the window at the little snow-covered lodges and tried to imagine how stunning the place would look in summer. He tried to imagine how different life would be for him in this little haven. Would he grow bored of the lack of bars, theatres, shops and sights that London held?

'What would it take for you to say yes?' Gabe asked, nervously.

Adam turned round to look at him, not realising that he was causing Gabe to worry with his lack of an answer.

'I'd match the salary Neve is on now, that goes without saying,' Gabe continued. 'It's very generous. And I'd make sure you had a proper house to live in, not just a room.'

'I'd want an assistant,' Adam said, surprising himself with his demands. 'A deputy manager, assistant manager or a PA, I don't care which, but I'd want someone here specifically to help me. This job is way too big for one person. I'm not surprised Neve has been struggling.'

'I'll get you one. As soon as the New Year is here I'll look for one. I'll make sure I get someone good.'

'I want a guaranteed day off every week, so I can continue my pilot's training.'

'OK, I have no problem with that. Actually, having another pilot on call here might lessen the load for Mikael. If there are courses or training you need to take, I'd pay for that.'

Adam nodded and then, as Gabe seemed to be in a 'saying yes' mood, he thought he might as well go for broke.

'When Ivy Storm's contract comes to an end next year, I want you to offer her a permanent position in the village.'

Gabe's eyebrows shot up at the bizarre request. 'Something you want to tell me?'

'Not really.'

Gabe smiled.

'I just know she wants to stay here and hates the prospect of leaving in a year's time.'

'And so you make her staying here a condition of you taking the new job? That's incredibly selfless and noble of you.'

'What can I say? I'm a noble kind of guy,' Adam said, clearly knowing that Gabe wasn't buying any of this for one second.

'Well, I have no problem with that. Her sales more than speak for themselves. The villagers love her and I haven't had any issues with her. I'll go straight down to the village now and ask her to stay if it means you'll say yes.'

'That's not necessary.'

Gabe stood up. 'Any more demands you want to ask for, a new Ferrari perhaps?'

Adam laughed. 'No, just those three conditions will be fine.'

'Why do I get the feeling that I've just been played? You had no intention of leaving here, did you?'

'I was going to come and see you about making the move permanent this afternoon.'

Gabe moved to the door, shaking his head. 'So we have a deal?'

'Yes, absolutely. I really appreciate the chance.'

'Of course, it might take a while for Neve to decide to leave, but I'm happy to have you here as long as it takes for her to come to her senses.'

'Well, I'm not going to push her out of her job, just so I can take over. If she chooses to stay and raise the baby alone, I'd be more than happy to stay here to assist her with the hotel.'

'Just as long as Ivy stays too?'

Adam grinned. 'That's right.'

Gabe walked out, still shaking his head.

Adam leaned back in his chair with a huge smile on his face. This day had suddenly got a whole lot better.

❋

Oakley stared into the swirls of steam coming from his hot chocolate. Neve had wanted some time alone and he strongly suspected she wanted to get him a Christmas present. Though he wasn't sure what present could correctly convey the 'I'm sorry I slept with someone else minutes after you left, please forgive me' sentiment.

He sighed. He didn't know what he was still doing there. He could have arranged for his helicopter to come and collect him straight after he arrived back from the hospital. By now he could be halfway back to America, but for some reason he couldn't work out, leaving Neve simply wasn't an option. But he had no idea where that left them. He loved her, he knew that, and loving someone meant forgiving them. They hadn't been together when she'd slept with someone else so technically she hadn't done anything wrong, but he knew it was going to take time before he could look past that. Problem was, they didn't have time. He was due to leave in less than a week. And what of the child that wasn't his and the man out there who had a claim over Neve's baby? How would he fit into the grand scheme of things? Nothing had gone according to plan since his arrival and he wasn't sure what he could do about it.

He took a sip from his deliciously creamy hot chocolate and rum drink and looked around the Christmas market. Although it was two days after the event, the place was still packed with guests, bustling from one shop to the next, their arms laden with bags of goodies and sweet delicious treats. The smells were wonderful, the savouriness of the hog roast combined with the sweet scents of the toffee, chocolates, fudge and pancakes were tantalising. The log cabins looked so pretty with their fairy lights in the windows, sending puddles of gold onto the snow-covered street. Snow fell in big fat flakes as it swirled around the guests and no one seemed to mind.

It was a lot colder here than he was used to and so he quickly finished his drink and headed inside one of the nearest shops to get in from the cold.

It was a shop filled with snow globes in all manner of shapes and sizes and the globes seemed to sparkle as he wandered through the spotlit-illuminated shop.

'Ah, Oakley Rey, I wondered when I'll be seeing you,' said a soft Irish voice from the darkness at the back of the shop. A very beautiful woman in her forties stepped out from the shadows, dressed in a long green velvet dress. 'Congratulations on your engagement, by the way. I presume you are here to fill in the wedding forms?'

Oakley stared at her in confusion. 'Erm, no.'

'Oh, let me introduce myself. I'm Mikki O'Sullivan, artist, snow globe maker and the official registrar on Juniper Island. When you and Neve get married here, I'll be the one to oversee the ceremony.'

'Oh, we're not getting married.'

Mikki cocked her head in confusion. 'But you're engaged?'

'No, not really.'

'I've seen the ring, on her finger no less.'

'Yes, I proposed and then. . . well, let's just say, everything that could go wrong did go wrong after that.'

But Mikki waved away his concerns with a flap of her hands, as if finding out the woman he loved was pregnant with another man's child was nothing of real consequence.

'There are always teething problems in a relationship, little hiccups here and there, but what matters is being able to get through those issues. When you put a ring on someone's finger, you are promising to love them through the rough and the smooth, the good, the bad and the ugly, to be there for them when times get tough. You don't run away when things get a bit sticky. She is carrying your child, now is not the time to get cold feet.'

Oakley didn't have the heart to correct her.

'I see you with your son, I see you playing on the beach with him and Neve is there, heavy with your second child. I see this as clear as you are standing before me.'

Oakley stared at her for a moment.

'You can see into the future?' he asked, incredulously. He would have laughed but she was standing there so serenely as if the words that had just come out of his mouth were not the most ludicrous thing in the world.

'Some say that, yes. I prefer to think of it as seeing your true path. Your destiny, if you like. Neve is your destiny and that is not something to take lightly.'

He swallowed down the sudden lump in his throat.

'Now, I've taken the liberty of filling out the form for you,' Mikki added, producing a form with his and Neve's names already printed on it. 'You will just need to sign and date it. Now if I were you, I'd backdate the form to the beginning of December. We are supposed to register an application to marry twenty-eight days before the ceremony unless there are extenuating circumstances. I imagine that you being a Hollywood star and filming schedules would hold some weight, but I can also say that snow and bad weather and Christmas bank holidays delayed the form being sent by post. Just sign here.'

Oakley opened his mouth to protest but at a glare from Mikki he did as he was told. Just because he was applying for a marriage licence, it didn't mean he would have to use it.

No sooner had he signed his name than Mikki had whipped the form away from him before he could change his mind and he quickly left the shop before she made him sign away one of his kidneys too.

Could any of what Mikki had said be true? That he and Neve had a future together? He didn't believe that someone could have the power to see into the future but Mikki was right about one thing. Marriage was for better or for worse and he had offered Neve that when he had proposed to her.

✻

Neve looked around the Christmas market with a smile. She couldn't believe she hadn't been down here to see all the progress that had been made. Almost every day since she arrived on the island a few months before had been spent sitting in her office, making calls, answering emails, and she had missed out on seeing the wonderful developments that Gabe and the boys had made. She knew about them of course, but even the photos she had seen hadn't done the place justice. The island was so small, there really was no excuse for not coming down and seeing it.

When she had visited in the early part of the summer, the houses had been stone cottages, the road had been little more than a dusty dirt track. Now all the houses were bedecked in wooden planks, continuing the winter ski lodge theme down here too as well as the accommodation up in the main part of the hotel. The shops were in what had been the front room of the house, with large leaded windows showing their wares inside. Fairy lights were strewn across the street, sending sparkling orbs across the snow. Each shop held something unique, mostly handmade and wonderfully Christmassy. She had bought all her presents for her family online but now she wished that she had bought something for them from the market instead.

She pushed open the door of one shop and walked inside. The glass Christmas ornaments twinkled and gleamed in the shop lights, twists of bright colours and glitter, sparkling in a multitude of patterns. Each piece was completely unique and each tree decoration was a different shape, in curves of gold, balls of green and drops of blues and purple.

Movement at the back of the shop caught her eye. Despite the cold of the day, Antoine, the man working at the back in a separate room, had no top on. He was muscled, dirty and filthy and had that sexy Poldark look to him. But despite his natural good looks, Neve was drawn more to what he was doing as he made the little glass ornaments. She stepped closer and watched as he pulled out a burning ball of glass from a furnace and blew into the pole holding it, making the ball wider. Using a tool, Antoine pulled at the end of the glass, making it longer, before he rolled it in tiny beads of multi-coloured glass and stuck it back into the furnace again, twisting and turning the pole as it melted in the heat. He pulled it out, rolled it on the table, pulling at little bits of it here and there, blew into it, twisted it, rolled it. Each time the piece was changing shape and, as the glass cooled, she could see all the different colours sparkling in the light.

'Hello, Miss Whitaker,' Antoine said, his eyes barely leaving the ornament he was making. 'Can I help you with anything?'

'No, I was just watching you,' Neve said, then blushed when he smiled to himself. This was a man who clearly knew how good-looking he was. She quickly corrected herself. 'The glass blowing is fascinating. I've not had a chance to look around all the shops yet. It's wonderful to see.'

'It is. And the people are all lovely. They were all very worried about you when they heard about your fall on Christmas Day.' He snapped the glass twist off the pole with a pair of pliers and, rolling it around in his gloved hands, he walked towards her, his dark eyes shining as he approached. 'I hope your arm doesn't hurt too much and there's no lasting damage.'

'Hopefully I'll be out of this cast in six weeks.'

'And you have someone up at the hotel to look after you?'

'Yes, she does,' came Oakley's stern voice from behind her.

Neve whirled round to see Oakley glaring at Antoine with ill-disguised hatred. She rolled her eyes and turned back to Antoine, who was still gazing at her with amusement.

'That's good. Here, why don't you take this with you, to remind you of your time in the village today? It's still quite warm but you can touch it.' Antoine held out his hand and placed the intricate twist of glass into her hands. 'It has the colours of the aurora so it's one of our more popular pieces.'

Neve held up the spun glass and watched the lights catch the flecks of colour. 'It's beautiful, thank you.'

He nodded and with another smile turned back to his workshop.

Neve walked out onto the street and Oakley followed closely behind. As soon as the shop door closed behind them, he turned on her. 'Is he the father of your baby?'

'Christ, Oakley, do you want to get a loudspeaker and shout it across the village? I'm pretty sure there's one or two people in the street who didn't hear you.'

She stormed away from him but he caught her up.

'Is he?' he repeated, more quietly this time.

'No, he isn't and I'm not talking about this with you here. You need to stop glaring at every man that I speak to.'

'You were practically drooling over him back there.'

'For your information, I was watching him blow glass and I would have been watching him with the same interest if he was a bald, fat man twice his age or even a woman.'

Oakley let out a sound of disbelief.

'There is only one man that I'm attracted to, one man that makes my heart skip a beat just by smiling at me, and that man is currently acting like a complete ass. You owe Adam an apology, by the way.'

'Yes, I do.'

She stopped at the lack of protest from him.

'I bought you some chocolate truffles,' Oakley said, handing her the paper bag as a peace offering.

She took it and sighed, popping one in her mouth and letting the creamy chocolate shell melt on her tongue. He smiled at her hopefully.

'It's delicious. Thank you.'

His smile brightened his whole face.

She reached up and ran her hand down his cheek, feeling the stubble under her fingers. He instinctively put his hands on her waist. 'Let's go home, we really need to talk.'

He looked at his watch and nodded. 'OK.'

A flash suddenly went off in their faces and then another and Neve looked around, blinking under the bright lights. One of the journalists who had come to review the hotel for the grand opening a few days before was taking photos of them. She frowned in confusion before she realised what was happening then she took a step back, knowing that Oakley wouldn't want his photo taken with her as he'd always been very careful not to be seen with her in public before, but he surprised her, looping an arm round her waist and holding her against him.

'Oakley Rey, Ben Eustace from the *Daily Oracle*. Is it true that you and Neve are expecting a baby?'

Neve gasped. How had he found out? But then she realised that any of the hospital staff could have gone to the press with their story. The hotel guests had probably seen Oakley wandering around too, though she knew at least that the hotel staff would have been loyal to her.

Were their pictures already in the papers? Were people looking at her and wondering what on earth Oakley saw in her? Were they judging her, judging their relationship? Were they deciding that she was too plain, too boring, too common for

Oakley? What would his mum think if she saw the photos of them together? What could they tell the press about their relationship? At the moment it was in tatters and she definitely didn't want to tell them that.

Oh God, what a horrible situation to be in. If Oakley told the press that the baby wasn't his, how would he explain the truth later? No one would believe that the boy was Oakley's once the press ran the story that he wasn't. If they got back together then people would always be looking at her like she didn't deserve to be with him because she had slept with someone else behind his back.

She looked up at Oakley and he must have seen the fear in her eyes as she shook her head.

'Let's go home, baby,' Oakley said, completely ignoring the photographer.

He took her hand and led her away.

'I see you're engaged,' the photographer called after them. 'When's the wedding?'

When they were far enough away, Neve turned to Oakley. 'You can't say anything to the press.'

'I never do.'

'There's something you need to know first.'

'I'm listening, Freckle.'

She looked back to see the photographer was still following them, albeit at a distance.

'I'll tell you as soon as we get home,' she told him.

CHAPTER 14

Neve's heart was hammering against her chest as she and Oakley walked up the stairs to her house. She knew he would be angry but she was hopeful they could get through this.

As she pushed open the door and stepped inside she was immediately met with a loud cheer and shouts of 'Merry Christmas'. She looked up and saw the smiling, happy faces of her mum, dad, Gabe, Pip, Wren and Luke all wearing gaudy Christmas jumpers.

'What's all this?'

Her mum, Lizzie, came over to give her a hug. 'Well, you missed out on Christmas, love, so we thought we'd have it now. We have all our presents, the board games, and Chef has even prepared us a proper Christmas feast.'

Neve smiled and turned to Oakley. 'Is that why you were so slow walking back?'

He grinned. 'Didn't want to get back before the big surprise.'

She was touched that they would go to all this trouble. She turned to Gabe. 'This is lovely, but I know how busy you must be getting ready for the New Year's Eve ball. Do you have time for this?'

He nodded. 'Of course, this is important. We always spend Christmas together and we didn't want you to miss out because you were in hospital. Besides, Wren wanted to do a proper Christmas with you.'

Wren came over to hug her and Neve awkwardly picked her up with one arm, her body complaining at the weight. Neve gave her a big squeeze. 'Was this your idea?'

Wren nodded. 'This way I get two Christmases.'

Neve laughed and Oakley took Wren from her, obviously concerned about her and her bruises.

'Oakley, Nanny said that Neve has a baby in her belly, is that true?'

He nodded and everyone suddenly went very quiet. 'It is.'

'I asked Nanny how the baby got there and she said that you put the baby there.'

He smiled.

'How did you put the baby in Neve's belly?'

Oakley cleared his throat. 'Well, when two people love each other very much then the man can put a special seed in the lady's belly and then the lady will grow and look after the seed until it becomes a baby.'

Wren stared at Oakley with wide eyes. 'How do you put the seed in her belly?'

Neve blushed, wondering at what point would be a good time to stop the conversation.

'I have the seed inside me and when we cuddle I put the seed inside her,' Oakley explained.

'So if the seed is already inside you, why don't you grow the baby?'

'Well, have you seen a seed for a plant?'

'Yes, it's very small.'

'And if I had one in my hand now, would it grow on its own?'

'No, it needs soil and water and sunshine to make it grow,' Wren said, knowledgeably.

'That's right. So I only have the seed, Neve gives the seed everything it needs to grow. She gives the baby food and water and lots of other important things to make the baby grow big and strong.'

'So you don't do anything to help make the seed grow once it's planted in Neve's belly?'

'No.'

'That doesn't seem fair that Neve has to do all the work.'

Neve suppressed a smile at the feminist attitude of her four-year-old niece.

'That's true. But the daddy has to look after the mummy while she is carrying the baby and then when the baby comes, they will both take it in turns to look after the baby.'

Wren nodded thoughtfully. 'Daddy and Pip cuddle a lot, will Daddy put his seed inside Pip?'

'Hey, Wren, why don't you sort out all the presents into piles so we know whose is whose?' Gabe suggested suddenly and Wren wriggled down from Oakley's arms and ran to the big pile of presents under the tree.

'I have a Christmas jumper for you both,' Neve's mum said, handing over two large paper bags from the shop in the village.

Oakley grinned as he pulled his jumper out of the bag, a large snowman face beaming out from the middle of it. Neve pulled her jumper out of the bag and looked at it. At the bottom, where her belly would be, were the words 'Mummy's Christmas pudding' over a picture of a small pudding.

'It's baby's first Christmas,' her mum explained, obviously over the moon at the prospect of being a grandparent again. 'We couldn't resist.'

Neve smiled and pulled it on, the pudding nestling directly over her little pregnant belly.

'Well, let's go and have some lunch and then we can open the presents,' Lizzie declared, shepherding everyone to the large dining room table near the kitchen.

Neve looked up at Oakley and he looked down at her pudding. 'You look adorable, Freckle,' he said, softly.

She smiled. They were going to be OK, she was sure of it.

※

Ivy placed a large sheet of glass on her easel and fixed it in place before wiping it down with a damp cloth. She hoped Adam would still be up for posing for her when he arrived. Because if it was going to end between them, she wanted a painting of him to remember the brief time in her life when everything was good and wonderful and perfect. And she was going to take advantage of everything he wanted to offer her now. She wouldn't look back on this time with him and regret anything she hadn't done.

Right on cue, Adam walked through the shop door with a huge smile on his face.

She moved to hug him, giving him a brief kiss as she ran her damp fingers through his hair.

'What's put you in such a good mood? Did you have a good day?' Ivy asked, as he pulled her tighter against him.

'It was busy as always, but I had some really good news. Gabe has asked me to take over the role of manager if Neve leaves.'

Her heart leapt. So that was it, he really was staying. 'That's fantastic, I'm so pleased for you. Is Neve leaving?'

'She might not. She might choose to stay here and raise the baby with her family but if that's the case, Gabe wants me to stay here permanently to help her with the hotel. But I have good news for you too. As part of the conditions for me staying here I asked Gabe to make your contract permanent and he agreed.'

Her heart soared. 'I get to stay here?'

'Yes, for as long as you want to and I promise you, if we ever break up, that won't be taken away from you. This is your home now.'

Tears filled her eyes. 'You have no idea how happy that makes me. When I split from my husband, the future looked so uncertain, I didn't know where I was going to live or what I was going to do. I came here for a reprieve, but I knew it was never going to be permanent. Thank you so much, you've given me my life back.'

Adam smiled. 'You're very welcome.'

He bent his head and kissed her and she wrapped her arms around his neck and kissed him back. He slid his hands up to her face, cupping the back of her neck gently, his touch so soft, his hands moving down to her shoulders and down her arms. He smelt so good, so delicious, Ivy wanted to run her tongue over his body and taste him all. She slid her tongue inside his mouth and a deep guttural moan escaped his throat as he pulled her against him.

She reached up and unzipped his coat and pushed it off his shoulders. Underneath he was wearing a soft grey jumper and a t-shirt. Her fingers travelled down to the hem and in one swift move she yanked both over his head. His mouth barely left hers for a second but his fingers quickly undid the zip on her hoodie and he slipped that over her shoulders until it fell to the floor and she was left standing there in her bra and jeans. As his hands traversed her skin and then moved to the top of her jeans, she pushed him back slightly.

He arched an eyebrow at her change in direction, his eyes dark with lust and need.

'We can pick this up after.'

He swallowed. 'After what?'

'After I've painted you.'

'You expect me to stand over there while you paint me after that kiss? How about you paint me after we've finished this kiss properly?'

He took a step towards her and she laughed, dodging his greedy hands.

'If you're good and stand over there for a few minutes, I'll make sure you're rewarded.'

He let out a soft grunt of frustration as he stepped to the other side of the room where Ivy was pointing.

'You have five minutes, then we're finishing what we started.'

Ivy quickly spread some white paint over the whole glass. Adam didn't need a background to his painting. He was the main attraction and she didn't want anything to distract from that. After pouring a blob of the deep cream colour she reserved for flesh, she added a drop of burnt orange to get his tanned complexion right. She glanced over at him, his hands on his hips as he waited patiently or rather *im*patiently. She smirked as she used her fingers to create the basic shape of his body, his arms, neck, chest and face, then added some dark blue paint for the very top of his jeans. Once the basic shape was there, she added details using her nails and the edges of her fingers, smoothing and blending the paint together to get the shadows and contours of his body.

She was so intent on the painting that she hadn't noticed that Adam had left his side of the room and was standing next to her, realising only when he pressed a kiss to the side of her head.

'Hey, you're supposed to be standing over there, being good.'

'I was never very skilled at that,' Adam said, his hands sliding around her waist.

She batted him away, slapping a handprint of paint on his arm.

'Hey!'

'Hey, yourself.'

'Talk me through what you do,' Adam said, as he moved back to her side. He planted a kiss against her throat, clearly trying to distract her.

'Well,' Ivy looked at him mischievously and then wiped both hands across his body, 'first I map out the basic shape of the person I'm painting. I draw the arms, the body...' she said, smearing the paint all over his shoulders, his stomach, his chest. 'I don't take my time over that, it's just the background colour.' She looked up into his eyes and could see he was amused with what she was doing.

'Then I'll take a slightly darker colour and start picking out the details,' she added, dipping her fingers into some more paint and then slowly tracing the lines of his abs, the muscles, picking them out with the very tips of her fingers. The feel of his hard flesh and the paint was incredibly enticing.

'And what if you make a mistake?' Adam said, suddenly tugging her against him so that the paint spread over both their bodies. 'What if you smudge the paint?'

She ran her painted hands over his face and in his hair as he ran his hands down to her bum.

'Sometimes when you smudge it, it can make the outcome so much better.'

'Is that right?' Adam said, his mouth mere millimetres away from hers.

Her breath hitched in her throat. 'Yes, when you blend unexpected colours and shapes, when you use different textures, or different parts of the body, you can get something utterly beautiful.'

'Well, let's see, shall we?' Adam muttered as his mouth came down on hers.

This time the kiss wasn't gentle, it was needful and full of lust and promise. She tugged at his jeans and he wriggled out of them, his body tight against hers.

Somehow they ended up on the floor, with Adam on top of her. He removed her bra and trailed his mouth over her breasts and down towards her stomach, gently sucking her belly piercing into his mouth, which made her stomach clench with desire. He knelt up and slowly undid the button on her jeans and carefully slid them down, taking her knickers with them. He trailed his mouth back up the inside of her legs, gently nudging them open with his shoulders, and when he kissed her at the very top of her thighs, she screamed out. She had never been touched there like that. Callum's idea of foreplay had been a quick fumble before he'd thrust away inside her like he was going for gold. But this, this was bliss. She'd never felt anything like it. Her orgasm, when it came, ripped through her so quick and so unexpected that she found herself shouting and crying and writhing under his hot mouth.

As the tremors subsided, she was vaguely aware of Adam sliding a condom on.

She looked up into his eyes as he braced himself over her. 'Is this OK?'

She hooked her legs around his hips and pulled him against her. 'Yes, God, yes. Don't stop.'

He smiled and slid so carefully inside her that it brought tears to her eyes. He was being so gentle and it was so completely unexpected. She had expected passion and urgency but instead he was tender and considerate.

'Are you OK, did I hurt you?'

'No, it's fine, everything is perfect.' She reached up and kissed him. He didn't move for a few moments, giving her body a chance to adjust to his.

As he kissed her, he very slowly started to move against her, sliding in deeper with every thrust. She arched against him, moaning against his mouth at the delicious friction between them.

He pulled back slightly to look at her. If there was any chance of guarding her heart against this man, he had just shattered that with the way he was looking at her as he made love to her. She was falling for him, she knew that. But right then, with Adam kissing and caressing her, buried deep inside her, she couldn't find it in her to be scared.

❄

Neve walked over to Oakley, who was sitting in the corner of the sofa, his arm sprawled out over the back. She plonked herself down next to him.

'Thank you for your help in organising today. It was wonderful,' she said.

The day had been magical, they'd eaten, played games with her family, opened the presents and eaten some more. What had been lovely was to see Gabe so completely happy with his new girlfriend Pip, who fitted into their family so easily. Wren adored her and the feeling was completely mutual. Oakley had fitted in so perfectly as well. He'd met Gabe several times before as Gabe had been at the hotel in London too, but he'd only met her mum and dad once or twice and he'd never met Luke before. But seeing the ring on her finger and knowing she was pregnant, they had all just accepted him as part of her life. Oakley played the part well, laughing and joking with all of her family. None of them knew the hidden tension between them. They had all left giving them both big hugs.

'It was my pleasure, Freckle,' Oakley said, his hand moving to her hair and absently running his fingers through her curls as he always used to when they sat together.

With the fire crackling nearby, being snuggled up by his side Neve felt blissfully and utterly content.

She passed him a paper bag with the gift she had bought him in the village. 'I wasn't sure what to get for the man who could buy anything he wanted.'

He took it and opened it up, pulling out the black beaded bracelet.

'It's obsidian,' she explained and he smiled. 'Which is for protection, to keep you safe.'

'Maybe you should wear this then, it might stop you falling down the stairs,' Oakley said, turning over the bracelet and letting the black glassy surface of the beads catch the light from the fire.

'I'm kind of hoping I'll still have my own Obsidian to keep me safe.' She looked up at him and his eyes were warm with fondness and love. 'I bought this because I thought you should have something to remind you of the time when all your dreams came true. I know that you'll never forget this time, playing Obsidian in a big Hollywood action film, but this is a reflection of all the hard work that got you here. I want you to know that I couldn't be happier for you, getting this job. I know it's everything you dreamed of and I'm so proud of you for achieving this. Which is why I hope you'll understand why I did what I did. I –'

'Freckle, this is great. Thank you so much, I love it.' He pulled the bracelet on and admired it on his wrist. 'But you should know that not *all* my dreams came true when I got this job. When I came here, the only thing I wanted for Christmas was you as my wife.'

Her heart ached for the unnecessary pain she had caused him. 'Oakley, I'm sorry.'

She leaned up to kiss him on the cheek, but he turned to look at her as she moved and she inadvertently kissed him on the side of the mouth. She pulled back slightly and looked into his eyes, seeing nothing there to say he wasn't happy with her kissing him. Emboldened slightly by this, she kissed him again. There was still no response but as she pulled away, his hand cupped the back of her head and pulled her back to him, his mouth taking hers in a passionate and needful kiss.

He moaned against her mouth as he tasted her.

She slid her good hand down his neck to his shirt and with some difficulty popped open one button. With his mind occupied with the kiss, she managed to pop open another and then slid her hand inside, caressing the smooth velvety warm skin. His kisses became more urgent.

She sat up and shifted so she was straddling him. With great difficulty she managed to undo another button as he watched her but when she moved her good hand to the next button, he reached up and stopped her. She thought he was going to help her rather than watching her struggle but when she looked up into his eyes the love and desire she had seen in them moments before had been replaced by a wariness.

'Freckle, I'm sorry, I just can't.'

Rejection slammed into her in a great wave.

'Of course not. I'm sorry, it was silly of me to instigate it.' She climbed off him, humiliation burning her cheeks and tears pricking her eyes. 'I'm a bit tired actually so I'm going to bed, goodnight.'

She hurried from the room before Oakley saw the tears.

'Freckle, wait. . .'

She didn't. She ran up the stairs hoping he would leave her alone.

She managed to slip her t-shirt over her head and remove her jeans then climbed into bed, facing out at the window as the tears slid silently down her cheeks.

A few minutes later, she heard footsteps on the stairs and then in the bedroom. She heard Oakley take his jeans off and then felt his weight as he climbed into bed behind her. He curled himself around her, just as he had on Christmas Eve, resting his hand on their child. He was still wearing his shirt and tight box-ers, she could feel them against her naked flesh. He swept her hair off her back and kissed her bare shoulder, softly.

'Goodnight, Freckle.'

She stared into the darkness in confusion. He had kissed her but he didn't want to make love to her although he was quite happy to sleep in the same bed with her and cuddle up to her. She didn't know what he wanted but it seemed he didn't know either.

CHAPTER 15

Adam lay in Ivy's bed, watching the snowflakes dance past the window in the early morning sunshine and enjoying the soft breath on his neck from Ivy as she slept next to him. Everything had changed so quickly. One minute he was looking forward to spending Christmas on an island in Scotland and having a bit of a break from the hotel in London and the next he was making the move permanent and waking up in the arms of a wonderful, beautiful woman after spending hours the night before making love to her.

In the blink of an eye, his life had changed and only for the better. He knew Ivy was holding back, that she was afraid of getting hurt again, but he hoped, in time, that she would grow to trust him.

He glanced at his watch and knew he would have to leave soon but he definitely didn't want to leave Ivy in bed for her to wake up alone, not after the amazing night they had shared. He ran his finger down her bare arm and she stirred and woke, staring up at him with bleary eyes.

'It can't be time to get up yet, it seems like we only went to sleep a few hours ago.'

'I think that's because we did only go to sleep a few hours ago. You're insatiable.'

She giggled and shifted so her head was on his chest, her arm wrapped around his shoulder.

'So do you honestly think Neve will leave?' Ivy asked.

'I don't know. Things are not great between her and Oakley. Gabe thinks she will move to California with him but I have a feeling she'll end up staying here. Her brothers are here, her niece as well. I don't think she'll want to leave them behind.'

'I can't believe she's pregnant, with Oakley Rey's baby too. That seems like something out of a movie. I haven't seen her for a while, is she showing?'

'Not really.'

'And with Joy ready to pop her second child, there will be five children on the island then. Does it make you broody for your own?'

There was something in Ivy's voice that suggested she was scared of his answer. He suddenly felt that this whole conversation about Neve and her being pregnant was laying the ground-work for something else, though he didn't know what.

'I'm definitely not broody,' Adam said.

'You don't want to have children of your own one day? I'm not saying with me, necessarily,' Ivy quickly clarified. She laughed nervously. 'I'm not saying, hey, we've just made love for the first time, let's get married and have babies. I'm definitely not saying that. I'm just saying, I don't know, just wondering if children were part of the big life plan.'

Adam smiled as she tried to talk her way out of the hole she had just dug. He didn't know what the right response was. He decided to go with a vague answer, he definitely didn't want to do or say anything that might push her away.

'I don't know, maybe, one day. If I do, great, if I don't that's fine too.'

'Really?'

He shrugged. It was a lie, he knew that. When his ex-girl-friend had announced she was pregnant it had been the happiest moment of his life. The thought of being a dad had been one of the best feelings he'd ever had. But he'd kind of accepted long ago that maybe he would never have a child of his own. He had enjoyed playing with Chester the other day and it had made him think what it would be like if he'd ever had a child of his own. It was hard to miss something you'd never had but he did feel like he had missed out on that part of his life.

He looked down at Ivy and realised that she seemed quite happy with his vague answer. Did she not want children herself one day? He decided to run with it. Right then, the prospect of having children together was very far away. This conversation seemed like a strange one to have so early in their relationship, but he got the sense it was a pivotal one.

'I work very long hours. It'd be hard to have a child when I'm so busy with my job.'

She hesitated for a moment before she spoke. 'I agree. I quite like my life as it is. I can sleep in late some days, go on holiday when I want. Children would get in the way of that.'

Her voice sounded forced, almost as if she didn't believe a word she was saying. He was sure, as she climbed out of bed and headed to the bathroom, that there were tears in her eyes. Had he said the wrong thing?

'Ivy, you OK?'

'Yeah, I'm fine, of course I am,' she said, without turning back to look at him. 'I'm just going to get a shower.'

The bathroom door closed and a second later he heard the water running.

He frowned. After the blissful evening the night before, he hadn't expected to come down from his high so soon, but he got the distinct impression something was very wrong.

✻

Neve woke to a cold and empty bed. She sat up and looked around and where Oakley had slept the night before was a note. She snatched it up and read it.

Freckle, I haven't left, don't worry. I just need some time and space to think. I've gone on the boat trip round the other islands, I'll be back tonight.

Love Oakley x

She sighed in frustration. Why couldn't the man just let her speak? She had been all set to tell him the night before with the obsidian bracelet. She had her little speech prepared with how happy she was for him and then she'd kissed him and he'd kissed her, rejected her, cuddled her and left her feeling so utterly confused.

It was three days before New Year's Eve, four days before Oakley was due to leave, and he still believed the baby wasn't his. She couldn't let this go on any longer. She wondered how long he had been gone and what time the boat left. Maybe she could catch him before he got on the boat.

She quickly got out of bed and attempted to get dressed. Damn, it was a lot harder than she thought. The day before Oakley had helped her but now she was on her own and rushing, even pulling on a pair of knickers was proving impossible.

There was a knock on the front door and then she heard it being pushed open.

'Hello,' Pip called. 'Neve?'

Neve grabbed a towel to cover her nudity and ran to the balcony overlooking the lounge.

'Hey, Pip, you all right?'

Pip laughed. 'I was going to ask you the same thing. Oakley told Gabe he was going out for the day. Gabe sent me round to see if you needed any help getting dressed or anything?'

She hadn't minded too much when Oakley had helped to dress her the day before, mainly because it gave her hope. If he could do that then maybe he still cared. She wasn't quite ready to let other people dress her like she was a baby but if she wanted to stop Oakley going on the trip then she would have to suck it up and allow Pip to help her. Pip could certainly dress her faster than her current attempts.

'Do you know if the boat trip has left yet?'

'Yes, about half hour ago. Why?'

Neve felt her determination to talk to Oakley deflate like a popped balloon. 'Because I really need to talk to Oakley.'

'Well, he'll be back tonight,' Pip said, helpfully.

'This won't wait.'

'Oh. I'm not sure what I can suggest. There are forty people on that boat, we can't exactly call the boat and ask them to turn around and come back.'

Neve sighed. 'No, I guess not.'

'The hotel has jet skis, don't they? I'm sure Gabe said they had a few they were going to hire out in the summer for the lake, you could take one of those.'

Neve thought about the practicalities of taking a jet ski out on the cold winter seas, chasing after the boat and using some kind of loudspeaker to get the boat to pull over. As dramatic as that sounded, in reality it would probably end up in disaster, especially as she'd never ridden a jet ski before. And if horse riding was on the 'no' list, then jet skiing probably would be too. She shook her head.

'What's wrong, Neve? Last night you and Oakley seemed to almost be faking being together. There's something not right and I'm not sure what it is.'

Neve sighed. 'Let me get dressed and I'll come down and tell you.'

'Do you need any help?'

Without the sudden urgency, Neve could take her time getting dressed and although she liked Pip, she wasn't sure their friendship quite extended to Pip seeing her butt naked just yet.

'No, I'll do it. Give me five minutes. Or maybe ten.'

❄

Pip looked at her in shock and Neve waited for the same lecture she'd got from Adam when she had told him what an idiot she was.

'Oh, Neve, I totally understand why you lied to Oakley.'

'You *do*?' Neve said. She hadn't been expecting that.

'Yes, you love him and you only wanted what was best for him. He didn't want this baby and raising one when he is in the biggest movie role of his life could be difficult and potentially limiting for him. I think it's really sweet that you put his needs before yours.'

Neve focussed her attention on her pancakes, knowing there was probably a lot more to it than pushing him away for the sake of his career.

'Regardless of the reasons why I did it, I have to tell him the truth. I can't let him carry on thinking he's not the father.'

'Of course you have to tell him. All I'm saying is I don't think he will take it as badly as you think he will. He will appreciate the reasons why you did it. He might be a bit miffed, but I can't see that he'll be angry. He stayed with you when he thought you were carrying someone else's baby, I can't see him walking away from you when he realises that the baby is his and you were never unfaithful to him in the first place.'

Pip had a point but the fear that had been niggling away at her for the last few days pushed its way back to the surface now.

'What if he is only staying because he knows the baby isn't his? What if he is relieved that he doesn't have this responsibility and when he leaves here on New Year's Day he'll never have to look back? What if me telling him the truth sends him running for the hills because he doesn't want our son?'

'Well then at least you'll know the truth and you'll be in no worse a situation than you are now. You can raise this baby on your own, you know that. Gabe did it with Wren and you can do it too. And we'd all help you. Raising a baby on your own has got to be better than raising it with someone who doesn't want a child so tell him the truth and then you'll soon see.'

Neve nodded. She would. Just as soon as she got him alone.

❄

Oakley stood on top of the boat alone, the wind rushing through his hair, as he stared out at the sea. After the motorised dinghies had ferried them out to the larger tour boat, the tourists had disappeared inside the lovely warm lounge area on the main deck. It had large glass windows to look out of, which was where all the guests were now, snapping photos of the rugged coastline. But Oakley needed the space to think and had headed up to the open top deck. The sea was rough and wild, the sky was grey, laden with the promise of more snow. It was quite spectacular in its raw, natural beauty, though he was hardly aware of any of it.

He had two things to decide and he needed to come back to Neve tonight with some answers in his head. It wasn't fair on her to drag this out any longer. She kept on expecting him to leave and with his rejection of her the night before and then cuddling up to her in bed afterwards, he understood he was confusing her. He didn't want to give her false hope and he knew if he'd let himself make love to her like he wanted to the night before and then left anyway, that would make him scum and he wouldn't play with her like that.

The press had released the story of his and Neve's dash to the hospital with rumours that she was pregnant with his child. He guessed that had a lot to do with the journalist or photographers who were still on the island and, judging by the articles, some doctors or nurses at Lerwick hospital hadn't been able to keep quiet either. His new manager was badgering him to release a statement to the press but he knew he had to decide what he was going to do first.

He needed to work out if he could move past the fact that she had been with someone else, but mostly he needed to know if he could raise a baby, be a dad to Neve's child.

The prospect terrified him. What kind of father could he really be? He had no memory of his own dad. His dad had left home before Oakley's first birthday and Oakley had never seen him again. What kind of person completely abandons their own child? Yet his greatest fear was that he might be the same kind of person, that it was inherent. Commitment had never been on his radar until he met Neve. He liked to party, go out with friends; he used to love the female attention being an actor would bring. He loved that lifestyle. Being with Neve changed all that. But would he eventually grow bored of playing the family man? Would he end up doing the same as his dad had done? Would he let Neve down in the same way his dad let his mum down all those years before?

What would being a dad mean? Could he cope with the sleepless nights and the crying? He worked such long hours, what would it be like to come home, after twelve hours on set, to a screaming baby and a tired and emotional Neve? Would she start to resent him when he was at work so much? Would it drive a wedge between them? But maybe she would come on set with him. He could help her so much more if she and the baby were there. Other actors brought their families on set from time to time. He had a big trailer where he relaxed on filming breaks, Neve could feed and play with the baby in there. He smiled at the thought of playing with his child in between takes, of showing off his son to the rest of the cast and crew. And the boy would be his son too, even if he wasn't Oakley's biologically; if he stayed with Neve, he would raise the baby as his own.

But what about all the things you should or shouldn't do with a baby, how would he know all that? If he thought the list of things Neve couldn't do or eat while she was pregnant was long, the list of things you shouldn't do with a baby was probably twice the length. Did babies sleep on their fronts or their backs, should you use a pillow or just lie them flat? How often did you feed them? When did you start them on solids? Breast milk or bottle milk? What was the correct way to hold them? He didn't know anything about babies or how to look after them. What if he was rubbish at all of that? What if he let Neve down just by being a useless dad? What if he tried his best and it wasn't good enough?

But then what was the alternative? The child wasn't his responsibility. He could leave on New Year's Day and never see Neve again and then he'd never have to deal with any of that. His stomach rolled. The thought of leaving her was, quite simply, unbearable.

❄

Ivy swirled the paint across the glass, not really paying attention to what she was creating but finding some comfort in the feel of the paint as the colours blended and twisted together.

Adam wasn't bothered about having children. She should be dancing and shouting for joy over that fact. If they stayed together there would never be a time that she would disappoint him or let him down because she couldn't have children. By the sounds of it he'd be quite happy if children were never part of their relationship. But she could find nothing to celebrate about that.

She was an idiot.

When Callum left her, all she'd wanted was to find a man who didn't want children. Then she could have a normal relationship and never feel like a failure, or never be waiting for the man to walk away from her because she couldn't have them. But now she had found one, a wonderful, funny, patient man she knew she was falling for, someone for who children simply weren't a priority, and it felt like a hollow victory. Because in reality she wanted a man to share the same hopes and dreams as her and share in the disappointments of those dreams not coming true too.

She glanced out at the street as Joy waddled past, holding Rebecca's hand. In the privacy of her own shop and with no one to see her, she let the tears fill her eyes. She wanted a baby more than anything and Adam would never understand that.

✳

After Gabe had turned Neve away from the office again, she made her way down to the ice palace on the pretext of going for a walk but in reality she wanted to see how they were getting on with the plans for the New Year's Eve ball. As she walked down the hill she smiled as the blue frosted glass walls of the ice palace sparkled in the early morning sunlight. When Gabe had told her of his plans to have a giant palace, seemingly made of ice, she had imagined it would look tacky and like something from a theme park. She couldn't imagine how it could possibly be in keeping with the wildness of the island but somehow it worked. It looked magical and although it was perfect right now against the snowy backdrop of the hills and trees, she knew it would look equally spectacular in the spring and summer, when it would gleam like crystals in the sunshine. The guests all loved it too, with several enquiring about hiring it for parties or weddings later in the year.

She pushed open the door and the first thing she noticed was the heat. Whenever she had been there in the days leading up to Christmas, the rooms inside had housed a magnificent ice carvings display, with ice reindeers, snowmen and other animals, and as such had to be kept at minus temperatures all day so the carvings wouldn't melt. Now the ice carvings had been stored in a huge walk-in freezer at the back of the palace while the display team worked on transforming the space into a ballroom.

The foyer of the ice palace was a grand affair in itself and she couldn't get over the change from a few days before. The floor was a white marble, the walls were silver and had large ornate mirrors hanging from every surface, reflecting the natural light that poured through the walls so beautifully, but what captured her attention were the two curved staircases either side of the room that she knew led up to a balcony that overlooked the proceedings in the ballroom and had spectacular views over the island too. The stairs and balconies were also made of glass, silver and mirrored panels, extending the wonderful ice palace theme inside as well as outside.

Neve pushed open the main door into the ballroom and stopped. She hadn't really seen it before it had been converted into the dark winter wonderland that housed the ice carvings, so she hadn't seen what it looked like normally – but this was a total transformation. The white marble floor continued in here and around the outside of the large circular room were white marble pillars leading up to a balcony. Giant swathes of silvery blue silk and chiffon were hung from the balcony so they billowed in the cool breeze coming through one of the open doors. Large glass windows and doors peppered the space in between the pillars, so the room was bright and airy, at least during the day. At night the room would be lit up by the ten spectacular crystal-drop chandeliers placed around the roof. Spaced around the edges of the room were wonderful potted trees with silvery white fairy lights strewn from the branches. It looked spectacular.

The display team were hard at work, a few of them polishing the floor right near the entrance with some huge buffering machines. A few were adding more lights to some of the naked trees, while others were bringing in tables and silvery chairs from the huge storage area at the back of the room.

In the middle was a large scaffolding platform and, to her surprise, Antoine was standing on it, hanging giant orbs of glass from the ceiling. They were obviously glass orbs that he had blown himself as they were beaded with silvery flecks just like some of the ornaments she had seen in his shop the day before. They would reflect the light from the chandeliers beautifully.

Antoine waved when he saw her as he finished hanging one of the orbs. He unhooked himself from the harness, climbed down and walked over to talk to her.

'These look wonderful,' Neve said. 'They really add to the ambience of the room.'

'They don't take too long to do fortunately. They're relatively simple to make, which is good as Gabe wanted a hundred of them.'

'They still must take a lot of skill. I wouldn't know how to start.'

He smiled at her, his green eyes soft and gentle. 'I could teach you.'

Wow. Was he flirting with her? She had a bruise on her head, a broken arm, she hadn't had the energy to do anything with her hair that morning beyond brush it, she was wearing comfy jogging bottoms as they were easier to pull on than jeans or her normal office attire. She looked a wreck. And to top it all off she was pregnant with another man's child and, as most of the village had congratulated her on her pregnancy yesterday when she had been walking around, she presumed he must know that too.

She cleared her throat. 'I'm no good at anything remotely creative, but if you're interested in passing on your skill, I think the guests would love to learn that while they were here. It would be another thing we could offer, I'm sure they would pay good money to learn that too. Why don't you speak to Gabe or Adam about offering it as a service? I'm sure they would be delighted with the idea.'

He stared at her with undisguised amusement. 'I'll think about that. It's not quite as fun with a room full of students as it is one on one.'

He *was* flirting with her. Good lord, no one ever flirted with her. She never had time for dates or boyfriends, or maybe she made sure she didn't have time because she never wanted to get hurt, but either way, her attitude of wanting to make sure everything was perfect in the hotel in London made sure she wasn't exactly the sweet and warm type that people were attracted to. Somehow, Oakley had seen through all of that and kept chipping away at the wall she had built to protect herself until it eventually came tumbling down. And Oakley was still here now. She had pushed him away and he'd come back to fight for her, she had told him she was carrying another man's child and he hadn't run away like she thought he would. Maybe she was giving off some kind of pheromone now she was pregnant. Maybe her body knew that she would be raising her baby alone and was sending off pheromones to men in search of a mate to look after her. Maybe that was what was attracting Oakley and Antoine.

She tried to look at Antoine objectively. If she wasn't pregnant, if there wasn't this mess with Oakley to sort out, would he be the sort of man she would date? Would she be turned on by a sweaty, muscly man who would teach her how to blow glass? Would he wrap his arms around her as he helped her to twist and shape the glass? Her stomach twisted at the thought of being with anyone but Oakley; even standing this close to Antoine now, she felt a stab of disloyalty and guilt and she didn't even know if she had any kind of future with Oakley. There would never be another man for her. If Oakley walked away, she would raise this baby on her own. The thought of falling into Antoine's arms seeking comfort and someone to look after her wasn't even something she could comprehend.

'Well, we can certainly offer one-on-one lessons if that's what you would prefer,' Neve said and then looked away around the room. 'This place is going to look wonderful for the ball.'

'It is. I'm quite looking forward to going. Do you have a date for the evening?'

Neve looked back at him in surprise. He wasn't even going for the subtle approach any more. She had to admire his tenacity.

'I'm not sure I'll be going, to be honest. After my fall the other day, standing for long periods of time doesn't really appeal. It hurts my back too much.'

'That's a shame. I was looking forward to having a dance with you.'

He wasn't going to give up. Time to nip this in the bud.

She smiled. 'That's very sweet. But if I was going to dance at all, it would probably be with my fiancé.'

His smile barely faltered. 'Ah, the man you were in the shop with the other day. I didn't realise you were engaged. Congratulations. Well, I must get on. I still have over seventy of these things to hang today. Hopefully I'll see you at the ball.'

He walked away, completely unconcerned by the rejection, and she shook her head with a smile.

She noticed Adam talking to one of the crew and she spotted Luke nearby, fiddling around with the cables for the tree lights. As she walked over to him, he stood up to greet her.

'How you feeling?' Luke said, brushing his hair from his face.

'I'm fine, aching, but fine. This cast is so itchy though. I want to poke something down the crack and give it a good scratch.'

'I wouldn't do that if I were you. You might damage something. How's the baby?'

Neve smiled and found herself unconsciously stroking her tiny bump. 'All good, I think. The doctor thought he was big and strong, so I'm trusting he's going to take care of himself in there.'

'Guess it pays off, having a superhero as a father.'

She laughed. 'I think it certainly helps. And you're going to be an uncle again. How do you feel about that?'

'Well, I'm certainly going to miss watching the little scamp grow up. I presume you'll be going to California with Oakley?'

Neve sighed. 'I have no idea what's going to happen. Things between Oakley and me are not exactly sunshine and roses at the moment. And even if we do work it out, I don't want to leave you guys – my job is here and I can't just leave Gabe in the lurch. But equally I never envisaged spending the rest of my life on this little island either.'

Luke wiped his hands as he looked around him, and as his eyes held on something across the room, Neve followed his gaze and saw he was watching Audrey hanging her little jars of lights that she sold in the village.

'You have to follow your heart and trust that it will lead you to the right place,' Luke said, his eyes on Audrey for a moment longer before he turned back to face Neve. 'Don't be stubborn and hold your job in higher esteem than your relationship. You could work in Gabe's hotel in California like you did before, if you still wanted to work in the hotel business. It's not so easy for Oakley to move his acting career to a little rock on the northernmost part of the UK.'

'I know,' Neve said, softly.

'And we'd come and visit and you could visit us. It's not ideal but love is never perfect. There's always lumps and bumps to navigate. It just depends if Oakley is the one to make all that effort for. You've been miserable since you broke up with him and now he's back and you're still miserable. Do you love him?'

Neve didn't hesitate. 'With everything I have.'

'It's clear he loves you too, so what are you so afraid of?'

'That I won't be good enough for him,' she said, without thinking.

'You're more than good enough for him,' Luke said. 'You're smart, generous, compassionate, beautiful, funny. In fact, I doubt he is good enough for you. Just because he's famous, it certainly doesn't mean he gets a pass in my book. He has to be someone truly special to deserve someone like you and I've not seen any evidence of that yet.'

'He *is* special. He's the most wonderful, kindest, most generous, sweetest person I've ever met. He makes me laugh. He knocked down my walls and made me happier than I've ever been. I pushed him away, Luke, and he came back to fight for me and I pushed him away again. He proposed to me and I threw up all these reasons why we shouldn't get married. I told him the baby, *his* baby, isn't his and he's still here after all that. He's definitely special enough.'

Luke smiled. 'Then you fight for him. If he's that wonderful, you fight for him too.'

Neve nodded. She just needed Oakley to come back now so that she could hopefully put things right between them once and for all.

＊

The boat came to a stop and the tiny lights of the jetty and the dinghies lit up the inky darkness. Oakley decided to hold back and let the other tourists go in the dinghies to Juniper Island first. All day he had thought of nothing but Neve. He had gone round and round making his mind up and then letting the fear of what kind of father he would be change his mind again but in the end there was only one solution and he knew that.

His phone rang in his pocket and when he dug it out he saw that it was his mum, Tamsin, calling. She had phoned him on Christmas Day but he had been too numb to speak to her then. Now she had no doubt seen the stories in the papers too and he knew he couldn't avoid her call any longer. Although if he was hoping that she was ringing to offer her congratulations he knew he would be sorely disappointed.

'Is it true?' Tamsin barked down the phone as soon as he answered.

'Hello, Mum, how are you?'

'Oakley…'

'Did you have a nice Christmas?'

'Is it true, is Neve pregnant with your child?'

'Yes.' He frowned at the lie and how easily it came but if he really was considering raising Neve's son, then the boy would be his and Oakley would love him as if he really was his own.

Tamsin was silent for a moment before she spoke. 'She needs to get rid of it.'

'What?' He hadn't heard right. The reception wasn't great and clearly he had misheard.

'She needs to get rid of the baby, this will ruin your career. If she cares about you at all, she will get rid of it. We can release a statement to the press about how she had a miscarriage, it will get the sympathy vote and—'

Anger ripped through him so fast that he nearly threw the phone overboard. When he spoke, his voice was low. 'That is the most disgusting thing you've ever said. I'm used to you being like a bull in a china shop when it comes to my career but this is my son, your grandson, that you're talking about like he's some piece of rubbish that we can just throw away.'

'Oakley –'

'No! I can't even talk to you right now. Don't call me again unless it's to apologise and to wish me congratulations.'

He ended the call and tried to steady his breathing, realising it wasn't just anger surging through him but a fierce protective streak too. He would never let anything happen to his son.

As he came to terms with these feelings and what they meant, he knew that his mum had inadvertently made the decision for him. He loved Neve and that meant loving everything about her, including her son.

✳

Adam sat at his desk as he read through a spreadsheet of sales figures, though he had studied the same column five times. Ivy had texted him earlier to say she was tired and would he mind if he gave that night a miss. He'd agreed, giving her the space that she wanted, but he was only going to give her tonight. He was going to go straight round there tomorrow morning so they could talk this out.

Although she had smiled and joked with him as normal as they had moved around getting ready that morning, he knew something had been very wrong and it had been the conversation about children that had done it. Did Ivy really want children and had she lied about it because she thought that he didn't?

Everything was so new and fragile between them and it seemed ridiculous to be having this conversation already but there was no way he was letting Ivy go either.

The phone suddenly rang on his desk and he snatched it up, hoping it was Ivy having changed her mind. He listened as the person on the other end spoke and his heart stopped.

CHAPTER 16

Neve was sitting behind reception waiting for the passengers from the boat trip to come back. It had grown dark, she had eaten dinner with her parents and there was still no sign of the boat returning.

Iris, the hotel's young receptionist and reservations manager, had let Neve sit behind the desk, out of sight of the customers but in front of a computer. Without Gabe, Adam or Luke to stop her, Neve had relaxed in front of a few emails and other little jobs that she felt needed to be done. But to her frustration, Adam had taken care of everything on her list of things to do that week so there really wasn't a lot left.

Idly she logged into her personal email account to see there were lots of Google alert emails about Oakley. She clicked on the one from Christmas Day first and to her surprise she saw photos of herself and Oakley being loaded into the air ambulance, shortly after her fall. Rumours from an unknown source claimed she was pregnant with Oakley's child.

She clicked on another article that somehow had grainy photos of her being unloaded off the helicopter in Lerwick. There were a few comments in the article from people too cowardly to give their names, confirming she was indeed pregnant and that Oakley had gone with her for the ultrasound.

She opened another article to see photos of her and Oakley in the village, one with her hand on his cheek while he stared down at her, his hand resting on their unborn child. Snow was swirling in the air between them and the look he was giving her was one of complete and utter love. This was such an intimate moment between the two of them and here it was plastered across the newspapers for the world to see. There was even a zoomed-in close-up of her belly and the paper was asking people to comment on whether they thought Obsidian Junior was inside there.

She scrolled down to the comments underneath the article and tears filled her eyes as she read them.

Oakley's taste in women has suddenly taken a downward turn.
Oakley Rey could have any woman in the world and he goes for someone like that?
This can't be true, he's supposed to marry me!
When a one-night stand goes badly wrong.
He looks angry. How much do you think he is paying her to keep quiet?
If I was Oakley, I'd demand a DNA test, she looks the type to sleep around.
I bet we have her kiss and tell story in the Daily Oracle next week.
I thought Oakley had better taste than that.
Entrapment!!
I bet he was drunk when he slept with her.

Neve quickly closed down the computer, not wanting to read any more. All these people sitting in judgement over her life, not having any idea what had gone on between her and Oakley, what kind of relationship they had. And all the comments about her not being good enough for him. It was everything she feared. She wasn't the only one who thought that, the public, his fans, they all thought it too.

She wiped the tears away furiously.

'What time is the boat due back?' she asked, hoping her voice wasn't betraying her feelings.

Jake glanced at his watch. 'About fifteen minutes ago.'

'They're probably just a bit delayed,' Iris said. 'I think they left here a bit later than planned and then they were going to stop at one of the southern islands for lunch, so maybe that took a little longer than planned. It's the first time we've done it so there's bound to be a few teething problems,' she added, practically.

Neve smiled. At seventeen Iris was far more mature than Neve had ever been when she was in her twenties. She couldn't imagine Iris giving away all of her money to a man who claimed to love her.

Suddenly she heard footsteps thundering down the stairs and she quickly ducked behind the partition at the back of the reception area in case Adam or whoever it was saw her.

'What's wrong?' Iris asked.

'The boat has got into difficulties. It's sinking.'

Neve stood up in shock. '*What?*'

Adam looked over at her but clearly didn't have time to question what she was doing there.

'I don't know any details, they just called it through and the reception is so bad up there, I could barely make out what they were saying. I'm heading down to the jetty now to see what's going on.'

'I'll come with you,' Neve said, hurrying round the edge of the reception.

'No, Neve, I need you here. We might need to call the coastguard or the RNLI and I need someone here for when the guests come back to deal with any complaints. Is Dr Brenick back from her holiday yet? If she is, give her a call if there are any injuries. She can deal with anything minor. We might need the air ambulance too. Look, I'll call you when I have some details.'

Adam turned away but she grabbed his arm. 'Adam, Oakley's on that boat.'

He paused. 'I'll let you know as soon as I know something. Try not to worry, it might not be anything serious. Get some of the boys to come down to the jetty too.'

With that he ran out the front door, jumped onto a snowmobile and sped off into the darkness, leaving Neve and Iris alone.

'What should we do?' Iris said.

Neve stared at the darkness. The sea was so cold at this time of year and the currents were so strong up the east side of the island where the jetty was. If anyone ended up in the water, they wouldn't stand a chance. And while she should have been concerned for the hotel guests and what it would mean to the hotel if several of their guests got hurt, the only person she was worried about was Oakley. The man she loved was on a sinking boat. The man she wanted forever with. Suddenly everything that had happened over the last few days seemed so silly and inconsequential. They were supposed to be together and she had ruined all of that. He wouldn't even have been on the boat if it wasn't for her.

'Neve,' Iris said.

She looked at Iris. 'Erm, call Dr Brenick from the village and I'll get some of the crew to get down to the jetty.'

Iris nodded and as she picked up the phone to call the doctor, Neve rang through to Gabe and Luke and the maintenance team on the walkie-talkies. Her hands were shaking, she could feel the tears pricking at her eyes. What was going on?

Two of the Land Rovers suddenly pulled up outside the hotel and several of the guests got out, laughing and joking with each other.

Neve ran out to meet them. 'Have you come from the boat trip? Is everything OK?'

'Yes, it was a great day,' said one of the men.

Neve stared at him in confusion. 'But we just had reports that the boat was sinking.'

'*Our* boat? I don't think so. They were still ferrying the last passengers off the main tour boat with the dinghies when we left, we were the first guests off.'

God, could it have been one of the dinghies that had got into trouble?

The guests all disappeared off to their lodges and Neve was left feeling utterly helpless. She ran back into the main reception to see if there was any news but Iris shook her head.

Neve picked up the walkie-talkie and tried to reach Adam but there was no answer. This was ridiculous.

Two more Land Rovers pulled up outside the hotel and Neve ran back outside again. She saw Poppy's mum get out, the driver running round to the boot to get Poppy's wheelchair.

'Do you know what's happening down there, we heard reports of a boat sinking?' Neve asked Peter, the driver.

Peter looked at her, bewildered. 'Everything was OK when we left.'

Neve wanted to scream. It was about fifteen minutes' drive to the jetty. How long had Adam been gone, five minutes, maybe ten? The incident must have just happened after these cars left. All the guests got out and there was still no sign of Oakley.

'How many more guests are there to come?'

Peter shrugged. 'We were told not to go back down as the other two cars would pick up the remainder.'

Poppy wheeled herself over to the discussion. 'Did you say the boat sank?'

Neve nodded. 'We heard the boat got into difficulties. Do you know how many guests were left on the tour boat when you left?'

'I think it was just Oakley, he was busy chatting to the crew. They all wanted their picture taken with him and Oakley was trying to persuade the captain to let him pilot the boat. Is he OK?'

'I don't know what's happening down there,' Neve said, desperation and panic clutching at her chest.

'Look, we'll head down there and see if there's anything we can do,' Peter said.

Neve nodded and they got back in their cars and drove off. She went back into the reception just as the walkie-talkie in her hand crackled into life.

Adam's voice came over the line but the reception was so bad she couldn't hear what he was saying.

'Adam, I can't hear you. Can you repeat your message, over.'

'. . . Oakley. . . hurt.'

Neve didn't wait for anything more, she ran back outside and climbed on the remaining snowmobile. She glanced down at her cast and nearly cried that she wouldn't be able to drive it properly. Before she could get off, Jake came running out and climbed on in front of her. She quickly wrapped her arms around him and they took off down the hill towards the jetty, taking a short cut across the grounds of the hotel instead of going the long way round that the road took.

She saw the road up ahead and saw one of the Land Rovers heading back towards the hotel. The snowmobile hit the road and took off towards the jetty.

Another Land Rover came round the corner and she flagged it down, asking Jake to slow down at the same time. The driver, George, stopped the car by her side and wound down the window.

'George, please tell me you know what's going on down at the jetty.'

'I don't know all the details, Miss Whitaker, but one of the dinghies got into trouble as they were bringing the last of the passengers and crew back from the boat. Everyone is fine though. As far as I can tell, no one was hurt.'

'Where's Oakley?'

'He was in the car that just passed.' George indicated the car that had driven by a minute before, heading for the hotel.

'Is he OK?'

'I think so. Like I said, I don't think anyone was hurt. Here, get in and I'll take you back to the hotel. It'll be quicker.'

She climbed off.

'Jake, are you OK to get back to the hotel?'

He nodded and she quickly climbed into the passenger seat. George put his foot down and headed back towards the hotel.

'Thank you,' Neve said with relief; going back uphill in the snowmobile was not going to be as easy as going downhill had been.

Oakley was OK. George said everyone was fine. He was OK, he had to be. But the panic wouldn't subside from her chest and she knew she wouldn't start to feel better until she had seen Oakley for herself.

George stopped the car outside the hotel and she ran into reception.

'He's gone back to the lodge,' Iris said.

Neve cursed as she ran back outside and back to the lodge as fast as she could. Was he hurt, was he OK? Surely if he was hurt they'd be taking him to hospital, not letting him go back to her lodge?

She ran up the steps and burst through the door. 'Oakley!'

There was no answer and no sign of him in the lounge or the kitchen.

'Oakley!'

He suddenly appeared at the top of the stairs, soaking wet and with only a towel wrapped around his waist.

Obviously seeing how upset she was, he came running down the stairs. 'Freckle, are you OK? What's wrong?'

'I heard the boat sank. Are you OK, are you hurt?' She ran her hands over his arms, checking him for injuries, but he didn't have a scratch on him. To her surprise and annoyance, tears of relief filled her eyes.

'Freckle, I'm fine. To say the boat sank would be a huge over-statement. We got into a bit of difficulty as the dinghy came back to the jetty. A few of the crew and I got a little wet, but no one was hurt, I promise.'

A sob escaped her throat and without thinking she reached up and kissed him. He pulled back slightly to look at her, wip-ing the tears gently from her face, and then he kissed her back. His kisses were gentle and soothing at first, his hands cupping her head in a sweet caress. But after a moment, his hands wan-dered down to her bum and he hauled her tight against him. He parted her lips with his own and tasted her with his tongue, the kiss turning urgent and desperate.

God, she needed him. After the angst of the last few days, she needed his hands on her, his mouth on her lips. If he could kiss her like this, maybe they would be OK.

He lifted her and she wrapped her legs around him. As the kiss continued, he carried her to the dining table, sitting her down on the edge.

She tugged at his towel, letting it drop to the floor as he made quick work of all her clothes, his mouth barely leaving hers for a second. As his mouth began to travel down her neck to her shoulder, clarity slammed through the desire-filled fog and she suddenly remembered she had to tell him the truth about his baby.

'Oakley, wait. I need to tell you something.'

'Hmmm?' Oakley's mouth drifted lower.

She closed her eyes at the feel of his mouth on her skin. 'You're not going to like it.'

'Then don't tell me, Freckle. Whatever it is, I don't want to hear it.'

His mouth continued his slow torture of her body.

'I can't not tell you, Oakley, it's important. Oh, God...' All thought and reason went straight out of her head as his lips moved even lower to her most sensitive area. His mouth felt hot and divine and he knew exactly what to do to drive her insane within a matter of seconds.

'Then tell me tomorrow.' The vibrations of his voice against her flesh did the most wonderful things to her insides.

'I really think I should tell you now,' Neve moaned, her voice strangled as she tried to find the strength to stop this before it went any further. But she had missed him so much over the last few weeks and she knew when she told him the truth he would be angry, so maybe she should just make the most of him now. She cringed about how cowardly she was being over this but with his mouth doing wicked and wondrous things to her, she was finding it hard to think of anything else.

'All I'm interested in knowing is whether sex is on the "no" list too,' Oakley said, standing back up and moving between her legs.

'No, thankfully that's not on the list,' Neve said, wrapping her legs around him and promising herself she would tell him as soon as they were finished.

'I can't hurt the baby?' Oakley asked, concern filling his eyes.

'No, definitely not.'

'Good.'

And with that, he slid inside her, filling her completely.

She shouted out, holding him tight as he moved against her. Cradling her against him, he lowered her to the table, kissing her, caressing her.

With a sudden groan of frustration, he pulled out of her and disappointment hit her in a huge wave. But the next thing he was pushing her gently backwards across the table and climbing up on the table on top of her. He slid back inside her again. He felt so divine, so hot, and as he moved against her she could feel herself building so quickly.

He pulled his mouth from hers to look at her, his eyes filled with love and adoration.

'I love you, Freckle.'

It was those words that sent her tumbling over the edge and he quickly followed.

❅

Neve was in a blissful, comatose state. She could see the early morning sunshine from the other sides of her eyelids, but she couldn't bring herself to open her eyes. After they had made love on the dining table, Oakley had carried her upstairs and made love to her again and then kissed her all over, sending her off into a blissful sleep. She was half awake now but the kisses were still continuing and slowly she came round more to what was happening.

She opened one eye and found him laying soft kisses over her belly. He smiled up at her when he saw she was awake and she knew now, when they were both so happy and relaxed, was the right time to tell him, crossing all her fingers and toes that Pip was right and he wouldn't be that angry about it.

'Oakley, I need to tell you something.'

'I need to tell you something too,' he said, laying another kiss on her belly.

'I have to go first,' Neve insisted.

Oakley laughed. 'Let's toss a coin to see who goes first.'

She tried to stop herself from groaning in frustration, he wasn't taking this remotely seriously and why should he? In his mind, what could possibly be worse than her carrying another man's baby?

'OK, forget that,' Oakley said. 'I'll go. I had a lot of time to think yesterday and over the last few days. I love you, Freckle. I told you that there was no problem too big that we couldn't make this work. I still want to marry you and I want to raise this baby as mine. I will love this baby because it's yours. He will want for nothing, neither of you will. And I'll help with all the night feeds and changing the nappies. Mikki told me that marriage is taking the rough and the smooth and she's right. I want to support you through this.'

Neve stared at him in shock. She hadn't been expecting this for one second. 'Oakley –'

'And if you track the real dad down and he wants to be a part of this kid's life then he can, I won't stop him. But I'll be the kid's proper dad. I'm the one that will play football with him and teach him how to play baseball and rock him to sleep every night. And we can still live here if that's what you want. My job is in California for the next few years but we can come back here after the job is finished or whatever you want, but the important thing is we're together, wherever we are. I want this baby with you. I know I was scared before, I know I didn't want children just yet, but I do want this now. I want to have a family with you.'

He wanted to be with her. He loved her so much that he wanted to raise a baby that, as far as he was concerned, wasn't his. He wanted them to be together like a proper family. It was everything she ever wanted. Every doubt about the permanence and durability of their love vanished. She *was* good enough for him, he had just proved that. Any fears that he wasn't serious about a proper relationship just faded away. He really did want forever. She had never really given him a chance. She had been waiting for him to let her down and that wasn't fair on him. They deserved a chance at being together and this time she was going to take it.

She rolled up onto her knees and kissed him hard. 'I love you.'

'I love you too and—'

She silenced him with her fingers over his lips. 'I love you and I hope you will understand that what I'm about to tell you, I did it for you. I did it because I love you so much.'

He frowned in confusion.

'Oakley, I lied to you,' Neve blurted out.

The smile faded from his face. 'You lied? About what?'

'The baby. I'm sorry, I'm *so* sorry. I did it for you. I could see you didn't want the baby, that you were scared about the responsibility and how it would affect your job, and I didn't want it to ruin your dreams so I lied. I told you the baby wasn't yours when he is. The baby is yours, Oakley. I haven't been with anyone else. You're going to be a dad.'

Oakley stared at her in shock and for the longest moment neither said a word. Then he climbed off the bed, still staring at her in horror. If she thought the pain he had been in before when he thought she had slept with someone else was bad enough, this was nothing to what he felt now.

He suddenly started to get dressed.

'Oakley, wait! Please understand that I made a terrible mistake but it was with good intentions. It wasn't nasty or malicious, I did it for you. I acted rashly and I shouldn't have done it.'

He pulled his jumper over his head and fastened up his boots. Then he stood up to look at her.

'You're carrying my son?' he choked out. 'The boy is mine?'

'Yes, I'm sorry.'

He started pacing the room. 'You lied to me. What if I'd left after you told me the baby wasn't mine, went back to America? I would never have known that I had a son. My son would never have known his father. You know how I feel about my dad, about him abandoning me and how upset that makes me feel that he never wanted me, that I was never enough to make him want to stay, and yet you would have put our son through the same thing, making him believe I never wanted him.'

'I would have told you.'

'When? When my son was five or ten or when he was eighteen and wanted to track me down?'

'I've been trying to tell you the truth. When we went down to the stables and I told you I hadn't slept with Adam, I was trying to tell you then and you assumed I'd just slept with someone else, and when we came back here before the surprise Christmas party, I told you we needed to talk. When I gave you the bracelet and we ended up kissing and then again last night after the boat. I've tried but everything kept getting in the way. I'm so sorry,' Neve said.

He was still pacing and he was barely looking at her. 'I can't believe you lied to me about our son. The hell I've been through over the last few days! All I could think about was whether we had any kind of future together, wondering whether you loved me at all if you could have been with someone else so quickly. And it was all a lie. The stress was for nothing.'

'Don't you understand? I did it because I do love you. You were talking about your job and how it was everything you ever wanted and how babies just weren't on your radar at the moment. I didn't want to ruin your life with a baby you didn't want. You looked so scared when I told you and I wanted to let you go, to free you of the responsibility.'

'That wasn't your choice to make,' Oakley snapped. 'Christ, my mum has spent my whole life making decisions for me and you know how much I resented that and then you decide to take the biggest decision of my life out of my hands.'

'I know, it was stupid. I reacted badly. As soon as I said it, I wanted to take it back.'

'But you didn't.'

'No, because five seconds after I said it, I fell down the stairs and knocked myself out.'

Oakley paced away again, pushing his hands through his hair. 'You didn't think I was good enough to raise your baby.'

'No, God no! I never thought that.'

'I wasn't sensible enough for you, didn't take life seriously. I was too busy enjoying myself. You never thought I was mature enough to be a dad.'

'Oakley, no, this isn't what it was about.' How could he ever think he wasn't good enough when she had always thought *she* wasn't good enough for him?

'Is that why you finished with me in the first place, because you found out you were pregnant and you didn't want me to be the dad?'

'No, I swear, I didn't know until about two weeks ago,' Neve insisted.

'And yet you didn't call me when you found out.'

'I was going to. I was just shocked myself and I didn't know how to tell you. It wasn't something that I wanted to do over the phone. I was going to wait until after Christmas and then I was going to fly out and tell you.'

He turned to look at her and she was shocked to see he had tears in his eyes.

'I might not know how to change a nappy or what temperature the milk needs to be heated up to, and I have no idea how to hold a baby or how to wind one, but I would be a great dad to our son because I would love him so much. I would read every god damn baby book there is and learn how to look after him. I'd love him as much as I loved you but you weren't ever prepared to give me that chance.'

Neve quickly stood up. 'That's not the reason at all, please. . .'

He backed away from her as if he didn't know her any more. 'I need some space, don't follow me.' He headed for the stairs.

'Please, don't go, we need to talk about this.'

Oakley didn't look back. He walked down the stairs and a few moments later she heard the front door close behind him.

She sat down on the bed and burst into tears.

CHAPTER 17

Adam knocked on Ivy's door, determined to talk to her before she went out for her early morning walk. He hated that there seemed to be this tension between them and he didn't know why.

There was no answer. He tried the door handle but for the first time since he'd met her the door was locked.

He knocked on the door again, just in case she was upstairs ignoring him, but there was no answer and no movement from inside.

'Adam, hello!' Deborah called from the shop next door. 'She's not in, I saw her go out for her walk about half an hour ago.'

Adam sighed, knowing she rarely took the same route on her walks and it'd be impossible to try and find her now.

'Why don't you come in for a cup of tea, dear, and a slice of cake?' Deborah suggested, gesturing for him to come in.

'Thank you, that's very kind, but I really need to get back to the hotel. There's a lot of work to be done ahead of the New Year's Eve ball in two days—'

'Nonsense, dear, there's always time for cake. This one is banana cake, it's lovely for breakfast.'

She turned and walked into the shop, not taking no for an answer.

Adam bit his lip and followed Deborah inside the shop, which smelt wonderfully delicious from all the melted chocolate.

Stephen was already walking around and turning all the chocolate fountains on and Adam knew that later the scents would spill out onto the street, attracting tourists in their droves.

'Go on back,' Stephen said, pointing to the back of the shop where the kitchen was. 'Just ask for a small slice, or she'll probably give you the whole cake.'

Adam smiled and walked into the kitchen, where there was a huge oak table and trays of fresh fruit were in the middle of being cut, ready for the tourists to dip into pools of melted chocolate. There were quaint flowered mugs hanging from a dresser and fairy lights strewn across the ceiling. Deborah was already cutting three extra-large slices of banana cake. She turned to the kettle as it came to the boil and poured the water into a big red teapot.

'How's things going with you and Ivy?' Deborah asked as if she had known him all his life and had every right to know all the details of his love life.

'Things are good,' Adam said, vaguely.

Deborah sat down and handed him his slice of cake. 'I noticed you spent the night several times this week.'

Adam had to stop his mouth from falling open as Stephen came into the kitchen too.

'Deborah, you shouldn't ask him things like that,' Stephen said as he took a big slice of his own cake.

'Oh, don't mind me, dear, I'm not going to judge. You young uns always get together a lot quicker than we did in our day. There was a lot more courting in my time, it's just the way of it now. I think it's wonderful that you and Ivy have found happiness together, even if it isn't forever. She needs someone to make her smile after all that unpleasant business with her ex.'

'I like her, I really do. It's early days for us, but I kind of hope what we have is going to be for the long haul.'

'You'll be going back to London though in a few months?' Deborah asked.

'Gabe has asked me to stay and I've agreed.'

'Oh. And are you thinking about marriage and children with her?'

Adam nearly choked on his cake.

'Debs!' Stephen said, incredulously. 'They've been seeing each other for a few days. It's too early for them to be thinking of that.'

'Ivy wants a child. I've seen the way she looks at Joy and Rebecca. She wants that more than anything,' Deborah persisted.

'Is that what she's said?' asked Adam, knowing straight away that his vagueness about having children the night before had been the thing that had upset Ivy.

'We've not talked too much about it. Just that her and her ex-husband tried for a while and it didn't happen. But I know she is desperate to have one. I don't think it would be fair to get involved with her if you don't want that too.'

Adam rubbed his head. He certainly hadn't expected a lecture when he came down there that morning.

'What makes you think I don't want that?'

'Your job means long hours. You've lived in London for the last few years with all the parties and shows. Not too much time for a child with that lifestyle.'

'There wasn't much time for parties and shows in my job as deputy manager either. My job does require long hours but if Ivy and I decide we want children in the future then we can work it out then. But really that is our business, not yours and as we've said, I've known her for less than a week, she could get bored of me and end things between us next week. I really don't think we need to worry about marriage and children just yet.'

'I just don't want to see her get hurt.'

'That's the last thing I want too,' Adam said, honestly.

'You obviously care for her so I'll say no more about it,' Deborah said. 'You certainly don't want us old fogies interfering.'

Stephen stared at his wife in shock at being lumped in with her as one of the interfering old fogies.

Adam smiled slightly to himself. Life was certainly going to be a lot different here than what he was used to.

❄

Oakley hadn't come back. Neve had waited and waited, hoping he would come back to her lodge, but there had been no sign of him. Eventually, when their baby had demanded that he needed feeding, she had got washed and dressed with great difficulty and headed over for breakfast.

She grabbed a plate with a pile of pancakes and fruit and sat down at the table with Gabe, Pip and Wren, who looked like a blissfully happy little family. Her mum and dad were there too.

Gabe's smile fell from his face when he looked up to greet her. 'What's happened?'

'I'm an idiot, that's what's happened,' Neve said, taking a big mouthful of pancake. She couldn't stomach the thought of eating when everything lay in tatters around her but she forced it down anyway because the baby needed it. When her family continued to look at her with concern she gave them all a very quick bullet-pointed version of what had happened since Oakley had arrived and how stupid she had been.

'Oh my darling, why would you do something like that?' her mum asked.

'It was for him, I did it for him,' Neve protested but she knew in her heart there was more to it than that. She knew that underneath all that was the fear of her not being good enough for him and therefore her baby wouldn't be good enough to keep him too. It was only now, after his noble proposition that morning, that all those fears had gone. She didn't care what the public said or the newspapers or even his mum. She deserved to be happy and she deserved to be with Oakley. But that realisation had come much too late.

Gabe took her hand, distracting her from her thoughts. 'You don't make things easy for yourself, do you? The man is crazy in love with you. He's angry, of course he is, but he'll come around. Just give him some space.'

'I'm sorry,' Pip said. 'I genuinely thought he might be a bit miffed about the lie, I didn't expect him to react like this.'

Neve sighed as she picked away at her pancakes. She had known that he would react badly to it, which was why she had been so worried about telling him. One of his big fears was that he wasn't a very good actor, that he had simply got where he was because people thought he was good-looking. Whenever he asked the directors, crew or other actors if the scenes he had filmed were OK, whether they were good enough, he said they always told him how wonderful he was. He'd often said the only person he could trust to be honest with him was her and now she'd let him down too.

She finished her pancakes and stood up. 'I have to go, I promised Poppy she could ride Knight. Oakley was going to ride Shadow alongside her. As Oakley is probably licking his wounds somewhere, Poppy will just have to make do with me leading Knight around the meadow instead.'

Gabe caught her hand. 'You're not going to ride Shadow, are you?'

'No, it's probably best that I don't.'

Neve wrapped herself up and walked down the track towards the stables. When she got there, she was surprised to see Oakley riding Shadow round the meadow at full pelt and Boris watching him as if Oakley were a god. She leaned on the fence next to Boris and joined in the ogling.

Oakley knew horses. She knew he'd first ridden one when he was only two years old. He could meet any horse and within seconds they were putty in his hands. He had this natural way with them. He was skilled as well – he could gallop, canter, jump, and do all those things bareback too. She watched him speeding across the meadow on the back of Shadow, twisting and turning with barely a nudge of the reins. He was truly magnificent to watch.

'Oakley said he wanted to burn off some of Shadow's pent-up energy before Poppy's lesson,' Boris said, not taking his eyes off the man himself.

Neve smiled that Oakley had turned up to do Poppy's lesson even though he was still angry. He really was a man of his word.

'I have Knight ready for you, as you asked,' Boris said. 'I've left the back on the saddle for now so she feels safer. Once she is more confident, we can always take it off.'

Just then, Poppy and her mum arrived. Poppy had the biggest grin on her face at the prospect of riding again. Or maybe it was the prospect of riding with Hollywood superstar Oakley Rey.

'Hi Poppy, are you ready to get started?' Neve asked, turning away from the meadow and leaving Oakley to attempt to tire Shadow out before the lesson started. She nudged Boris and he quickly dragged his attention away from Oakley and went to retrieve Knight from the stable.

'I can't wait. It's been so long since I've ridden, I hope I can still do it.'

'I'm sure you'll be great. How long has it been?'

'Three years.'

'OK, so we'll just go really slowly to start with. Get you used to being in the saddle again. We might spend a few minutes on the lunge, just so you're comfortable, and then hopefully you can ride on your own and maybe we can even have you trotting by the end of the session. Now I don't have a hoist, I'm afraid, so are you OK if Boris lifts you into the saddle?'

Neve knew how important it was for paraplegic riders to be independent and not babied, but she hadn't anticipated offering lessons this early into the opening of the hotel and hadn't got everything she would need just yet.

'No, that's fine. I'm just so happy to be riding again.'

Boris lifted her carefully into the saddle and Poppy immediately grabbed the pommel to steady herself as she rearranged herself and her legs into the right position.

'So, we have several straps on the saddle and stirrups to ensure your legs are in the right place. If I do one side, can you do the other?'

Poppy nodded, visibly shaking with excitement. She watched carefully as Neve attached the strap around her foot and the stirrup, fastened a Velcro strap just below her knee and across her thigh and then did a belt up around the waist, anchoring her to the back of the saddle. Poppy repeated the process herself on the other side and Neve checked they were all done up correctly. Knight stood patiently throughout the whole thing, but he'd had many paraplegic riders on his back and for him this was the norm.

'OK, do you feel safe?' Neve asked.

Poppy nodded.

'I'm going to lead Knight for a little while. We'll go for a little walk inside the meadow, just so you can get used to it again. Let me know if you want to stop. Just keep a hold of the pommel for now, don't worry about the reins.'

Neve took the reins and led Knight slowly into the meadow. Knight plodded along carefully, clearly conscious that Poppy was nervous. Oakley came trotting over on Shadow and fell into step on Knight's other side. He didn't say anything and she appreciated that he was letting her take the lead on this, even though he was more than capable of teaching Poppy himself. Neve looked back at him but his eyes were on Poppy and Knight, not even acknowledging she was there. She glanced up at Poppy, who was sitting perfectly in the saddle as if she had been riding all her life and had not had a break for three years or no longer had the use of her legs.

'You have a great seat,' Neve observed.

'It feels so weird to be walking again, it feels like I have my legs back,' Poppy said.

'Do you want to pick up the reins?'

Poppy nodded and picked them up, holding them perfectly.

'That's great,' Oakley encouraged.

Neve carried on leading Knight across the length of the field but slowly loosened her hold on the harness slightly, letting Poppy take more control.

'OK, when we get to the corner of the field are you happy to turn Knight yourself and we'll walk along the top of the field?'

Poppy nodded keenly. Neve took a step away from Knight but continued to walk alongside him. Poppy held the reins tighter.

'You won't need to pull too hard when you get there, Knight will respond to the gentlest of touches,' Neve explained.

As they approached the corner, Poppy pulled gently on the right rein and sure enough, Knight responded beautifully. They continued their slow plodding path through the snow as they walked along the perimeter of the field towards the top corner, where Poppy's mum was waiting, ready to take some pictures.

'Mum, I'm riding again. Look at me, I'm riding,' Poppy cried.

'You're doing great, Popstar,' her mum called back.

They turned through the corner again as her mum fired off a couple of shots and as Neve passed right in front of her, she heard her whisper, 'Thank you.'

Neve smiled at her, her heart soaring. It felt so good to be doing this again, she wondered why she had spent so many years putting it off.

❋

Neve leaned on the fence and watched Poppy ride. She had spent a while letting Poppy walk, correcting her where necessary, though it was very obvious she knew what she was doing. Neve had taught her a few voice commands and they had spent a while on the lunge, alternating between trotting and walking at Poppy's command so she could get used to the feel of it and taking control of Knight. Poppy had been a complete natural. After that Neve had asked if she wanted to trot Knight around the field and handed the lesson over to Oakley, as he could trot alongside Poppy on Shadow and offer instructions where Neve would be unable to keep up. They had been trotting backwards and forwards, chatting and laughing, for the last half hour. Boris had set up some cones and Poppy and Oakley were currently racing each other up the small slalom course.

Her mum, clearly having taken over a thousand photos, came to stand with her.

'How much do I owe you for the lesson, by the way? I asked at reception about it last night and the receptionist said you weren't offering lessons at the moment.'

'We're not,' Neve said. 'Consider this a bit of an experiment. I've trained Knight with paraplegic riders, so I know what I'm doing and it was something I wanted to do here, but we haven't started doing it yet. And please don't worry about money, I'm just happy to see Poppy having so much fun.'

'Well, you're very good with her. I definitely think you should offer more of it in the future. There are many people that would love to ride up here. And if you offer Oakley Rey as part of the lesson, I'm sure it would be very popular.'

Neve laughed. 'Sadly he'll be going back to California in the New Year.'

'Well, thank you again for today, you have no idea how much it means to her.'

Neve looked over at the huge grin on Poppy's face and thought she might have some idea.

Oakley and Poppy came trotting over and both slowed to a walk as they came through the gate. Poppy started unstrapping herself from the saddle and Oakley dismounted and then carefully lifted her down and placed her in her wheelchair.

'Here, I'll take care of the horses,' Boris said, appearing from the shed where they kept the snowmobiles.

He led them both away, disappearing into the stables.

'Thank you so much, I had the most amazing time,' Poppy said.

She and her mum said their goodbyes and disappeared back up the track, leaving Neve alone with Oakley.

'Thank you for coming today,' Neve said.

Oakley nodded and then walked up the track after Poppy.

'Wait, Oakley, can we please talk?' she called after him.

'There's nothing to talk about.'

Neve caught up with him and he stopped. 'You have every right to be angry with me. What I did was horrible but don't let this silly lie ruin our whole relationship.'

'You're the one who did that, Neve, not me.'

Anger flared up in her. 'So you're walking away? You were prepared to stay and look after the baby when you thought he wasn't yours, but now you know he is, you're going to turn your back on him?'

'I have every intention of being a part of my son's life, I just don't think I can be part of yours.'

He turned and walked away again.

Neve stared after him, feeling like she had just been slapped.

'OK, go back to California. We'll be fine here without you. I can raise my baby on my own, we don't need you.' She yanked the engagement ring off her finger and threw it back at him. It landed in the snow and Oakley barely glanced at it as he turned around, he didn't even stop walking.

'That was exactly the plan all along, wasn't it? You had no intention of letting me be a part of his life. You pushed me away and I was an idiot for thinking that we could ever make this work again. You wanted everything perfect and there was no way I was ever going to be good enough to meet those high standards, no matter what I did. Well, you got your wish, Neve. My helicopter is coming to pick me up tomorrow. I'll be back for the twenty-week scan and I'll be back for the birth, but for him, certainly not for you.'

With that he turned away.

Neve stared after him in shock. She had ruined everything. They'd broken up. It really was over.

Up ahead on the track she could see the press photographer lurking in the bushes and taking more pictures of them. She hated that they had just inadvertently given him more ammunition.

She took a few steps forward and stared down at the ring that sparkled in the snow. She picked it up and held it in her palm. It felt heavy, filled with a life of love and laughter that she had carelessly thrown away. She slipped it in her pocket, a reminder for herself when for the briefest of moments everything in her life was good and perfect and wonderful before she had destroyed any chance of being happy again.

CHAPTER 18

Ivy wiped clean yet another painting she had messed up and sighed. She was thinking about this too much. Adam was good and kind and patient in the face of all her craziness, not to mention amazing in bed. She would just talk to him, she would be honest and tell him what she felt and then she would know where he stood once and for all. If he decided to walk away from her then it was better it happened now before either of them got too deeply involved.

She glanced out at the street where Audrey was standing on the doorstep of her shop opposite, looking as if she was waiting for someone.

Abandoning the sheet of glass, Ivy walked across the street towards her.

'You OK?'

Audrey nodded and opened the shop door for Ivy to follow her back inside. Her shop was empty of customers and Ivy noticed a load of boxes stacked up by the door.

'I'm just waiting for Luke to come and collect me and these boxes to take to the ice palace. He's obviously running a bit late.'

Audrey made the most gorgeous lamps, fairy lights inside jars of glittered water in all manner of different colours. She called them 'Aurora Jars', after the Aurora Borealis, and they were a big hit with the tourists. Ivy knew Gabe had commissioned her to make lots to adorn the inside of the ice palace, which were going to look great for the ball.

Ivy noticed that Audrey was pacing nervously across her shop. 'What's wrong?'

Audrey turned to face her. 'I... I was going to ask Luke to go to the ball with me but I've talked myself in and talked myself out of it several times in the last few minutes.'

'You like him?' Ivy smiled. She liked the idea of Audrey finding happiness even if her own love life was a big fat mess.

Audrey sighed. 'I've fallen in love with him.'

'Oh.'

Ivy didn't know what else to say. Love was such a complicated, terrifying and wonderful thing. She wanted that with Adam as much as she wanted to run away and hide from it.

'It's crazy,' Audrey continued. 'I don't think he is ready to fall in love again. He was hurt so badly by his ex-wife and I don't know whether he will ever open himself up to the possibility of a relationship again. The man is grumpy and rude to everyone around him, even his own family, but with me... I don't know, he's not exactly cheerful but he seems different with me. I wonder if he likes me too. We've spent so much time together in the months leading up to the grand opening and he came round here on Christmas Eve to give me this present.' She held up the necklace that had the marcasite and opal star hanging from it. 'And he said I was his light in the darkness and then got all embarrassed and left. Then I saw him on Christmas Day just before Neve fell, and he kept on talking about how much he liked having me as a friend, that he would never want to do anything that would damage our friendship and lots of other stuff about being mates and I got the impression he was warning me off, that he didn't want anything more from me than friendship. And now I'm contemplating asking him to go to the ball with me and I know I must be stupid or crazy because if he says no, I'll be devastated and maybe it's better that I just don't know.'

Audrey finally fell quiet.

'Well, I think I'd rather know,' Ivy said. 'A marriage ending is heartbreaking regardless of the reason and Luke has more reason than most to be upset over how his marriage ended. I was destroyed when mine came to an end but I wouldn't shy away from the possibility of love again.'

Ivy stopped because that was exactly what she was doing with Adam. Hinging her future happiness on the prospect of not having children or even Adam's feelings towards that was stopping her from ever moving forward. If she could never have children then she needed to accept that and move on. And although that was easier said than done, she couldn't be sad for the rest of her life either. She quickly changed the subject before she could dwell on it any longer.

'Let's have some chocolate before Luke comes. Chocolate always makes any situation better. Do you have any of that big box left the hotel gave each of us?'

'Yes, it's in the small cupboard by the fridge,' Audrey said, staring out onto the street again.

'I'll get it,' Ivy said, and wandered out into the kitchen. There were several small cupboards by the fridge and it took her a few moments to locate the right one and when she did, she realised she couldn't reach the chocolates as they were placed on the very top shelf out of reach of temptation. She grabbed a chair and stood on it to grab the chocolates just as the shop door swung open. Still standing on the chair, she peered round the edge of the kitchen door to see that it was Luke, towering over Audrey like a giant bear.

'I've been thinking, I was wondering if you wanted to come to the ball with me?' he blurted out and Ivy nearly did a little dance of happiness for Audrey, though she would have probably fallen off the chair if she had.

Audrey stared at him in disbelief before she finally spoke. 'You're asking me to go to the ball with you?'

'Yes.'

'I was just about to ask you to come to the ball with me.'

Luke stepped closer, a rare smile filling his face. 'You *were*?'

'Yes, but then I got scared that you probably wouldn't want to go with me and now you're here, asking me to go with you,' she babbled and Ivy couldn't help but smile at them.

'Well, will you?' Luke said.

'As friends?' Audrey asked.

Luke hesitated. 'Yes. No, not friends. Well, maybe. . .' he tucked a lock of hair behind her ear. 'Maybe very special friends.'

Ivy watched Audrey break into a huge grin. 'I'd love to.'

Luke smiled too and then he took a step back. 'Let me give you a hand with these.'

It took a few minutes for them to load the boxes into the back of the car and, as Audrey came back to close the shop door, she gave Ivy a discreet thumbs up. She jumped in the car and it sped off in the direction of the hotel and the ice palace.

Ivy put the chocolate box back and hopped down from the chair.

If only her own love life was as simple to sort out.

※

There was a knock on Neve's door later that day, after she had spent the rest of the day lying on the sofa, feeling sorry for herself. She opened it and was delighted to see Oakley standing on her doorstep. Maybe he had forgiven her though that hope was quickly quashed when she saw his angry face.

'I'm not here for you, I'm here to read to my son.'

Neve blinked in surprise.

'I bumped into Finn and Joy in the village and they lent me some children's books. I know that babies can hear voices and music in the womb and it's important that my son hears my voice too.'

Neve swallowed down the lump of emotion in her throat. She didn't dare explain that babies couldn't hear until at least eighteen weeks, she was just glad he was there.

'OK,' she said, quietly.

She sat down at one end of the sofa and Oakley sat awkwardly next to her for a moment. She didn't say anything, she didn't know what she could say. She had ruined everything and she didn't know how to fix it.

Oakley shuffled around so he was lying on his front and his face was next to her stomach. He picked up one of the books from the bulging bag and opened it to the first page. He cleared his throat, obviously embarrassed about reading in front of her.

'Just pretend I'm not here,' Neve suggested, gently.

'Oh, I *will*,' Oakley muttered, angrily, and Neve looked away so he wouldn't see the hurt on her face.

She jumped suddenly, when she felt his hands on her, gently rolling up his shirt she was wearing and exposing her tiny baby bump. He ran his fingers softly over the bump, which was hugely intimate, and he must have realised that because he immediately stopped.

'So, little bear, you got really unlucky and ended up with me as your dad. I'm not good at the practical stuff, I'll probably fail spectacularly at changing your nappy and I'll probably make your bath water too cold because I'll be scared about getting it too hot. I won't always be around a lot as I'll be in America and your mommy will be over here but I promise to love you with everything I have and I'll come and see you as often as I can. I'm going to read you a few stories now. You'll have to let me know which books you like.'

Oakley started reading about a daddy bear who couldn't sleep and Neve smiled at the wonderful singsong tone of voice he used. He even used different voices for the characters. He was a complete natural. Once or twice he turned the pictures towards the bump as if the tiny baby had the powers to see through the walls of the womb, though knowing his dad's superpowers he probably could.

He got to the end of the story and immediately picked another book from the bag. Judging by how many books were inside, Oakley planned to be there a while. He could stay as long as he wanted as far as she was concerned. Hopefully for the rest of the night.

He opened the book and started reading *The Gruffalo* to the bump. She wanted this life with him, she wanted to raise their son with him, to have him there to read the baby stories every night. She couldn't deny their baby that. Even if they weren't together, she needed to make sure the child had this wonderful man in his life, not just once every few months but every day.

He got to the end of *The Gruffalo* and picked up another book, clearly not leaving any time for her to talk to him, but for once she was happy to be quiet and listen to him.

He started reading a book called *Guess How Much I Love You*. As he read the first page, which was about a baby hare trying to tell Big Hare how much he loved him, Oakley reached out again and rested his hand on her bump. As Baby Hare and Big Hare competed with how much they loved each other, tears filled Neve's eyes and fell down her cheeks. Sobs tore from her throat but Oakley carried on reading but as he turned the pages she noticed he was crying too, his voice was choked, tears filling his eyes, and by the time he reached the last page and Big Hare declared that he loved Baby Hare to the moon and back, Neve was nearly full-on wailing.

Oakley tossed the book to one side and pulled her into his arms as she sobbed against him.

'I'm so sorry,' she cried into his chest.

'Don't cry, Freckle, it kills me to see you cry. It was never going to work between us, you know that. My job would mean I'd be travelling a lot and your work is important to you here. And I was too immature for you. We're too different. We had fun and it was silly of me to want something more than that. But we're going to have a child together so we need to be friends if we're going to make this parenting thing work but we can't be more than that.'

'I ruined everything.'

'No, it never would have lasted. I was trying to force it and you kept pushing me away. You knew we weren't meant to be together, that was why you were so reluctant to come with me to America, but we can still be friends. I'll come over here as often as I can and maybe you can bring our little bear over to see me occasionally. I'd pay, of course.'

Neve could do nothing but cry as he gently extricated himself from her arms and stood up.

'I'm staying in Mistletoe Lodge in the village tonight and my helicopter is picking me up early tomorrow morning so I better get my things and leave now.'

She watched as he moved upstairs and came down a few moments later, stuffing his clothes in his bag.

'Will you let me know what date your twenty-week scan is?'

She nodded numbly.

He leaned forward and kissed her on the head. 'Take care of yourself, Freckle.'

And with that he walked out of the house and didn't look back.

❋

As Adam strolled through the village towards Ivy's house, he looked up at the vast sky that seemed to stretch on forever. In London he never saw the stars and sky as clearly as this. There was too much pollution to ever be able to sit back and enjoy it. Everything felt so much cleaner here. Coming here was the best decision he had made in years so he knew he had to make this work with Ivy. He refused to let it fizzle and die before it had properly started.

As he approached Ivy's door, he was sure he saw the curtains flicker next door, where Deborah was no doubt watching him with her beady eyes. He felt like giving her a cheery wave but decided against it.

The door was unlocked and as he could see Ivy moving around in the workshop out the back, he let himself in. She looked up and smiled at him, which he took to be a good sign. Ivy wiped paint off her hands and then walked over to him, sliding her hands round his neck before he'd even uttered a word.

'Hi.'

'Hello,' Adam said, mystified by this sudden change in direction. The morning before things had been so tense, even if Ivy had pretended everything was fine, and last night she hadn't even wanted to see him.

'I'm an idiot,' she said, leaning her forehead against his chest so she didn't have to look at him.

'You're definitely not that.' He tilted her chin back up to face him.

'I'm so scared of the future that I'm stopping myself enjoying the present.'

'I obviously said something to upset you yesterday morning, want to tell me what it was?'

She nodded. 'We need to talk, I know that. I haven't been in a relationship since my divorce and I just don't know how to deal with all the fallout from that marriage. I'm so scared of getting hurt again and of you walking away from me just like Callum and I feel like I'm overthinking everything. I know I'm not making any sense.'

'Not really, but you're not going to scare me away.'

'You seem to have infinite patience. Why don't you come and have a shower with me?' She smiled as she stepped away from him and took his hand, leading him upstairs. 'We can talk after, I promise.'

He smiled. 'After what?'

Ivy laughed. 'After the shower, of course. Get your mind out of the gutter, I'm not that kind of girl!'

Adam caught up with her, wrapping his arm around her stomach and kissing her neck. 'I think, after the other night, we've already established you *are* that kind of girl.'

Ivy giggled and wriggled from his grasp and ran up the stairs ahead of him. He laughed and ran after her.

✳

There was another knock on Neve's door later that evening. She had cried for hours since Oakley had left, her eyes were red and sore and she felt so exhausted. She didn't have any hope that the person at the door was Oakley, all hope had now gone. So she wasn't disappointed to see Gabe and Pip standing there.

Pip took one look at her face and immediately stepped forward and enveloped her in a big hug.

Gabe shuffled them both in and closed the door behind them, then he was hugging her too.

'It's really over,' Neve said, wiping away her tears. 'There's no way back from this now.'

Pip took her hand and led her to the sofa, sitting down next to her, and Gabe sat on her other side.

'He hasn't left yet,' Pip said. 'He came over here, flew thousands of miles to fight for you. Now it's your turn to fight for him.'

'What can I say that I haven't already said?' Neve asked, hopelessly.

'Luke said you were worried that you weren't good enough for him,' Gabe said.

'I did think that,' she admitted.

'Why on earth would you think something like that? You're an amazing, fantastic person. Oakley would be very lucky to have someone like you in his life.'

'Some of it came from his mum. She said I wasn't pretty enough or famous enough to go out with Oakley. She said that if I cared for him, I would let him go as he deserved to have someone much more glamorous in his life.'

'She did not say that?' Pip said, her eyes wide and angry.

Neve nodded, sadly. 'And as I was feeling vulnerable when I first started going out with him after what happened with Zander and fearful that it would happen all over again I allowed myself to think maybe she was right. I started to have doubts. Zander dumped me for someone beautiful and famous and I could suddenly see myself falling in love with Oakley and it happening all over again. His mum said that I had nothing special enough to keep him interested, that I was nothing more than a novelty to him after all the dancers, models and actresses he'd slept with over the years and that novelty would soon fade away. She said the best thing I could do for him was to finish things with him. I didn't want to hold him back in his career because of his association with me and all the travelling he would do to come and see me, so when his time came to an end in London, I thought the best thing for him was for me to let him go.'

'Does he know she said all that stuff to you?' Gabe asked.

Neve shook her head. 'I didn't want to come between them. I know he resented her interfering with his work but he's still close to her.'

'But he needs to know. All of this dumping him, pushing him away, came about because of her. If you have any chance of saving your relationship, he needs to know the truth.'

Neve hesitated.

'You were so happy with him and then she came to the hotel to visit him and you were never the same after that,' Gabe continued.

'She caused your fear of the past repeating itself to rear its ugly head,' Pip added. 'The one thing that I learned from what happened with Gabe, I think the one thing we both learned, is that you can't let what happened in your past define what happens in your future. If we had both let our fear of the past happening again stop us from getting involved with each other, we would never have what we have now and I would have missed out on this incredible loving man being in my life, my soul mate.'

Gabe grinned at her, reaching across Neve to take Pip's hand. 'Oakley's mum might have been the catalyst but that fear that you weren't good enough was there for her to be able to poke at in the first place. Don't let it rule you and don't let it ruin your life. If you do then Zander wins all over again.'

Neve stared into the flames of the fire. They were right. She wasn't going to let Zander win, and she wasn't going to let Oakley's mum win either. She and Oakley belonged together and she had to do everything in her power to get him back.

❄

It was the very early hours of the morning when Adam got out of bed, leaving Ivy to sleep. Outside of the confines of the duvet it was cold and, not entirely sure where his clothes had been thrown, he grabbed her pink towelling robe and pulled it on before heading to the kitchen to make himself a drink. They hadn't talked. They had kissed and made love and laughed, but Adam couldn't escape the feeling they were just papering over the cracks.

He poured himself a cup of coffee and as his feet were cold against the wooden floor, he pulled his boots on and padded down the stairs. He looked around the workshop at all the paintings stacked up against the wall, ready for framing or displaying in the shop. Ivy had so much talent. At the back of the shop were loads of photos, some in frames, others pinned to the walls. He stepped closer to take a look as he sipped his coffee.

There were several landscape photos of the island and several others of various unknown locations; some of them looked very tropical and others extremely remote and barren. She clearly used them for her inspiration.

There were other photos of people in frames and he picked one up. They were photos of one young couple and their children in various stages of growing up. He realised these weren't just photos of random people but obviously people that Ivy knew and cared about. As he looked around the back of the room, he saw there were loads of them, particularly of the children.

'My nieces and nephews,' Ivy said, from behind him.

'They look beautiful. I bet they're real characters,' Adam replied, turning and noticing she was wearing his jumper, which came down almost to her knees, and big bear paw slippers.

'They are.' She stepped closer and picked up a frame of a lanky boy, covered in mud, with a rugby ball under his arm and the biggest grin on his face. 'Archie is ten and the most amazing artist. He does comic book graphics and drawings and he is so talented at it. He creates all his own comic books and makes up the stories. I'm sure he'll be working for Marvel or someone like that one day.'

Adam smiled at the fondness she obviously had for her nephew as he handed her a photo of a little blonde girl dressed as a pirate.

'That's Quinn, she's seven and I'm sure she'll be on the stage when she's older. She sings all the time, loves getting dressed up and is the most confident child I know. The one you have there is of Imogen, Rachel and Drew. I love them all to pieces. Do you have any nieces or nephews?'

He nodded. 'Oliver is eight and Megan is five.'

Ivy smiled, sadly, and put the pictures of Quinn and Archie back on the shelf and Adam knew he had to be honest with her.

'I always wanted a child of my own. My ex-girlfriend got pregnant and I was over the moon. I went out and bought all the stuff straight away, a cot, the car seat, all the nappies and baby clothes, probably a hundred teddies. When she miscarried we were both absolutely devastated.'

Ivy stared at him with wide tear-filled eyes.

'I'm so sorry.'

'It's OK. I was heartbroken. We never recovered from that and we broke up soon after. I threw myself into my job and I've not been with anyone since. I tell myself and anyone else that asks that I don't really mind if I don't have children as it's easier than telling people how disappointed I am that it never happened for me.'

'You broke up with your girlfriend because of the miscarriage?' Ivy said, her voice no more than a whisper.

He nodded and to his surprise she took a step away from him and then another, staring at him as if she didn't know him any more.

'I think you should go.'

She walked to the front door and flung it open.

'Wait! *What?*' Adam said, beyond confused.

'You need to leave. This. Us. It was a terrible mistake.'

'What are you talking about? I don't understand.'

She walked out onto the street and he followed her.

'Ivy, what's wrong?'

She put her hands to her face and screamed into them in frustration. 'I'm such an idiot! I did it again, I fell for it again.'

'Ivy, please, talk to me.' He reached for her but once more she stepped away from him.

'I don't want to see you again.'

Ivy walked back into the shop and closed the door, locking it behind her. Adam stood out on the street in shock as he watched her move back upstairs. It took him about five seconds to realise that the only things he was wearing were her dressing gown and his boots.

CHAPTER 19

The sun hadn't even risen when Neve banged on Oakley's door. She had spent hours trying to come up with the perfect speech to get him back but still she had nothing and she was running out of time. There was no movement from within and she suddenly got scared that he had already left.

She turned the handle and was relieved when the door opened. She let herself in just as Oakley came running down the stairs, wearing only his jeans. Halfway down he stopped and stared at her. He looked dishevelled and as if he hadn't slept either.

'The door was open,' Neve explained, lamely.

'Security is lax round here.' He came down the last few stairs and stood in the lounge, his hands in his pockets.

'I thought you might have gone.'

'The helicopter comes at half nine, that's not for another five hours yet.'

'We need to talk.'

He gestured to the sofa and she sat down. He sat down on the sofa opposite her.

She had to say something, anything to give them another chance. She thought of what she could say, something that would make him forgive her. A hundred possibilities ran through her mind but none of them seemed good enough.

'You're wearing the ring again,' Oakley said, gesturing to the diamond, which was back in its rightful place.

She stared at it. 'It's a reminder of everything I've ever wanted.'

'Which is?'

'You. I love you. And I don't think we wouldn't have lasted. We are meant to be together. You're my forever and there will never be anyone who means as much to me as you do. Of course there will be bumps in the road, there always are, but as you said when you came here to get me back, there is no problem too big that we can't work through, because if we love each other then that's all we need.'

Oakley stared down at the floor, shaking his head slightly.

Fear and desperation ripped through her. 'You were right, I was pushing you away, but it was never because you weren't good enough for me. I was scared that I wasn't good enough for you.'

He looked up, staring at her in confusion.

'You're this big famous actor, you have women falling at your feet, you could have anyone you wanted. I never believed you would want me forever. Zander told me he loved me, then he became this famous Olympian and he ditched me. I was scared of it happening all over again and I couldn't cope with losing you. But you have to understand that I was deliriously happy with you. Zander was my past but you were my future and then...' she hesitated but she couldn't possibly make this situation worse. 'Your mum told me that I wasn't pretty enough, glamorous or famous enough to go out with you. She said that I wasn't special enough to keep your interest. She said you deserved better than me and if I loved you at all, I should let you go as going out with me would ruin your career.'

Oakley's face turned to thunder, his voice was low when he spoke. 'I don't believe this.'

'It's true, I swear. I didn't want to hold you back. This was your dream come true and I wanted that for you so I pushed you away. And selfishly I wanted to protect myself from you when, as your mum put it, you came to your senses and dumped me.'

'She had absolutely no right to say those things to you or to make you feel for one second worth less than you are. I can't believe all of this came from her.'

Neve shook her head. 'It was an old wound and she just ripped off the plaster and made it bleed again, but it was already there.'

'You were everything for me. There wasn't a single seed of doubt in my head that you weren't perfect for me in every way. And you let my mum and Zander take that away from us.'

'I know, I never gave us a chance. I was so scared of the future that I wouldn't allow myself to enjoy what we had. I was so scared of you breaking my heart that I pushed you away and I broke my heart anyway. I want to give us a chance now.'

'I'm not Zander, I don't know what I can do to get you to trust me—'

'I trust you. I didn't, but I do now. When you said you wanted to marry me and raise my baby as yours when you thought you weren't the father, I knew that you loved me. You have no idea how much confidence that gave me. You weren't staying with me because I was pregnant with your son, you were staying because you loved me so much. Every doubt and fear I had went away when you said that. Your mum, the press, all the assholes that wrote nasty comments about the photos of us, saying I wasn't good enough for you, they can all go to hell because you wanted forever with me and I could finally see that.'

'So the lie was a test, push me away and see if I come back?' Oakley said, clearly getting angrier by the second.

'God, no, that wasn't the plan. I never intended to lie to you, that was a gut instinct to your horrified reaction to me being pregnant. I was trying to protect you. I knew you didn't want a child, I was trying to set you free. It absolutely wasn't a test, it wasn't me thinking you wouldn't be a good father, it was me trying to do what I thought was best for you. I didn't want to stand in the way of your dream job. I'm sorry, it was a terrible mistake.'

He sighed, pushing his hands through his hair as he walked away from her, pacing the room.

She stood up. 'I still love you, I still want this to work. And if you can find it in you to forgive me and you still want to marry me then my answer is yes. I'd marry you right now if you'd have me and I'd move with you to California.'

He turned round to face her. 'You'd move to America with me? You'd leave your family, your job?'

'Yes, wherever you are, that's where I want to be. You're the most important thing in my life and, as long as I'm with you, nothing else matters. But even if you don't want to be with me any more. . .' her voice choked. 'If you don't love me any more and we can't be together. . .' she swallowed a sob. 'I want our son to grow up knowing his dad. I want him to see you every day, not two or three times a year. You are a wonderful, loving, kind and generous man and you will make a fantastic father to our son. I don't want him to miss out on that. If you don't want me then I'll still come to America so you can be part of our son's life. I can sleep in a different bedroom or, if you don't want me in your house, I can get a house nearby so you can see your son whenever you want. And. . .' she wiped a tear from her cheek. 'You won't have to see me at all, if that's what you want. You can just send some PA to come and collect him and bring him back and you'll never have to see or speak to me ever again. There's no way I want our son missing out on having you in his life, so I'll do whatever it takes to make sure you're a part of it in any way that you want to be.'

She wiped the tears from her cheeks.

'You'd come to America even if we weren't together?' he asked, incredulously.

'I want the best for our son and you being in his life is the best thing for him. I'd have to sort out visas and I have enough money put aside to start my riding school. That would be enough to buy a small house somewhere, if you didn't want me any more.'

Neve couldn't help the sob that escaped her throat. The thought of being in America all by herself, raising a baby without her family to help her, was a terrifying one, but she hoped it would show Oakley how serious she was about them, that she would give up everything for him. She hoped that if she was living nearby then maybe one day he would be able to forgive her and they could have another chance at being together but even if they couldn't, being alone was the price she would have to pay to ensure her son knew his father and was part of his life. It was all her fault, so she owed her son that much.

Tears filled her eyes and she was surprised when Oakley wrapped his arms around her and held her as she sobbed against him.

'The fact that you would do that for me means so much, but if we weren't together, you'd be all alone out there and I couldn't ask you to do that.'

The crying intensified and there was nothing she could do to stop it. After everything she had said, it had made no difference. He still didn't want her.

'Shhh, don't cry, Freckle.' He pulled back to look at her. 'We'll figure this out somehow. Fortunately money isn't a problem for me. I can fly over every weekend if need be. We'll sort it out. You look wrecked, have you slept?'

'No, I couldn't.'

He scooped her up and carried her up the stairs. Then he sat her down on the edge of the bed and undressed her as she continued to cry, and then encouraged her to get under the covers. He covered her and then lay next to her on top of the duvet.

'Go to sleep, Neve, you need to look after our little bear.'

She carried on crying. That's all she was to him now, the mother of his child, not someone he loved or cared about any more. She closed her eyes and when she felt his arm go round her, holding their son, she cried herself to sleep.

❄

Adam slammed a fist onto the door in frustration. He'd been knocking on Ivy's door for ten minutes or more; it was quite clear she wasn't going to let him back in.

'Hey, Adam, what are you doing?'

He turned to see Oakley staring at him in confusion. Adam sighed in defeat and came to sit on the bench outside Ivy's house.

Oakley came to sit next to him. 'Nice dressing gown.'

Adam sighed.

'I owe you an apology,' Oakley added.

With his mind only on Ivy and what had just happened it took Adam a few moments to realise Oakley was talking about accusing him of sleeping with Neve.

'It's OK, I think I would have reacted like that too if I'd thought that someone had got Neve drunk and slept with her.'

Oakley looked at him in surprise.

'I care about her too and no, not in any kind of romantic way – we're just friends – but that doesn't stop me caring about her. What's going on with you two?'

Oakley sighed. 'I don't know.'

'I hear she told you the truth.'

'She lied to me. I'm not sure I can get past that.'

'Do you love her?'

'Of course I do but—'

'There are no buts here. If you love her and she loves you, which I know she does, then make amends with her. She shouldn't have lied, she knows that and you have every right to be angry at her, but don't let that anger ruin what you have. The sad thing is, she thought she was doing the right thing for you. She is head over heels in love with you, and you were offering her marriage, a house, riding stables and everything she ever dreamed of and she was prepared to turn all that down for you because she knew a baby was not something you wanted. She was scared it would interfere with your dream job. She lied to free you of your responsibilities. It wasn't selfish, it was anything but selfish. In fact the only one being selfish here is you. You're prepared to walk away from her, the woman who you love and who is carrying your child, because your feelings have been hurt. You need to grow up. No one is perfect, everyone makes mistakes, but being in a proper relationship means forgiving each other for the mistakes that you make, not walking away at the first sign of trouble.'

Oakley stared out at the snow-laden trees for a moment. 'If I want advice, I don't think I'll be taking it from a man sitting outside his girlfriend's house in a bright pink dressing gown at five in the morning.'

Adam's patience snapped. 'Then go, sod off back to America. We'll take care of Neve. *I'll* take care of her.'

Oakley turned back to glare at him. 'If you lay one hand on her I'll—'

'You'll *what*? Do you honestly think that when you go back to America and start screwing around with all these famous women that she has seen you with in the newspapers over the last few weeks that she'll sit at home like a virgin and never touch another man again? She's a very beautiful woman and it won't be long before she moves on. You walk away from her this time, there'll be no coming back from that. She won't forgive you for that. Antoine has already been sniffing around her and there will be others. Someone who will love and cherish her regardless of the mistakes she makes. Someone who will be here for her son, who will raise your son as theirs. Is that what you want to happen just because she made one little mistake?'

Oakley didn't say anything for a moment then he stood up to leave. 'I've got some clothes you can borrow, if you don't want to walk back to the hotel dressed in that.'

Adam took one more look at Ivy's front door and stood up too. He followed Oakley back to the cluster of lodges at the end of the village which had been converted to guest accommodation.

Oakley shushed him as they walked into the house.

'Is Neve here?' Adam hissed, as they walked up the stairs.

'Yes, which is why I couldn't sleep.'

Adam walked into the bedroom behind Oakley and saw Neve curled up fast asleep, in the middle of Oakley's bed. Though she was mostly covered in a blanket, her bare shoulders peeped out the top and it was quite clear she was probably naked.

He watched as Oakley covered her shoulder up with the blanket and she stirred slightly, reaching her hand across the empty bed, clearly looking for him. She frowned slightly when her hand fell on nothing but cold sheets.

Oakley handed some clothes to Adam.

'Thanks.'

Oakley nodded, unable to drag his eyes from Neve.

'I certainly wouldn't be wandering around outside in the cold in the middle of the night if I had a beautiful naked woman to keep me warm. If I had someone like that in my bed, I don't think I'd ever leave.'

Adam went into the bathroom and quickly got changed. When he walked back into the bedroom, Oakley was already climbing into bed next to Neve and pulling her into his arms.

'Oakley,' Neve whispered, clearly still half asleep.

'I'm here, baby,' Oakley said.

Adam smiled and left them to it. Hopefully they would sort themselves out. If only his own love life was that easy to fix.

He went downstairs and stepped out into the night. He glanced over to Ivy's house, which was now in complete darkness. He would talk to her tomorrow.

❄

Neve woke up later. Judging by the sunlight pouring through the windows it was late in the afternoon. Panic shot through her before she realised she could feel hot breath on her neck and the feel of a large hand wrapped around her stomach. She turned round in his arms to find Oakley lying in bed with her, fast asleep. He looked so peaceful. She leaned forward and kissed him on the lips.

'I love you,' she whispered.

Instinctively the hand that was around her waist pulled her in closer to him and she snuggled against him, closing her eyes and wishing that moment could last forever.

Oakley's eyes suddenly snapped open as he realised where he was. He looked at her warily but he didn't move away from her and he didn't remove his hand from her waist either.

She leaned back slightly, giving him some space. 'I thought your helicopter was coming at half nine.'

'He couldn't get here. Too much snow,' Oakley explained.

Overhead she heard the sound of the plane coming in to land and Oakley blushed at being caught out in the lie.

'Snow affects planes and helicopters in different ways.'

Hope bloomed in her heart. Had he cancelled his flight? She wouldn't push him any more. She had said everything that she could say but the fact that he was lying in bed with her, holding her, proved he still cared about her. He was angry and he had every right to be but maybe, just maybe, he could move past that and forgive her so they could have a future together.

'When are you leaving?'

'I don't know. Maybe tomorrow.'

'It's the New Year's Eve ball tomorrow.'

'Yes, it is.'

She ran her fingers down his jawbone, relishing the feeling of his stubble against her skin. 'And you promised you would dance with me.'

A slight smile played on his lips. 'I did, didn't I?'

'Though I need to get a new dress for tomorrow. I'm getting too fat for most of my dresses.'

'You're not fat, Freckle. You're beautiful and you're carrying my child. There's nothing sexier than that.'

'Well, everything is starting to get a little tight, especially around the breasts.'

Oakley lifted the duvet to look at them. 'They are getting bigger, aren't they?'

'Hey!' Neve laughed and grabbed the duvet from him and covered herself back up. 'You don't get to look at these again, I'm not that kind of girl. Only men I'm in a relationship with get to see these.'

Playfully he tried to tug the duvet away from her fingers. 'I'm an ex-boyfriend, that's got to count for something.'

She frowned, not liking the direction the conversation was going. 'I've got lots of ex-boyfriends, does that mean they can all come round and have a look?'

'No, they bloody can't!' he laughed.

Neve got out of bed, taking the duvet with her. 'You've got the same rights as all my exes over my body, you don't get to look at or touch it if we're not in a relationship and you've already made it clear that you don't want that. If I come and live with you in America so you can be a part of our son's life, you don't get to make love to me or kiss me whenever you like and then cast me aside again because we're not actually together. You're either with me or you're not, there's no in between. In fact, you won't get to see me naked again unless we're married and then I'll know that you won't be able to leave me the next time we have a stupid row.'

To her surprise, he was still smiling as he lay on the bed, watching her. He got out of bed and started getting dressed.

He walked up to her and she backed up to the wall as he crowded her with his wonderful body.

He brushed a strand of hair from her face. 'One of the things I fell in love with was this fire in you. This no-nonsense, not-taking-any-crap attitude. I love that. I'm glad to see it's still in there. There's been far too many tears lately, though I know I'm almost entirely to blame for that.'

He leaned forward to kiss her but she stopped him.

'No kisses either? OK.' He smiled as he walked past her, heading towards the stairs, seeming completely unperturbed. 'I better see what I can do about that then.'

She stared after him in confusion, watching as he walked down the stairs. 'What?'

Without another word, he walked out the door.

❉

Ivy stood outside Adam's office and raised her hand to knock on the door before changing her mind. She knew that he would come down to her house later on, demanding an explanation for why she kicked him out wearing only her robe, and she wanted to explain to him here rather than have him in her home again. If they properly broke up – and she strongly suspected they would – she wanted to be able to walk away from him, not have to get him out of her house again.

She plucked up the courage and knocked. A few seconds later the door was flung open. Adam stared at her for a few moments and then gestured at her to come in. She walked in and he closed the door behind her.

He sat down behind the desk and waited for her to speak, clearly still angry over what had happened the night before.

She took a deep breath and ensured that when she spoke her voice was strong and not clogged with emotion. 'My husband broke up with me because I couldn't give him a child.'

He stared at her for a second and then his face softened. 'Ivy—'

'He was a charmer, just like you, said all the right things, brought me flowers. He was sweet and attentive. It wasn't until we were married that I realised what an absolute ass he was. He wanted children so badly, sex came to be only about producing a baby. We tried everything. He encouraged me to lose weight, I had to take all these vitamins and supplements and we did all the sexual positions that were supposed to be the position where we were most likely to conceive. We used all the ovulation kits to see when was the optimum time to have sex. We even tried IVF and when I still didn't get pregnant, he divorced me, citing unreasonable behaviour from me as the reason. The fact that I couldn't produce a child was unreasonable to him.' She swallowed. 'To hear that you finished with your girlfriend because she miscarried—'

'Hang on, that wasn't the reason we broke up!' Adam stood up. He stared at her for a moment, then moved around the desk and took her hand, leading her to the sofa. He gently tugged her down next to him. He sighed. 'She blamed me for the miscarriage. We'd made love the night before she lost the baby and she said it was my fault our baby died. She never got past that. She wouldn't talk to me, wouldn't let me touch her. She moved out of my house and told me she never wanted to see me again. I tried to get her to come back but she refused.'

Ivy stared at him in horror, suddenly glad she was sitting down because her legs were shaking. She'd got it all wrong.

'I felt so bad afterwards,' Adam continued. 'It didn't matter that all the research, all the articles I read, all the doctors I spoke to said that sex was not the cause of the miscarriage, I still carried around that guilt for years. She's happily married now, three beautiful children by all accounts. She moved on where I never felt like I could.'

She swallowed. 'I'm so sorry that you went through that and I'm sorry for jumping to the wrong conclusion last night. Everything still feels so raw after my divorce and last night I could suddenly see it happening all over again. You want children and I can't give you any.'

Adam put his arm round her shoulders and hugged her to his chest.

'So this is what all this has been about, your fear that I'm going to leave you because you can't get pregnant?'

Ivy nodded.

'And have you been to the doctors about this?'

'Yes, I've been poked and prodded and tested for every possible thing. There is no medical reason why I haven't been able to get pregnant.'

'Could there be something wrong with your ex-husband? Was he tested?'

'Yes, at least I think so, but his new wife is already pregnant, something he had great pleasure in telling me, so clearly the problem lies with me, not him.'

'Maybe you just weren't compatible.'

Ivy shrugged. 'It's possible.'

Adam kissed the top of her head and her heart fluttered against her chest. The fact that he was still there with his arm round her gave her hope.

'Ivy, I like you a lot. Probably a lot more than like actually. It's really early days for us and neither of us can tell whether we will last a month, let alone a year, but I have a really good feeling about it. There's a connection here I haven't felt with anyone before. If we get married and we both want children in the future and it doesn't happen naturally without all the vitamins and ovulation charts, we can look at IVF again and if that doesn't work or you don't want to go through that again, we can always adopt. There are many babies out there in the world who need a loving home. And if all else fails we can get lots of little fur babies instead. I love dogs, how do you feel about them?'

Ivy smiled, tears filling her eyes. 'I love them. I always wanted a spaniel, but Callum was allergic to fur.'

'Well, we have a plan. We'll get a whole litter of puppies to occupy our attention and spoil rotten. Look, if I'm with you, I'm with you for you, for how you make me laugh, for your generosity, your fiery nature, your passion for your art, your insanely good sandwich-making skills, not your baby-making abilities. I accepted long ago that I was probably never going to have children so if it doesn't happen I'm OK with that, just as long as I'm with you.'

'Really?'

'Truly.'

Ivy felt herself almost sag with relief. 'God, I've been so worried about all of this. I know things are still so new with us and to start talking about children already is craziness but I didn't know when was the right time to bring it up. You have a right to know what you're getting involved with. I didn't want to get a year down the line or wait until we're married and then drop the bombshell that I can't have children. That wouldn't be fair on you.'

'I appreciate it must have been difficult for you, but if we're going to work then you have to tell me when something is bothering you. Don't shut me out.'

'I won't, I promise.'

Adam kissed her briefly on the lips, stroking a finger down her cheek before he stood up. Ivy guessed it was time for her to leave so he could carry on with his work. She watched him move to the door and lock it.

She let out a laugh as he came back to the sofa and leaned over her, his hands either side of her head.

'Now I hear that one of the ways to make a baby is getting the technique right.'

She grinned as she undid the buttons on his shirt. 'Is that right?'

'So I think we should practise now so when the time comes we know what we're doing.'

His mouth went to her throat and she let out a soft moan. 'I think that sounds like an excellent plan.'

CHAPTER 20

Neve hadn't seen Oakley for the rest of the day. She'd wandered round the village, visited her horses, Shadow and Knight, and she'd even gone for a walk down to the ice palace and the lake, but she hadn't even seen him from a distance. She'd gone back to his lodge but he hadn't been there, so after dinner she made her way back to her lodge.

Pip was waiting for her on the steps.

'How's it going?' she asked as Neve let them both into her house.

'With Oakley? I have no idea. I've told him I love him, I've told him that I'd move to America with him, I've told him how sorry I am, but he was still referring to himself as my ex-boyfriend earlier today right before he tried to kiss me and walked out the door.'

Pip shook her head. 'Talk about mixed messages. Would you really go to America with him?'

Neve didn't hesitate. 'If we're together then yes. I honestly don't know what we're going to do if we're not. I offered to move out there regardless but he said he didn't want me to be alone. But I want him to be a part of his son's life. His job is there and he can't move it as easily as I can. It makes sense for me to go.'

'He still loves you. He's crazy about you, anyone can see that. Just give him some time to get over the lie. I'm sure he'll come round.'

'We haven't got time, Pip. He leaves on New Year's Day, we need to sort it out before then.'

'He won't leave without sorting it out. Are you going to the ball?'

'As manager, I kind of have to. I'll need to oversee it all, make sure everything runs smoothly. I know Adam will be there to take care of things but this is a big event and I feel like I should be there to help if need be. I need a dress though, everything is getting a bit too tight.'

'Let's go shopping tomorrow, Gabe says there's a great ball-gown shop in Lerwick. We could take the plane or the boat over. I need something to wear too. I have a really small selection of clothes and definitely nothing fancy enough for a ball.'

'I have a few dresses you could borrow.'

'That's kind, but I really want to buy something new. I want something spectacular for Gabe.'

'Why, is he wearing a dress too?' Neve teased. 'How's it going between you two anyway?'

Pip's whole face lit up into a huge smile. 'I have never been so utterly happy in my entire life as I am now.'

'You make him that happy too.'

'I know it sounds silly, but he's my soul mate. It's like we were meant to be together.'

Neve smiled. 'It doesn't sound silly at all. I feel the same way about Oakley.'

'I just want tomorrow night to be really special for us. It feels like it's the start of a whole new chapter in our lives. A new year with endless new possibilities.'

'So we need the perfect dress to signify this,' Neve said. 'Fine, we'll go dress shopping. It's not like I'm allowed to do any work at the moment anyway.'

'Great, I'll see you tomorrow.'

Pip left and Neve changed and got into her bed. She grabbed her phone and scrolled down to Oakley's number. She hadn't phoned or messaged him for weeks. She didn't even know if he had the same number any more. She quickly wrote out a text message.

I'm not sure where you are but I love you.

She pressed 'send' and stared at the screen, waiting to see if there would be any reply. After half an hour with the phone screen staying resolutely blank, she put it on top of her bedside table and curled up and went to sleep.

❄

Neve sat down to breakfast with Gabe, Pip and Wren the next morning.

Gabe reached out and took her hand. 'Are you doing OK?'

Neve shrugged. 'I'm not really sure, to be honest. I think I've cried all the tears I have. I have no idea whether me and Oakley have any kind of future together. He walked out yesterday afternoon and—'

'Came to see me.'

Neve blinked. 'He *did*? What did he say?'

Gabe rubbed the back of his neck awkwardly. 'He took the last plane to Lerwick last night.'

Neve stared at him, her waffle suddenly dry in her mouth. She swallowed hard. 'He's left?'

'No, he's coming back. Today, I think. I don't know. Has he not spoken to you at all?'

'No, what's he doing in Lerwick?'

Gabe frowned. 'Well, the good news is I know he spoke to that photographer as well. I have no idea what Oakley told him, but whatever it was, it ensured the photographer packed his bags and flew out to Lerwick first thing this morning too.'

'What's happening in Lerwick?'

Gabe looked around awkwardly. 'I have some emails I need to send. I'll catch you girls before you leave. And Wren, me and you are going to help Luke with some of the ponies today, so I'll see you shortly.'

With that he stood up and left the table.

Neve looked at Pip. 'What's going on?'

'I don't know but we're going to Lerwick shortly too. It's not that big a place, and Oakley is quite easy to spot. Let's go and ask him.'

'He's gone to see Annabelle,' Wren sang, while she tucked into her pancakes.

'Who's Annabelle?'

Wren shrugged. 'Oakley spoke to her in Daddy's office. He was very excited about seeing her.'

Neve stared down at her breakfast and then back at Pip. 'Eat up, we have a plane to catch.'

❄

Lerwick, as the only town on the Shetland Islands, was actually a lot bigger than Neve imagined it would be and tracking Oakley down was going to be harder than she first thought. There were certainly no hordes of screaming teenage girls running down the streets after a famous Hollywood star.

Pip must have realised the same thing. 'We might as well go to the dress shop, I have a map Gabe drew for me.'

They found the shop on a little side street filled with row upon row of beautiful ballgowns. The assistant was very friendly and helped Neve and Pip pick out a range of different dresses she assured them would complement their figures perfectly and, with several scraps of satin underwear, they were bustled off to the changing rooms.

Neve pulled on a negligee that barely came down past mid-thigh and stared at herself in the mirror. Was she supposed to wear this under the dress? It gave next to no support to her ample breasts, and although it clung beautifully to the rest of her body, it looked more the sort of thing used to seduce someone in the bedroom. No one would get to see this under her dress so she didn't really see the point.

Just as she was about to take it off, she heard the whispered squeals of two of the assistants outside the cubicle and froze.

'I can't believe he's here.'

'He's so hot!'

'Did you see the way he looked at me, I think he likes me.'

'Bloody Oakley Rey, here in our little shop!'

Before she knew what she was doing, she opened the cubicle door and pulled back the curtain to the staff-only area, where the two girls were jumping up and down with glee.

'Where is he?' Neve asked, not in the mood to play any more games. If he was here, she wanted answers.

The girls straightened their faces. 'Who?' asked the very pretty blonde.

'Oakley Rey, where is he?'

'I don't know what you're talking about,' the other girl said.

Neve sighed and turned around, walking straight out of the female changing area and into the men's. A few men were there trying on suits and tuxedos and looked a bit surprised when she marched straight past them to the room at the end, which seemed a frenzy of activity.

She marched straight in and there was Oakley standing in the middle of a large room being attended to by almost every female and male assistant that worked in the shop. He was dressed in a tuxedo that fitted him perfectly and he looked like a star, but more than that, he looked sexy as hell and all thought and reason went straight out of her head.

His eyes locked with hers in the mirror and he turned around, bringing the attention of all the assistants down on her.

'Miss, you can't be in here.' One of the assistants stormed towards her.

'It's OK,' Oakley said. 'She's a friend. Could we have a few minutes alone?'

Friend. That hurt more than it should.

The assistants left them alone and Oakley walked towards her, taking her in.

'Is that the dress you plan on wearing tonight, because if it is it certainly has my vote.'

Neve looked down at herself and cursed that she was still wearing the stupid negligee.

'What's going on? Why are you here and why are you dressed like James Bond?'

He cocked his head. 'I promised you a dance at the ball tonight. You know me, Freckle, I always keep a promise. I need a suit if I'm going to waltz you round the ballroom tonight.'

She felt so confused. 'What's going on, Oakley? Yesterday you were lying in bed with me, flirting with me. Now you're here, buying a suit just so you can keep a promise and dance with me. Are we. . .' She trailed off, not wanting to ask the question she needed answering most of all for fear of his reply.

'Freckle, I fly out tomorrow afternoon, we start filming again the night after and I can't not be there. I want to make sure things are good with us before I leave. Over the last few days I've been hard on you and I want to make that right. You don't need that stress when you're pregnant. And as we're having a baby together, we need to be friends if we're going to make this work.'

Friends was not the outcome she was hoping for but it was something.

'Does that mean you forgive me for lying to you?'

'There's nothing to forgive, it was a mistake.'

'But. . . But does that mean that we can—'

'It means that I'm going to dance with you tonight, it means that afterwards I have a tiny little surprise I want to give you before I leave. And when I leave tomorrow, I'm really hoping we'll be on friendly terms.'

He studied her, concern and hope flashing in his eyes.

'We'll always be friends. I will always love you, Oakley, but if you can't give me more than friendship then I'd be more than happy to be your friend.'

Oakley gathered her into a big hug, holding her tight. She couldn't help the emotion from clogging in her throat.

He pulled back slightly and kissed her on the forehead.

'And I meant what I said, I'll come to America and raise our child there so you can see him whenever you want.'

'We'll talk about that later and how we can make that work. I don't want to take you away from your family.'

She didn't want to tell him that, although she would miss her brothers and Wren, Oakley was her family now, even if they weren't together.

She stepped back out of his arms. 'I better go. I need to find a dress and get back to help with any final preparations for the ball. I'll see you later.'

'You can count on it.'

She smiled, sadly, and he didn't take his eyes off her as she left the room.

Neve hurried back to the cubicle and sat down on the bench. She had one more night with him and she had to make it count.

❋

Oakley burst out of the house later that night and ran down the street towards the airport. He knew he had five minutes until the last plane to Juniper Island left. He didn't know what would be the checking-in policy at such a small airport but if he could just make it on time, they might possibly hold the plane for him.

Annabelle had taken a lot longer than he expected and then the thing Adam had asked him to pick up had taken a while to sort out too.

He had to be there to dance with Neve. He had to prove to her he was a man of his word. Everything hinged on tonight and the only way he was going to pull it all off was if he was there to dance with her before midnight.

Clutching Adam's present for Ivy against his chest and carrying the suit bag in his other hand, he ran as fast as he could, but before he even made it as far as the airport building, he heard the sound of engines powering up on the runway on the other side of the fence. To his horror he saw the small plane roar down the runway and up into the night sky.

That was it. There was no way to get back to Juniper Island now.

❋

It was gone eleven o'clock and Neve had barely been able to take her eyes off the doors to the ballroom all night. Despite his promises, there had been no sign of Oakley all evening. She didn't know if he was still in Lerwick or whether he was on the island somewhere. Earlier that afternoon she and Pip had caught a plane and he hadn't been on that. The last boat and plane had been and gone that evening with no sign of Oakley on either. But somehow she knew that he wouldn't go back on his word either.

The ballroom looked spectacular. The lights in the coloured jars and on the trees sparkled, the floor gleamed, the music was beautiful. The night had gone without a hitch. All the guests looked stunning in their ballgowns and tuxedos as they swept each other around the dance floor, their dazzling masks making the whole affair look exotic and exciting, as if everyone had some kind of secret.

In the middle of the floor Adam was sweeping Ivy around the room and she was laughing at something he was saying to her. They looked very happy together. Gabe was dancing with Pip and Wren, looking happier than she had ever seen him. Neve glanced over to a darkened area of the room, near the store cupboards, and smiled when she saw Luke kissing Audrey in the shadows. Luke needed someone lovely in his life and Audrey fitted the bill perfectly. Even her parents were dancing away happily, looking at each other as if they were the only ones in the world. Everyone had someone but she had spent most of the night alone.

Gabe approached, looking dashing in a black tuxedo and a silvery blue mask. He sat down at the table with her, taking his mask off.

'Maybe he isn't coming,' he said, gently.

'He'll be here.'

Gabe nodded. 'What's going on with you two?'

'I have no idea.' She paused, hating what she was going to say next. 'I'm moving to America.'

Gabe sighed and nodded. 'I thought you might be.'

'My son needs a dad and Oakley will make a wonderful father. I can't deprive either of them of the chance to be in each
other's lives.'

He moved to sit next to her, slinging an arm around her
shoulders. 'I'm going to miss you so much.'

'I'm going to miss you guys too, but I'll come over as often as
I can. I'm sorry to let you down.'

He frowned. 'You're not letting me down. At all.'

'But this place has just opened and—'

'And Adam will take over. I'm here too. I'm not saying that
it won't be difficult without you, you're so good at your job and
Adam will have very big shoes to fill, but in no way are you letting me down. You have to do what's right for you and your
child. I don't think spending the rest of my life on a remote Scot-
tish island was ever part of my game plan, but things change
when you have children and you have to do what's best for them.
I only want you to be happy and if you are, then I'm happy too.'

Neve leaned her head on his shoulder. 'Thank you.'

'And if things go badly with Oakley or you miss English bacon too much and you want to come home, you will be welcome back any time.'

Neve smiled. 'Yes, bacon is an issue I hadn't thought of. I'll
have to take whole suitcases back over with me every time I
come to visit.'

They were silent for a while and Gabe leaned his head on top
of hers. 'When are you thinking of leaving?'

'Not yet. We have the big Fire and Ice Festival in January and
our first wedding on Valentine's Day. I don't want to leave Adam
with all that stuff to deal with. I know he's very proficient and
experienced, but things are different up here than they were in
London. I want to make sure he's OK before I leave. I need to
do a proper handover, not just drop everything and run. Maybe
I'll leave end of February, after my twenty-week scan.'

He nodded.

The doors to the ballroom were suddenly pushed open and Neve stood up, something inside her knowing instinctively that it was Oakley.

Her breath caught in her throat as she spotted him. Despite the fact that he was wearing a turquoise and gold mask, there was no mistaking him. His gaze found hers straight away and he moved towards her. There were murmurs of interest as several people clearly recognised him but he had eyes only for her.

As he approached, he caught her hands in his and kissed her on the cheek. 'I'm sorry I'm late, Freckle. The jobs I needed to do took longer than I would have liked. I missed the plane and I had to make alternative arrangements that included hitching a ride with a fishing trawler and a helicopter ride from some very nice Navy men for who I now somehow have to get a walk-on part in the Obsidian movie in order to repay them. But I'm here, I hope I didn't keep you waiting too long.'

'I knew you'd come.' Neve couldn't help but smile.

'I promised you a dance. Now let's do this, because I have another promise I need to keep before midnight. Several, in fact.'

She frowned a little. What other promises did he need to keep? Would he be dancing with anyone else?

But before she could ask any questions, Oakley took her hand and escorted her onto the dance floor. With one hand in hers and the other on her waist, he started to sweep her around the floor. He was clumsy and very ungraceful but being in his arms was the only thing that mattered. She wanted that moment to last forever. He took her hand and spun her out and then back towards him as if it was some kind of rock and roll dance, which made her laugh. The music came to an end and changed to something much slower. He smiled and shifted her closer into his arms so that he was hugging her as he moved slowly around the dance floor. She leaned her head on his chest, listening to his heart.

'You look so beautiful tonight, Freckle.'

He held her tighter and as the song came to an end he whispered in her ear. 'I love you so much.'

She pulled back slightly to look at him; his eyes were filled with so much love and tenderness.

Suddenly there was an announcement from one of the staff over the microphone. 'Ladies and gentlemen, the fireworks over the lake will be starting at midnight. If you want to make your way down to the lakeside now, hot drinks will be available.'

There were murmurs of excitement as all the guests slowly filed out but Neve was glued to the floor, wrapped in Oakley's arms as she stared up at him. He'd said he loved her. Could they really get back together? Would he put what had happened behind them?

As they were left completely alone in the middle of the ballroom, she reached up and kissed him. This time he didn't hesitate, he kissed her straight back. Something shifted between them, a need and urgency. If he was leaving and this was goodbye then she wanted to make love to him one more time and from the way he was kissing her, he felt the same.

'Let's go upstairs and we can talk in private,' Oakley said, taking her by the hand and almost dragging her out of the room. She giggled at his desperation to be alone with her too, though she'd much rather go back to her lodge and reconcile their differences in the privacy of her home.

She quickly kicked off her heels and ran up the stairs after him, her hand firmly in his.

They reached the top and she pulled him towards her, kissing him hard. He didn't pull away, instead he kissed her back, wrapping his arms around her and shuffling her back against the wall as he slid his tongue inside her mouth, tasting her. He let out a moan of need. She wrapped her hands round the back of his neck, caressing his hair before she let them fall to his shoulders and slowly started to slide off his jacket.

He suddenly snatched his mouth from hers. 'Freckle, we can't.'

Her heart fell in disappointment.

'Not yet anyway, I have several promises to fulfil before we can do that.'

'What do you mean?'

He led her to the doors that led to an observation room over-looking the lake, though he didn't push them open.

'Freckle, I've been an ass over the last few days and I'm sorry. I hate that you lied to me but I know you did it for all the right reasons. But we all make mistakes and I made the biggest one of my life the day I let you go. I came back here vowing to get you back, I should have known you would make me work for it, but I learned a long time ago that if you really want something then you have to fight for it. We will argue and fall out, you're feisty and demanding and I'm stubborn and prideful, but we love each other and that's all that matters. I promised you there was noth-ing that could stop us being together, that whatever problems came our way we would face them. I promised that I would love you and take care of you and our child forever. I also promised Gabe that I would do everything I could to make you happy. I intend to fulfil those promises. We're getting married.'

She stared at him in shock. He wanted to be with her, he wanted to marry her.

'We're getting *married*?' Neve whispered.

'Yes, right now.'

CHAPTER 21

Her heart roared in her chest. 'Wait, do I not get a say in this?'

'No, Freckle, not this time.'

'But—'

'Do you love me?'

'Yes, but—'

'Do you want to spend the rest of your life with me?'

'Yes, of course, but—'

'Then we're getting married now before you try and push me away again, before we have another stupid row and I storm off. What we have is forever and once you have that ring on your finger, once you're my wife, you'll know no matter what happens, there's no getting rid of me. I'm in this for the long haul, baby. I never wanted forever with anyone until I met you. Now the prospect of my life without you in it is completely unbearable. I need you, I love you. You're the other half of my heart. Will you marry me?'

Neve had no words.

'Mikki O'Sullivan is in there waiting to marry us, she made me sign the registration papers earlier in the week. To be honest, I'm not sure how legal this is. Crazy lady from the village who claims to see into the future says we can marry without the twenty-eight days' notice due to extenuating circumstances, but she's all we've got. We can do it all over again properly in a few months, we can have a big party and I'll buy you a great big meringue dress if that's what you want, you can have a hundred bridesmaids and a St Bernard who carries the rings, you can have whatever you want, but I'm not leaving here tomorrow unless you're my wife. If I go and we're not married, doubt will slowly start to creep in, you'll come up with some other silly noble reason why we shouldn't be together, so just say yes now and we can get married and we can get back to what we were doing five minutes ago.'

Neve's throat was dry. 'Mikki is our official registrar for the hotel. She forced me to sign the registration forms earlier in the week too. If she says it's legal then. . . it's legal.'

'So, looks like it will be official after all. We can still do the big ceremony thing if that's what you want, but let's do this now before you come up with any more excuses.'

'I need my family, I can't get married without them.'

Oakley pushed open the door and Neve looked inside. Her parents, Gabe, Pip, Wren, Luke, Audrey, Adam and Ivy were all waiting for her. Mikki was waiting at the far end of the room, by the large glass windows overlooking the lake. The room was filled with flowers, lit only by candles and fairy lights and the light of the star-filled sky outside.

She turned back to face Oakley. He'd had all this planned.

'Say yes, Freckle, and me and you and our little bear will be a proper family, just as you've always wanted.'

'Are you doing this because I'm pregnant?'

Oakley stepped closer, wrapping one arm round her waist and pulling her against him. He caressed her cheek, his thumb dancing over her freckles. 'I'm doing this because I love you with everything I have.'

Tears filled her eyes. 'Then yes.'

Oakley sighed with relief and before she could say another word, he took her hand and marched her up to the window, standing before Mikki.

The ceremony was very short, no readings, no songs or poems, but she couldn't take her eyes off Oakley throughout the whole thing. She kept waiting for the panic or the fear and doubt to take over and cause her to stop the proceedings, but it never came. This was right: she knew that with every fibre of her soul, she and Oakley were meant to be together.

Before she knew it, Mikki pronounced them husband and wife and Oakley took her in his arms and kissed her like she was the oxygen he needed to breathe.

There were a few minutes where her family and friends all fussed around them, giving them both hugs and congratulations before they all rushed outside to help with or watch the New Year's fireworks, leaving them alone, overlooking the lake and the island beyond. Neve felt numb with shock. She was married. She had woken up this morning thinking there was no way back for her and Oakley, that they would never be together as anything but friends, and now she was married to the man she loved.

'I love you, Mrs Rey,' Oakley said and her heart roared at the sound of her new name. 'You're very quiet.'

'I'm still in shock over your sneaky tactics. What did you say to that press photographer to make him leave, by the way?'

'I told him we were getting married on New Year's Day in Lerwick and he could have exclusive photography rights if he left us alone on the island after we got married.'

Neve laughed. 'I can't quite believe we're actually married.' She stared down at the wedding ring, a twist of platinum and obsidian. 'This is beautiful.'

'I had a ring designer make it specially, Annabelle Brent on Lerwick. It took her bloody ages though, which is why I was so late.'

'I love it.'

She moved to the window to look out over the lake and Oakley moved behind her, wrapping his arms around her belly and peppering kisses over her neck.

Down by the lake, Neve could hear the guests starting the big countdown to the New Year and the start of the fireworks.

'This is a clean slate for us, Freckle. After midnight, we're going to look forward to our future. We won't dwell on the things that have happened over the last few weeks, us splitting up, the lie, or my overreaction to it. We're starting fresh as of now.'

She nodded. 'A new beginning.'

The night sky exploded into a blaze of colour, the fireworks competing with the moon and stars to light up the night sky. Sparkles of ruby, emerald and sapphire danced and fizzed across the inky darkness, reflecting off the lake beautifully.

She turned her back on the riot of colour and wrapped her arms round Oakley's neck.

'If we're drawing a line under our pasts tonight, how about we go back to my lodge and give last year one hell of a send-off?'

Oakley smirked and, taking her by the hand, led her out of the room and down the stairs. They had reached the front door before Neve realised she had kicked her shoes off somewhere, but as she looked around for them they were nowhere to be seen. Oakley wasn't to be deterred though. He took off his jacket and wrapped it round her, doing up the buttons. It completely dwarfed her. He removed his shoes, took off his socks and kneeled down to put them on her feet. She giggled as she watched him and then he stood up and put his own shoes back on before scooping her up into his arms.

'Oakley, you can't carry me all the way back to my lodge.'

'Knowing what's waiting for me back at the lodge, I have some incentive, but fortunately I won't have to.'

He used his back to push open the door and Neve laughed at the snowmobile that was waiting for them, complete with a newlywed plate and ribbons and tin cans tied to the back. After placing her astride the snowmobile, he climbed on in front of her. She wrapped her arms around his chest and he took off in the direction of her lodge. When he got to the lodge, he repeated the process, but this time he carried her through her door and straight up the stairs to the bedroom.

He kissed her, helping her out of his jacket as she helped him out of his shirt. His hands moved to her back and slowly unzipped her dress and then let it pool at her feet. His hands wandered over her body, caressing and slowly taking off the rest of her clothes. When she was naked, he lifted her and laid her on the bed. He quickly removed his own clothes as she watched keenly.

'Do you think it will feel different, making love as husband and wife?' she asked.

Oakley climbed on the bed onto his hands and knees and then crawled up so he was leaning over her.

'I think it will be the best sex we've ever had,' he said, smiling down at her.

'Really? Well, don't let me stop you.'

He kissed her, nudging her legs apart he slid inside her. She wrapped her arms and legs around him, holding him close.

'Happy New Year, Mrs Rey,' he whispered against her lips and as he kissed her again he proved just how happy he really could make her.

⁂

Adam walked up the hill from the ice palace holding Ivy's hand. It was gone two in the morning and the last guests had finally disappeared off to bed. After the fireworks, which were supposed to mark the end of the New Year's ball, many of the guests had returned to the ice palace and decided to carry on partying. And Adam had stayed to supervise things, offering the musicians more money to stay, apologising to the bar staff who were having to work a bit later, and finally pulling the plug on the event, half hour before. All the while he would much rather have gone off to celebrate the start of the New Year with Ivy in a much more private and intimate setting.

'I'm sorry about tonight.'

Ivy looked up at him with a big smile on her face.

'I had the best time tonight, we danced. . .' She smiled mischievously. 'We kissed.'

He grinned. After the second half of the party had gotten underway and all the staff seemed happy enough to work a bit longer, he and Ivy had snuck upstairs and shared a celebratory kiss that had got so heated it had very nearly turned into something more. As Adam knew how inappropriate it would be for the newly appointed hotel manager to be making love to his girlfriend somewhere where they might get caught, he'd somehow managed to hold back before they'd gotten too carried away.

'I'm sorry my job stops me from spending as much time with you as I would like,' he continued. 'I'm getting an assistant soon so things will be a little easier in a few weeks.'

She leaned into him and he kissed her on the head. 'Do you know how utterly happy and content I feel right now? For the first time in a very long while, I'm looking forward to the future and what it might hold. And you gave me that hope. I will never mind when you're busy with work. I know you always go above and beyond what's required in your job and I love that about you. And I'll always be grateful for that attitude because it was that that brought us together. The day when a little old lady got lost on her walk and instead of sitting in your office and delegating a search party, you came out to look for her yourself. And you found me and then you saved me in more ways than you can possibly imagine.'

'You saved me too. I spent so long burying my head in my job that I never looked up and realised there was a life worth living out here. You gave me that.' They were approaching the main reception now. 'I thought we'd spend the night in my room tonight, the village seems too far away.'

Ivy smiled. 'That's fine by me.'

He led her inside and up the stairs to the second floor. As he walked in he looked around the bedroom, but could see no sign of the present he'd asked Oakley to pick up for him. Damn it. He'd had no time to speak to Oakley after he'd arrived and before he'd married Neve, but he had hoped that he wouldn't let him down.

'I'm just going to use the bathroom,' Ivy said.

Adam nodded, still scanning the room.

She disappeared and Adam quickly clambered over the bed to peer down at the other side. He smiled when he saw the black spaniel puppy, fast asleep in a cardboard box, lined with blankets and cuddled up to a furry hot water bottle. There was a bowl of food and water nearby and newspapers on the floor surrounding the box. Oakley had thought of everything. He was going to be a great father to his son.

Ivy came out of the bathroom dressed in his robe, her long dark hair tumbling down one shoulder, and Adam sat back quickly, leaning against the headboard as he watched her. As she approached the foot of the bed, she slid the robe off, revealing she was naked underneath. His mouth went dry.

She climbed up the bed towards him and straddled him. As she kissed him, picking up exactly where they had left off an hour before, Adam nearly forgot all about his secret gift. She slid his shirt off, running her fingers down his chest as he let his hands explore her body. As she stopped kissing him for a moment, moving her mouth to his neck, clarity pierced his mind.

'Wait, I have a present.'

'It can wait,' Ivy said, as she resumed the trail of her mouth down to his shoulder.

Knowing the puppy could wake at any time, he shook his head. 'Let me give it to you now. Close your eyes.'

Ivy sighed slightly at having her plans thwarted again, but she duly closed her eyes.

Adam leaned over the side of the bed and scooped up the tiny bundle of fur. The puppy stirred and let out a squeak as she yawned.

Ivy's eyes shot open and then widened in shock as she stared at the puppy in his hands.

'I thought we could practise at being parents with this little girl. She's ten weeks old and she's called Hope.'

Tears filled her eyes as she took the little puppy and cradled her in her arms. 'She's beautiful.'

Hope licked the inside of Ivy's elbow and she snuggled down into the crook of her arm, her eyes closing and going back off to sleep.

'I thought she could live with you but we could walk her together every morning and when she gets bigger and needs more exercise, we could walk her together in the evenings too. I'd help with all her training as well.'

'That sounds perfect,' Ivy said, barely able to take her eyes off the sleeping puppy.

Adam smiled, knowing he had definitely done the right thing.

He took the puppy off her and popped her back in the box, next to the hot water bottle. Hope didn't stir; clearly exhausted from her long day travelling from Lerwick.

As he sat back against the headboard, Ivy kissed him. 'I think I'm falling for you, I know it's only been a short while, but—'

'I'm falling for you too,' he whispered against her lips and she smiled.

She kissed him again and he could feel her hands going to work on his trousers. A few moments later he was buried deep inside her. He groaned against her mouth as she moved. He held her hips, pulling her tighter against him. As she pulled back slightly to look into his eyes he knew it was a lie to say he was falling for her. He had already fallen.

❄

Oakley woke the next morning with Neve lying on his chest, her chin resting on her hands as she watched him. His beautiful wife. There was a sense of complete and utter contentment in his heart. Things hadn't worked out as he intended; although he had come here to get engaged, he hadn't figured he would be leaving already married and with a child on the way, but somehow the future looked so much better already. Neve was his wife and he was going to be a dad and he could find nothing but joy and excitement at that prospect. They were going to be a proper family and that was something he'd never really had before.

As he moved his hands to stroke her, he realised they were trapped. He looked up and found his wrists tied to the headboard with the towel belt from Neve's dressing gown.

He laughed as he gave his wrists a tug; they weren't coming free unless she released him.

'Now you have to stay here,' she giggled. 'I'll bring you food and drink and I'll force you to be my sex slave.'

'I don't think you'll have to force me, Freckle, sex with you is definitely no hardship.'

'Was last night the best sex you've ever had?'

He smiled. 'Making love to my beautiful wife, I don't think it'll ever get better than that.' He gave his hands another half-hearted tug. 'Although if you want to try something a bit kinkier, I'd be up for that.'

She laughed.

'Pervert.' She bent her head and kissed his chest. 'Do you really have to go?'

'Yes, Freckle, I do. What time is it?'

'You've got a while yet.'

Oakley looked over her shoulder at the clock on the wall and sighed. He had a few more hours and that was it. 'You could come with me,' he tried.

'You know that I can't. Not yet. I need to be here for the wedding on Valentine's Day, after that I can come and join you.'

'I understand. I'll come over for your twenty-week scan at the end of February and then we can go back to America together. I know it'll be hard for you to leave your family but this move doesn't have to be forever. I'm filming at the studios in California for the next two years but there's a month filming in London too so we can come over here then and whenever we have a break from filming we can fly over here for a few days. I think I have a break in July too. We could bring our little bear over then to meet the family. Once I've finished work on this film, we could move back here for a while. My agent has got me a part in a film set in Scotland, we can use this as a base when I'm filming there. We'll make it work somehow, Freckle,

I promise you that. I'll even fly your family over whenever you want to see them.'

'I know, it's OK. I will miss them but you are my family now and wherever you are, that's where I'll be too.' She leaned over him to kiss him and as her lips met his he tugged at the belt holding his wrists, desperate to touch her.

She pulled back slightly, smiling at his predicament.

'I love you,' Oakley said. 'And these next eight weeks will be hell without you, so untie me now so I can make the most of the time I've got left.'

Neve laughed and then leaned over his head to do just that.

✻

Oakley's lips against hers was like a drug she was never going to get enough of. Neve wrapped her arms around him and tightly closed her eyes so she wouldn't have to see the helicopter waiting for him on the helipad. He moved his hands down to her waist, holding her belly and caressing his thumbs over her tiny bump. Letting him go was going to be so hard to do but at least it was only for two months.

He pulled back slightly and kissed her forehead and she knew her time was up.

'I love you,' she said, needing him to know what she felt for him, though those words didn't even come close.

'I love you too, Freckle. I will miss you so much, but we'll talk every day, I promise.'

She grinned. 'I know, I know, we'll make it work.'

He laughed. 'We will.'

He kissed her briefly on the lips and knelt down and pressed a kiss to her belly. 'Be good for your mummy, Little Bear.' He turned to Gabe and shook his hand. 'Take care of her for me.'

'I will.'

Oakley flashed her a smile, picked up his bag and walked over to the helicopter. She watched as he climbed on board and fastened himself in his seat. Tears filled her eyes.

'Why are you not going with him?' Gabe asked.

'You know why.'

'Not really. You've just got married to the man of your dreams. Right now you should be going on honeymoon and instead you're letting your husband leave without you. I know him working every day at the film studios isn't an ideal start, but California isn't a bad place to spend the first weeks of your married life. He won't be working every day, you could spend romantic weekends in some beautiful beachside resort.'

Neve stared at him as the helicopter's rotors powered up.

'There's so much work that needs to be done. I want to stay and help Adam with the transition and I don't want to just leave you when there's so much going on at the hotel over the next few weeks.'

Gabe shrugged. 'You could work remotely – most of the work that needs to be done doesn't actually need you to be here. The table plans and menus for the wedding, the correspondence for the Fire and Ice Festival, all of that can be done from anywhere in the world as long as you have access to a laptop and Wi-Fi. Adam can handle anything that needs dealing with here in the hotel, and he'll have an assistant soon. I'm here and there are other members of staff that can step up and help too. If we need anything we can reach you by phone or email. Let's face it, you spending the next eight weeks crying at your desk because you miss him isn't going to be that much use to me. Having you happy, rested and loved up, even if that's on the other side of the world, is going to be much better for getting things done.'

Neve looked back at the helicopter as the pilot went through some final pre-flight preparation.

'You've been through hell over the last few months since you split up with him. Don't put yourself through that again, go with him.'

The rotors seemed to speed up and the helicopter suddenly lifted a few feet off the ground. Oakley waved and before she knew what she was doing she was running forward, frantically waving at him to come back. His face fell and he quickly said something to the pilot. The pilot touched back down on the ground and without waiting for the rotors to stop, Oakley unbuckled himself and ducked down as he clambered out of the helicopter and ran straight to Neve, taking her in his arms.

'What's wrong?'

'Do you have time for me to pack?'

Oakley studied her for a moment and then his face split into a huge grin. 'For you, Freckle, I have all the time in the world.'

EPILOGUE

Neve stared down at Juniper Island as the plane came into land. It was Christmas Eve and snowflakes swirled through the air, covering the whole island with a sparkly blanket.

She and Oakley had spent a month there after Ted was born in the summer when the trees were green and flowers grew from every available surface. She had forgotten how beautiful the place looked when it was covered in snow.

The plane touched down and came to a halt. Immediately Oakley started to dress a sleeping Ted in a thick, furry all-in-one coat that had a hood with little ears. She smiled fondly at him as Oakley fastened him back into the car seat: her little Teddy Bear.

Oakley saw her watching them. 'What?'

She stood up and kissed him. 'I love you.'

Oakley grinned. 'Well, that's good because you're never getting rid of me.'

The door opened and a gust of snowflakes drifted through into the plane. Oakley took her hand and led her down the stairs.

Adam was waiting for them at the bottom, with Hope sitting loyally by his side, apparently taking her role very seriously as formal guest greeter, even if they weren't proper guests.

Neve hugged him. 'We're not late, are we? I can't believe all the flights were grounded due to a little snow. Americans are supposed to be hardy sorts and ready for harsh winters.'

Oakley laughed. 'The worst snowstorm in over a hundred years, it was a bit more than a little snow. Over six foot of the stuff dumped itself on the ground in less than two hours. People lost whole cars in the snow.'

'We've had bad snow here too but fortunately nothing like that,' Adam said. 'And no, you're not late. They're waiting for you. How's the little bear?'

Adam took a peek at the sleeping Ted and smiled. 'Come on, let's get you all out of the cold.'

They got in the Land Rover and Adam made sure their bags were stowed in the back.

'Do you guys need to freshen up and get changed before we go to the ice palace?' he asked, getting into the driver's seat as Hope hopped into the passenger seat.

'No, we knew we would be cutting it fine with our plane arriving so late, so we came already suited and booted. Underneath all these coats, of course,' Neve smiled, as she watched Oakley buckle Ted's car seat.

'Go slowly, eh, mate,' Oakley said. 'These roads look very icy.'

'It's OK, I'll take it easy, and it's only a minute away,' Adam said, not minding Oakley's overprotectiveness at all.

True to his word, Adam took the very short distance to the ice palace really slowly.

'We're upstairs,' he said.

They all got out and climbed up the stairs. When they reached the top, they quickly got out of their coats. Neve took off her tracksuit bottoms and unfolded her dress, which had been tucked up by her waist. She quickly changed out of her snow boots while Oakley stood waiting for her, looking dashing in the tux he had worn to marry her a year before.

Neve opened the door and saw her parents, several villagers and Gabe and Luke milling about at the far side of the room.

Gabe beamed when he saw her and ran to greet her, gathering her up in a huge hug.

'I'm so glad you're here,' he said.

'I wouldn't miss it for the world.'

He released her and Luke gave her a huge hug too. Luke had the biggest smile on his face and no wonder, she'd seen the enormous engagement ring he'd bought Audrey when they had Skyped her a few days before to tell her the news. She glanced around to greet her parents to see they were already fussing over Ted. She smiled when she saw Oakley chatting and laughing with her dad. Last week they had attended a film premiere together where the fans had been screaming his name and here he was on a tiny island in Scotland, carrying his son, chatting to her parents, obviously just as at home here as he was on the red carpet.

Neve went over to say hello to Joy and Finn and was just admiring Audrey's engagement ring when a voice behind distracted her.

'God, sorry, I needed to pee! Did I miss anything?'

Neve turned to see Ivy waddling into the room, her huge pregnant belly protruding out in front of her.

'Ivy, oh my God, when did this happen?' Neve said, unable to take her eyes off the huge belly.

Ivy laughed. 'Well, about nine months ago.'

'You were pregnant the last time we were here, why didn't you tell me?'

'I didn't know. I thought I was just putting on some weight. I always assumed that this would never happen for me, so I didn't even spot the signs. Adam knew before I did. I took ten pregnancy kits before I believed him that I was.'

Neve hugged her. 'I'm so happy for you.'

Adam stepped up behind Ivy, wrapping his arms around her. 'Doesn't she look beautiful?'

'In all the times we spoke over the last few months, you didn't think to mention this to me?'

'I thought I'd tell you in person,' he grinned, stepping back to address the room. 'Ladies and gentlemen, if you'd like to take your seats.'

There were murmurs of excitement as everyone sat down and Gabe and Luke moved to stand at the front.

Oakley sat next to her, slinging an arm round her shoulders and kissing her head. 'What are you grinning about?'

'Last year everything seemed so bleak for all of us. The hotel was just about to open but none of us was truly happy. And now Luke is engaged to Audrey, Adam and Ivy are going to have a baby, we've been blissfully, happily married for a year and Gabe is about to tie the knot with his childhood sweetheart. Everything has come together.'

Oakley glanced over at Adam, who was looking adoringly at Ivy and stroking her bump while he talked quietly to her. 'I'm happy for him. God, looking at her makes me broody again! I can't wait to have another child with you.'

Neve smiled and having no fear this time of his reaction, she took his hand and placed it over her belly. 'You won't have to wait too long.'

He stared down at her and then down at her belly.

'I found out last night. I was going to do something romantic and tell you in some sweet way but. . .' she shrugged.

He broke into a huge grin and kissed her hard. 'I love you,' he whispered.

Before she could answer the music started and the doors at the back opened. She turned to see Pip enter the room in an elegant silver dress, her eyes only on Gabe as she walked towards her future husband. Wren was following her and while she wasn't wearing a *Frozen* dress as Gabe had said she wanted to do, she was wearing a blue bridesmaid's dress with snow-flakes round the hem. Wren waved at her as she passed and Neve waved right back.

Oakley nuzzled into her ear. 'I want a little girl this time.'

Neve laughed. 'I'll see what I can do.'

ACKNOWLEDGEMENTS

To the wonderful Kakslauttanen arctic resort in Finland, the real-life Stardust Lake Hotel. The incredible beauty of this resort, the glass igloos and the log cabins were the inspiration for both of the books in the *A Town Called Christmas* series.

To my family, my mom, my biggest fan, who reads every word I have written a hundred times over and loves it every single time; my dad, my brother Lee and my sister-in-law Julie for your support, love, encouragement and endless excitement for my stories.

For my twinnie, the gorgeous Aven Ellis, for just being my wonderful friend, for your endless support, for cheering me on, for reading my stories and telling me what works and what doesn't, and for keeping me entertained with wonderful stories and pictures of hot men. I love you dearly.

To my friends Gareth and Mandie for your support, patience and enthusiasm. My lovely friends Jac, Verity and Jodie, who listen to me talk about my books endlessly and get excited about it every single time.

For Sharon Sant for just being there always and your wonderful friendship.

To my wonderful agent Madeleine Milburn for just being amazing and fighting my corner and for your unending patience with my constant questions.

To my wonderful editor Claire for putting up with all my crazy throughout the whole process, for replying to every single email and for listening to me freak out with complete and utter patience. My editor Celine Kelly for helping to make this book so much better; my copy editor Rhian for doing such a good job at spotting any issues or typos. Thank you to Kim Nash for the tireless promoting, tweeting and general cheerleading. Big thanks to Natasha Hodgson, who is a huge help with the proofreading and the eBook files and getting them exactly how I want them to look – I love the snowflakes! Thank you to all the other wonderful people at Bookouture: Oliver Rhodes, the editing team and the wonderful designers who created this absolutely gorgeous cover.

To the CASG, the best writing group in the world. You wonderfully talented supportive bunch of authors, I feel very blessed to know you all – you guys are the very best.

To the wonderful Bookouture authors for all your encouragement and support.

To all the wonderful bloggers for your tweets, retweets, Facebook posts, tireless promotions, support, encouragement and endless enthusiasm. You guys are amazing and I couldn't do this journey without you.

To the Kielder Observatory, who gave me some great information on the Northern Lights and how to predict when they appear.

Thanks to Andi Michael who helped to name Oakley's superhero character Obsidian. Thanks to Mikki O'Sullivan who bid the most in the Clic Sargent Get in Character auction and who gave her name to the crazy lady in the snow globe shop.

To anyone who has read one of my books and taken the time to tell me you've enjoyed it or written a review, thank you so much.

Thank you, I love you all.

LETTER FROM HOLLY

Thank you so much for reading *Christmas Under a Starlit Sky*. I had so much fun creating this story and I hope you enjoyed reading it as much as I enjoyed writing it.

One of the best parts of writing comes from seeing the reaction from readers. Did it make you smile or laugh, did it make you cry, hopefully happy tears? Did you fall in love with Neve and Oakley, or Adam and Ivy? Did you like the gorgeous Juniper Island, the Stardust Lake Hotel and the town called Christmas? If you enjoyed the story, I would absolutely love it if you could leave a short review. Getting feedback from readers is amazing and it also helps to persuade other readers to pick up one of my books for the first time.

To keep up to date with the latest news on my new releases, just click on the link below to sign up for a newsletter. I promise to only contact you when I have a new book out and I'll never share your email with anyone else.

www.bookouture.com/holly-martin

I have one other book set on Juniper Island and in the *Town Called Christmas* series, so if you enjoyed this book and haven't read *Christmas Under A Cranberry Sky* yet, I hope you will love reading it too.

Thank you for reading and I hope you have a magical Christmas!

Love Holly x

@hollymartin00

hollymartinauthor

www.hollymartinwriter.wordpress.com